CONSEQUENCES

THE FUTURE WILL REVEAL THE PAST

CONSEQUENCES

THE FUTURE WILL REVEAL THE PAST

JIM PROCK

Thunderbird PRESS

The author acknowledges the following photo and graphic credits: Map of China and "Go" Board Game photos courtesy of Shutterstock.com; Fortune Cookie graphics courtesy of 123RF.com/413 Fortune Cookie Clip Arts, Stock Vector; Author photo courtesy of Lifetouch® Inc.

Published by:
Thunderbird Press
P.O. Box 524
Rancho Mirage, CA 92270
thunderbirdpress@dc.rr.com

Library of Congress Control Number: 2019911532

Prock, Jim
Consequences: The Future Will Reveal The Past

ISBN: 978-1-7328760-2-6
1. Fiction, Political, Romance

Printed in the United States of America

To my wife, Sue

We dreamed of children,
and they give us pleasure
beyond the gifts that each provide
in different, yet special ways
and fill our hearts with joy.

We dreamed of grandchildren,
and our cup runs over
with the love that they share without condition
and remind us of why we started on this journey.

JP

This is a work of fiction and historical fiction containing references to political leaders and entertainment personalities, both living and dead. Non-historical characters, names, places, organizations and events are the product of the author's imagination or are used fictitiously. Any resemblance to actual events, places or people, living or dead, is purely coincidental.

A family tree of Chinese and Chinese-American characters, a list of characters, and a list of abbreviations are provided in an Appendix at the end of the book.

CONTENTS

INTRODUCTION TO CHINESE HISTORY xi

PART ONE **THE PAST** 1
CHAPTER 1 The Invitation May 11, 2017 3
CHAPTER 2 The Escape September 26, 1938 7
CHAPTER 3 The School October 2, 1938 27
CHAPTER 4 The Struggle March 19, 1947 37
CHAPTER 5 The Mission September 17, 1962 49
CHAPTER 6 The Dream September 21, 1964 65
CHAPTER 7 The Return June 12, 1965 89

PART TWO **THE FUTURE** 103
CHAPTER 8 The Transition February 1, 2016 105
CHAPTER 9 The Suspicion January 21, 2017 127
CHAPTER 10 The Intelligence March 2, 2017 145
CHAPTER 11 The Interview March 27, 2017 165
CHAPTER 12 The Exposé April 12, 2017 179
CHAPTER 13 The Cover April 17, 2017 193

PART THREE **THE REVELATION** 207
CHAPTER 14 The Receptions May 11, 2017 209
CHAPTER 15 The Clues May 15, 2017 221

PART FOUR **THE CONSEQUENCE** 235
CHAPTER 16 The Aftermath November 7, 2017 237

APPENDIX 239
Family Trees 241
Characters 242
Abbreviations 245

ABOUT THE AUTHOR 249

INTRODUCTION
TO CHINESE HISTORY

The following synopsis identifies several significant events that occurred during the past one hundred years of Chinese history, including some that are referenced in this story.

CHINESE RULE AND WAR (1912–1949)

The rule of China dates back over five thousand years. After its first three thousand years or so, several Imperial Dynasties ruled China. In 1912, Sun Yat-Sen's Kuomintang (KMT) political party and his fellow revolutionaries, succeeded in establishing the Republic of China (ROC), taking control of what is now China, Mongolia, and Taiwan. After failing to maintain control of the new government, Sun was exiled to Japan. He returned to China in 1925 and started a rival nationalist government in the south, supported by the recently formed Communist Party of China (CPC). Sun died in 1928, and Chiang Kai-shek, the new right-wing leader of the KMT, successfully led a military campaign in the north, establishing yet another new nationalist government. Later, Chiang expelled the left-wing CPC members from the KMT.

A civil war ensued in which the Chinese Workers' and Peasants' Red Army, later known as the People's Liberation Army (PLA), an arm of the CPC under the command of Mao Zedong, fought against the National Revolutionary Army (NRA) of the KMT, led by Chiang Kai-shek, Mao's adversary.

After a pause in the conflict during China's war against Japan, the civil war resumed in 1945 with the CPC, supported by the Soviet Union, battling the KMT, supported by the United States.

The CPC finally defeated the KMT in 1949, and the civil war ended when Mao Zedong proclaimed the existence of the People's Republic of China (PRC).

Chiang Kai-shek retreated to Taiwan with a plan to defeat Mao's form of communism and return to his homeland as a nationalist. The U.S. continued to support Chiang until 1979 when the United States of America and the PRC recognized each other, and the United States established an embassy in Beijing.

Today, the U.S. continues to recognize the PRC as the sole government of China, while Taiwan's government functions as the ROC. Both regimes continue to claim jurisdiction over all of China; however, the United Nations only recognizes the PRC.

HONG KONG (1941–1997)

After centuries of dynastic rule in China, war broke out between China and Great Britain in 1839 over diplomatic relations, including the export of opium by the British to Hong Kong in an attempt to balance trade. In the end, China ceded Hong Kong to Great Britain as a British Crown Colony in 1841.

Japan invaded Hong Kong in 1941, concurrently with its attack on Pearl Harbor. Its occupation ended in 1945 when the Atomic Bomb was dropped on Japan. Thereafter, Great Britain continued to govern Hong Kong until 1997, when the governance of Hong Kong was transferred to the PRC under separate administrative rule.

KOREAN WAR (1950–1953)

U.S. relations with the PRC were contentious after 1950 when the Korea War broke out involving China, North and South Korea, and the U.S. After a long and bloody series of battles, the parties signed an armistice agreement in 1953. A rumor that the U.S. might use nuclear weapons may have contributed to the signing of a cease-fire agreement, although there is also no doubt that there were significant casualties on all sides, especially among the Chinese and Koreans. The war never officially ended, and the armistice continues today.

VIETNAM WAR (1955–1975)

The Vietnam War began officially in 1955 as a civil war. China supported the communist North Vietnamese throughout the war, while the U.S. supported the South Vietnamese in an attempt to combat communism.

After a cease-fire agreement in 1973 and the withdrawal of American forces from Vietnam when hostilities finally ended in 1975, the North Vietnamese forces entered South Vietnam. Since 1976, the country has been unified as the communist Socialist Republic of Vietnam.

LAND REFORM AND
THE GREAT LEAP FORWARD (1958–1961)

Throughout its history, China has sought to avoid the concentration of land ownership by landlords in favor of the peasants who work the land. The conclusion drawn by Mao Zedong was that the welfare of peasants should become the central objective of the communists' program and the basis for its political power. The result was a continuing series of land reform policies.

In 1958, Mao Zedong started his "Great Leap Forward" plan to rapidly develop agricultural and industrial output in order to compete with other nations. Private holdings were banned, and state-run communes were organized to increase grain production for export and show the success of the plan. The plan failed, and his plan ended in 1961.

CULTURAL REVOLUTION (1966–1969)

The Cultural Revolution began in 1966 as Mao's grand plan to remove every trace of pre-communist China and gain absolute control over the government. Capitalism and the cultural and traditional elements of Chinese history were destroyed. Individual thought became a crime, and guilty persons were punished severely, while life was increasingly characterized by military rule, terrorism, purges, persecution, banishment to labor camps, and death.

The plan ended in 1969 when it became a severe setback for the CPC, the government, and the people.

MODERNIZATION (1978–2014)

Deng Xiaoping never held a top office in the CPC or the government, but he led several movements, beginning in 1978, to transform the economy into a socialist market economy. Deng opened China to foreign investment, the global market and limited private competition. Deng's four main goals, called the "Four Modernizations," were to strengthen the economy, agriculture, scientific and technological development, and national defense.

Deng found similarities between socialism and capitalism. He wasn't afraid to adopt the advanced management methods applied in capitalist countries, as he felt that socialism and market economies were compatible. He was somewhat concerned about right-wing deviations, but he was more concerned about left-wing deviations. In other words, he felt it was important to stick to the socialist plan.

China's considerable economic growth owes its success largely to the pragmatism of Deng's theory.

The task faced by Deng was twofold: to promote modernization while preserving the ideological unity of the CPC, and to control the difficult process of reforms.

U.S. DIPLOMATIC RELATIONS WITH CHINA AND HUMAN RIGHTS (1979)

Since 1979, the U.S. and China have enjoyed full diplomatic relations, although human rights in China have continued to be a major concern of the U.S. The problem was exacerbated in 1989 with the treatment of Chinese citizens during the Tiananmen incident when students voiced their grievances with the government and were met with severe military force. The Chinese government continues to remain hostile to dissidents.

WORLD TRADE ORGANIZATION (2001)

Despite human rights protests in both China and the U.S., an agreement was signed in 2001 admitting China as a full member of the World Trade Organization (WTO). Its current membership of 160 includes both China and Chinese Taipei that includes the offshore Customs Territories comprised of the islands of Taiwan, Penghu, Kinmen and Matsu.

Since its admission to the WTO, China's population and economic growth has continued to stagger the pundits. By 2013, China had over 1.3 billion people, with over 120 billionaires. Moreover, China owns some $1.3 trillion in U.S. securities, making it the largest holder of U.S. debt.

CHINESE LANGUAGE AND SPELLING

Standard Chinese, also known as Mandarin, Putonghua, and Guoyu, is the sole official language of China. Mandarin is the language spoken in and around Beijing that provides the basis for Standard Chinese.

In China, the surname (the family or last name) is stated first, followed by the personal name (the given or first name) as in "Sheng Tom," rather than "Tom Sheng." A polite salutation would be Mr. Sheng. If Mr. Sheng were married, his wife would not use his family name.

Spellings of geographical names on various maps and references may appear differently here and there, as different naming systems were developed over time in order to adequately translate Chinese characters for use by non-Chinese. Since 1958, many English names of geographical entities in China reflect the Pinyin romanization system, based on the Latin alphabet. Pinyin is also used to enter Chinese characters into computers, and it became an international standard in 1982.

PART ONE

The Past

CHAPTER 1 ~ The Invitation

MAY 11, 2017

The passengers on Air China's overnight flight from Beijing to Los Angeles were asked to keep their window shades closed as the cabin lights were dimmed to accommodate those people who wanted to continue sleeping. The attendants were quietly collecting the remaining items from the breakfast meal that had been served an hour and a half before their expected arrival time.

The smell of coffee still coming from the galley reminded Jinli of his college days, when he first picked up the habit. He had returned to his cultural habit of drinking mostly tea, as the vast majority of Chinese do, but he always relished an occasional cup of coffee when it was available.

He had gotten very little sleep during the flight, mulling thoughts of his college days over and over in his mind.

When the pre-landing announcement was made, Jinli adjusted his sleeper seat and raised his shade just high enough to see out. As he looked down, he noticed the flicker of scattered lights coming on, signaling the end of another day in Los Angeles.

The plane's engines revved when air traffic control ordered the pilot to initiate a go-around, and after a few minutes, he was looking west toward the sunset over the ocean. He raised the shade to its full height for a better view.

The sun had dropped nearly all the way below the horizon, and the clouds floating above the water were painted with a multitude of pink and orange hues. Narrow blue rays emanating from the sun reached into the sky, piercing the clouds like big searchlights announcing a big movie premiere, just as he remembered them back in 1962.

The beauty of the scene mesmerized him. Then, in the blink of an eye, the ever-elusive "green flash" he'd heard about but never seen produced a momentary small green spot that touched the upper rim of the sun's disk just as it disappeared below the horizon.

He closed his eyes, attempting to etch the picture in his mind.

His wife had dozed off in the seat next to him so he reached over gently as he placed his hand on Shuchun's arm. Their visit to the United States promised to be quite an experience for both of them.

Guang Jinli, the first-ranked Vice Premier of the People's Republic of China for finance and economic development, had accepted an invitation from the new American President to meet in Washington, D.C. and discuss several trade issues with his Treasury Secretary, Dr. Winston Lee.

But first, Guang's trip would include a stopover in Los Angeles where the vice premier was scheduled to deliver this year's graduation speech at the University of Southern California, his alma mater, and receive the Honorary Doctor of Laws degree that he had been awarded.

Jinli planned to show Shuchun around Los Angeles during the day after the graduation, and then fly on to the capital in the morning of the following day.

But at the moment, he wasn't thinking of Shuchun. His thoughts had turned to Su Lin Wong, the girl he abruptly left behind in Los Angeles on the day after he finished college there, fifty-two years earlier.

In spite of their overwhelming love for each other, he had faced an impossible dilemma.

Su Lin had told him that her parents despised communists and would never accept him. And if that wasn't enough, she was a faithful evangelical Protestant, and wondered if he believed in God, much less Jesus. She said she would bring unforgiveable shame upon her family if her parents ever learned that she was in love with someone with his politics and lack of faith.

Jinli, on the other hand, had promised his father that he would return home immediately after he graduated. Going back was a tragic thought he couldn't bear.

He was in a no-win situation.

If he returned to China, her heart would break, and if he stayed, he would break his promise.

When he said goodbye to Su Lin at the airport, he wondered if he would ever see her again.

In 1937, eighty years earlier, the relationship between the U.S. and China was much different. The President of the U.S. was not focusing on trade issues with China, but on China's ongoing war with Japan.

Japan had adopted a policy of imperial expansion in the 1930s with a series of incursions onto the China mainland seeking access to China's raw materials to support its modernization, and control of China's food producing areas to accommodate Japan's overpopulation.

By the middle of 1938, the Imperial Japanese Navy had gained control of the entire Chinese coastline, blocking the mouth of the Pearl River delta area between Hong Kong and Macao. Then, in early September, Japan's 21st Army landed troops nearby and began moving inland to attack the port city of Canton.

CHAPTER 2 ~ The Escape

SEPTEMBER 26, 1938

Chen Wei rode his cargo bike into a village near Shilling Town on the outskirts of Canton to attend his last class. When it let out, he went shopping and bought a few last-minute supplies for the long trip ahead. As Wei headed back home in the dark, his lantern illuminated the narrow dirt path leading to his father's farm.

When he walked through the door, his father, Chen Yongmin, stopped him dead in his tracks. "You come home late every night and can't get up in the morning! Where have you been? You've been skulking around here for months!"

"What do you mean?" Wei shot back.

"You know what I mean. I know you've been up to something."

"If you must know, I've been attending night school classes in the village. I've been studying communism," he said proudly.

"Communism? Are you serious?" He was startled by his son's defiance. After all, Yongmin revered President Chiang Kai-shek and hated the communist rabble-rousers.

"Tonight I had to stay late to buy some things for my trip," Wei added.

"What trip? What things? And how did you pay for them?"

"I sold some of our excess rice seed. My sisters are married now and have gone to live with their in-laws, so we have fewer mouths to feed. You won't need all the seed you've been accumulating."

"Son, that's not your seed to sell. That's stealing."

"Not really … As your only son, I should share in the proceeds from what we sell, but you don't share. Besides, you must know what's happening."

"So, what's happening?" Yongmin yelled back.

"Father, you know the Japanese have been bombing in the delta area below Canton for a few weeks now, and they're knocking on our door. You act as if life here will go on tomorrow as just another normal day. The situation is really serious, and I'm getting ready to leave, even if you're not."

Shaking his head, Yongmin admitted, "I know they're coming, but I don't think there is anything we can do about it."

"Well maybe not, but I plan to do something."

"And what is that exactly?"

"I can't change the situation here, but I want to become part of Mao Zedong's movement and help him however I can. He has our best interests at heart, and he has a plan to rectify all the injustices suffered by our people. I know he failed once and was driven out of Jiangxi when Chiang defeated his Red Army forces, but Mao and what was left of his army evaded their pursuit in a circular retreat that covered over six thousand miles to the west and north. Now they're in the mountains of Yan'an. Lots and lots of young people were inspired by Mao's heroic effort and they're headed that way right now. Regardless, I think his defeat was only temporary, and I want to join up."

"Join up?"

"Yes, but it's not what you think. I won't have to join the army if I can get into his new Communist Party School up there. I'm convinced the communist message is the right one. It makes sense to me. I want to learn everything I can about it and participate in Mao's future plans as a cadre.

"Chiang Kai-shek is a dictator. He claims to be a nationalist, but he isn't doing enough to resist the Japs. He already let Manchuria fall to them, and now he's just trying to protect himself by chasing Mao around and neglecting the rest of us. Maybe he has Mao on the run right now, but I think Mao will ultimately prevail and take control of all of China. Can't you see how exciting that is? We will all be better off when the fighting is over."

"So you've got it all figured out, huh? What does a twenty-year-old farm boy know about politics? The KMT under President Chiang has made great strides in unifying our country, but your Mao Zedong is really mucking it up. You know Mao is an Atheist, right? I didn't send you to Christian school for nothing. Haven't you learned anything?"

"I know that politics and religion don't mix," Wei replied.

"Son, you aren't old enough or smart enough to know what will happen in the future. That's for sure. Just try to be happy, and forget all this political nonsense."

"Well, I haven't been going to school for nothing. I read a lot and listen to all points of view wherever I can find them—in the news and in conversation, and I can tell you that our situation here is dire."

"Big word ... 'dire' ..." Yongmin remarked, and he threw his head back and laughed.

"Yes, dire!" Wei said. "I'm even told that my old teachers at the Mission School are scared. Time will tell if I'm right or not."

"Yes, provided you don't get yourself killed in the process. I can't prevent you from leaving, Son, but I hope you'll reconsider. We're right in the middle of our fall planting season, and I'll be left with no one to help me if you leave. What's more, I would never be able to keep the land in our family without a son to take over when I can't work anymore."

"Well, Father, my mind is made up." Wei said. But then, a thought crossed his mind. "Will you go with me?"

"Go with you?"

"I don't think you understand at all what I've been saying. The invaders will be on our doorstep pretty soon, and your life may be in jeopardy if you stick around. Do you know what happened in Nanking? The Japs went wild! Those dogs … the way they treated our people … especially the women. What do you think they will do after they invade Canton? It's only twenty miles from here."

"I'm willing to take my chances," Yongmin said quietly. "Our family has been a part of the Chen clan for generations, and I've farmed these rice paddies my whole life, just like your grandfather, and his father, and his father before that. I don't know anything else. Besides, Jap soldiers will need food, won't they?"

Later that night, Wei packed his school bag with a blanket, some warm clothes, his canteen, a folded camouflage ground sheet, a notebook and a map of Southern China. Then, he slid his knife into its sheath and stuck it in the bag where he could reach it easily. In case he might be searched by the KMT during his trip, he left his copy of *The Communist Manifesto* by Karl Marx hidden under his bed. He found some empty tea tins and put some slices of his mother's *bak kwa* that was left over from the previous Chinese New Year into them and added the tins to his supplies. The dried meat would provide some energy along the way when no other food was available.

Early the next morning Wei ate millet porridge and drank tea for breakfast. Then, he put his bag in the basket on his bicycle and started to mount it. He paused for a moment and turned to look at his mother, who was watching him. He noticed a tear trickle down her cheek, but he knew she would not cry; her subservient role as a woman did not permit any expression of sadness. As Wei started to leave, Yongmin whispered something in his ear. With a loving heart Wei waved goodbye, and headed off to the railway station in Canton. He was determined to leave the farm for a better life. *Yan'an might not be the answer,* he thought, but he hoped it would be a long way from the war, and that his schooling would help to shape his future. Still, he felt sorry for his father and only wished that he had accepted the offer to join him.

With the speed of the big British Vulcan 600 series steam engine, the six hundred forty-mile trip to the end of the line in Wuchang would take about twelve hours. Wei had planned to take the early morning train in order to get there before dark. He had never been anywhere close to that far away from home before, so he knew that traveling alone would bring its challenges and potential danger if he arrived after the sun went down. He had heard plenty of stories about passengers being robbed when they weren't paying attention.

Wei approached the ticket window and said, "One ticket to Wuchang, please."

"We only have fourth class cars left, you know," came the response. "A lot of military are going north so you'll have to take what you can get. The cars aren't comfortable, but they'll get you there, barring an accident. Maybe you heard that an engine fell into a bomb hole a while back. Cars wound up all over the place."

Wei dismissed the man's caution and paid for the cheap ticket. He would not allow any bad news to affect him. Any remorse he had felt earlier was gone. The heady feeling of independence and adventure overwhelmed his conscious thinking.

He climbed into the wood-sided, open-air boxcar that was normally used by farmers traveling in and out of the city. It smelled of fertilizer and manure. But today, in addition to a few farmers, the passengers were mostly NRA army officers in full battle uniform with backpacks and bedrolls, armed with pistols and rifles with fixed bayonets.

The officers spoke about heading north to Wuhan to join the central forces that were preparing to defend the area. Chiang Kai-shek was determined to resist the Japanese at any cost, having lost badly in the battle of Shanghai. Wei had heard a lot of stories about army personnel switching their allegiance to rival armies, so the comments he overheard came as no surprise to him, especially when he learned that Chiang's objective was to consolidate several armies for an impending engagement.

They must realize they're facing an uncertain fate, Wei thought. Their armies haven't stopped the Japs yet!

Then his thoughts turned back to Canton, and he winced as he came to the sudden realization that it was being left without much protection. Nevertheless, he still felt strongly about his decision to leave.

An officer in his line of sight seemed puzzled by his reaction to their conversation, and he stared at Wei while talking with his comrades. Conscription into the service had begun, and Wei was sure the soldiers wondered why he hadn't joined the army, or been forced to join.

Wei took a deep breath and looked the other way as he attempted to avoid any suspicion of eavesdropping.

At the first water stop, some farmers got off and Wei managed to move to a better spot near the back of the car, out of sight of the officers. It was also out of the way of the inevitable soot that the coal-fired locomotive kept belching from time to time.

As the train pulled away, Wei pressed his face against the open space between the slats in the side of the car to look around, feeling a little like a dog trying to stick his head out of a car window to take in some fresh air. He marveled at the beauty of the scenery as he glimpsed the rolling hills and the rice paddies and lotus ponds dotting the landscape. The sight took his mind off his present circumstance for a little while.

When the train started climbing into the mountains, the fog increased, and the occasional light rain fell over him like a soft blanket. Fortunately, the temperatures were still fairly mild in advance of the cold winter he knew he would face later on.

Wei decided to try and get some sleep to avoid making contact with anyone. The trip would be long, and he certainly wasn't interested in conversation—especially if it involved politics or war.

His attempt failed as he was constantly being jostled against the side of the car, and the clickety-clack sound of the car's wheels kept him awake.

He wondered what his options would be after he reached Wuchang, but he was not concerned. He would find his way.

As the train slowed again to take on water at the Chaling station, Wei planned to jump off, relieve himself quickly, and then regain his seat before someone else got there. Unfortunately, men with the same idea delayed him and as he reboarded, there was only one remaining empty spot left between two men seated on a bench in the back of the car.

Wei had attended China Inland Mission School that was headed up by a missionary from the American Presbyterian Mission so he immediately recognized the men as Americans, or perhaps British. As they pulled away, one of the men leaned over and spoke to him, introducing himself as Clarence Hopkins from the English Wesleyan Mission.

"And your name is …?" he asked.

Wei had learned to respect his teachers so he smiled and responded graciously. "Sir, my name is Guang Wei."

Wei had decided to adopt his mother's family name, Guang, to differentiate it from that of his father, lest he somehow became associated with the KMT. He was proud to be joining their opposition.

"I'm happy to meet you, Wei. And may I introduce my associate, Walter Harness."

"Where are you headed?" Walter asked.

This was just the kind of thing Wei had wanted to avoid, but he answered anyway. "I'm headed up North, sir." He was reluctant to say exactly where he was headed or why.

"Well, Wei, Clarence and I are headed up north ourselves," Walter said. "We were stationed in Liuzhou, but we have been reassigned to the Kong Chuen Hospital & Mission Compound near Canton. A lot of trouble is expected down there, and when it materializes, they will need our help with refugees.

"First, however, we are going up to Xian to see the Tang Chinese Stele, called the Nestorian Monument. It revealed that Christianity was established in China in the year 635 AD, and it's the historical basis for our mission here in China."

Here we go, Wei thought to himself.

"In our study of the Book of Revelation, we concluded that the Gospel was undoubtedly spread to the East as traders and merchants traveled the Silk Road from Rome to Xian. There are a number of accounts of Emperor Taizong embracing a Syrian Missionary named Alopun, who was permitted to grow his church in the Xian area. The church eventually disappeared after two hundred years or so, but it reappeared hundreds of years later. Do you know about the Stele?"

Wei's ears perked up when Xian was mentioned. It was directly on his planned route, at the base of the mountains below Yan'an.

"Yes, I know something about it. My teachers taught me well."
"So, you were taught by missionaries?"

"Yes sir, I was."

"Well, if you're headed our way, we'd be happy to give you a lift. We'll be meeting an associate missionary of ours in Hanyang and driving from there. We'd love to have you join up, if you want to go with us."

Seizing the opportunity, Wei replied, "I am going in that direction, so I'll tag along with you if you're serious. I didn't know what I'd do after I got off the train, so I appreciate your offer."

"No problem at all, Wei, we'll be happy to help," Walter replied. "You'll provide good company for some tired old men!"

Secretly, Wei couldn't bear the thought of hearing the message of the Christian Gospel repeated over and over again during the six hundred fifty-mile trip to Xian, but the offer was too good to be true.

Then, Walter probed Wei again for an answer. "Did you say you are headed to Xian?"

Wei hesitated and then said, "No sir, I didn't, but my family is originally from that area. My father can't travel, so he asked me to look in on my grandfather who we understand is pretty sick. We never thought he would ever reach old age. I think he's at least seventy-five now."

The men looked at one another, nodding their heads as they smiled.

The three of them exited the train at the end of the line at Snake Hill and purchased tickets for the steam ferry connecting Wuchang with Hanyang on the North side of the treacherous Yangtze River.

As they disembarked the ferry at the Turtle Hill terminal in Hanyang, their associate, John Huckleberry, hailed them as he stood off to the side of a staging area while hundreds of soldiers were assembling there, preparing to move out.

Wei and the three men exchanged hellos and quickly departed for the Wesleyan Mission where John was stationed. It was located nearby, behind the walls of the city.

Homeless refugees were still arriving there from the North, following Chiang Kai-shek's orders to flood the area south of the Yellow River to slow the Japanese advance. The dikes had been opened on the river's Southern banks at Huayuankou, and millions of villagers had either drowned or became homeless as their land was inundated. The survivors who escaped the indiscriminate aerial bombing of their columns as they walked south, away from the river toward Hanyang, were severely malnourished by the time they got there.

The new arrivals were housed wherever John's staff could make room for them, and those who could not be accommodated in other shelters nearby were left begging on the streets.

Wuhan, a city which includes the districts of Wuchang, Hanyang and Hankow, had promised to be a safer area than where the refugees started out, but they would soon find out later that it decidedly wasn't true; Wuhan was just a stopping point of hesitation on the way to their annihilation.

The missionaries' quarters were quite small, but clean, set apart from the areas of the mission where the refugees were housed.

John and his three guests had a quiet dinner in near total darkness to avoid detection by enemy planes that would soon be making their normal night bombing runs in the area. After praying for an end to the hostilities and a safe journey, they turned in early. Morning would come soon enough, and they hoped to leave at daybreak.

Wei said goodnight, found his room, and made the first weekly entry in his journal. His short notes were an attempt to capture his feelings about everything going on around him, and he would follow that practice faithfully for the next forty years.

He didn't get much sleep, as the flashes of light coming through his window, followed by the ensuing sounds of bomb blasts, kept him awake much of the night. To compound the problem, the shrill, undulating noise of ambulance and police car sirens pierced the air like a parliament of screeching owls.

As they prepared to depart the next morning, the bombing continued as the Japanese bore down on the city, already having taken several surrounding areas. The key industries that had moved in from Shanghai before that city was taken were moving inland again, along with private-sector businesses from all over the Wuhan area.

John said that Chiang Kai-shek's government headquarters had been relocated from Nanking to Hanyang some time earlier, but that Chiang had moved the capital, this time farther inland to Chongqing. This time it was established in Chongqing to prepare for another defense of Wuhan. He said he heard that Chiang was amassing a staggering one-million-man army to resist the anticipated attack.

Clarence was a student of American History, and noted that an army of that size would be double that of the combined troop strength of the Union and Confederate Armies in the American Civil War!

Wei silently questioned if he had made the right choice to leave his family and his home virtually unprotected as the Japanese moved in, but his only objective now was to get to Yan'an.

16

John had originally suggested they take the train north to Zhengzhou in Henan and connect with the train going inland to Xian. After assessing the pattern of the Japanese advance, he had changed his recommendation and offered to drive them to Xian. The distance would be shorter as the crow flies, but the journey would be much more difficult.

But now, he felt he should stay behind to handle the refugee crisis that was bound to get a lot bigger, and reluctantly chose to stay at the Mission. Consequently, he demanded that the three of them take his Buick and leave, which they did without much of an argument.

Clarence took the wheel as they pulled away from the Mission. They wove their way through a maze of equipment-laden trucks and an assortment of rickshaws, bicycles and cars, all piled high with their owners' belongings, as ordinary citizens fled the attacks. Those with no means of transportation were walking. Given the heavy cross-traffic, Walter wondered aloud if the escapees had any destination in mind, or if they were frantic to go somewhere, just anywhere they thought would be safer.

In spite of all the turmoil, they managed to clear the city limits within an hour and head toward Xian. As they reached the outskirts of town, a dirt road began where the pavement ended. It was filled with ruts made by farmers' narrow-tired, two-wheeled freight carts, and Clarence struggled at first to stay out of the ditches. But fortunately, the summer rains had disappeared and there was no appreciable mud or dung to hinder his progress.

Clarence was able to concentrate on his driving, as there was not much conversation during the first few hours of the trip. John's burden of caring for more and more refugees was overwhelming everyone's thoughts, and the time passed in silence.

As they moved along, the fading sounds of the bombing diminished until the memory of them vanished from their consciousness.

After three days on the road, they arrived in Shanglou at the foot of the Qin Mountains, where they stopped for dinner, more fuel, and a final night's rest before tackling the last leg of their journey.

From there, it would be a fairly short, but rough and treacherous drive through the Lantian mountain pass at 4,200 feet, until they dropped down into Xian at about 1,300 feet on the landlocked Loess Plateau.

They were up early the next morning, ready to go.

The road was very steep in some sections, and passing local peasants transporting their goods in carts pulled by draught animals made the climb even more difficult.

There was still evidence of the old gallery roads with timbers for a roadbed sitting on supporting poles, embedded in the cliffs of the mountainside. Iron chain railings or stone balustrades lined the side of the road in some areas to protect people from falling into the Bahe River flowing alongside.

Wei tried not to think of the danger and focused his eyes straight ahead.

Walter cautioned Clarence to pay attention to his driving, but remain on the lookout for golden snub-nosed monkeys high in the trees, or giant salamanders slithering on the ground near the water. A waitress in town had told him they were the most common animals in the mountains, but that they might also see some Ibis or other birds, and maybe a Takin or two. She said that those goat antelopes come down from the high elevations for better grazing when the temperatures start dropping as winter sets in.

"Look!" Wei said. "Along the edge of the river down there. I saw one. Man, are they ugly. Oops, he just disappeared."

"We're not stopping to look," Clarence announced. "We're on a mission."

The vistas along the way were breathtakingly beautiful, with the Lishan Mountain to the East and the towering Mount Taibai to the West. "I can't believe how beautiful these mountains are," Wei noted. "We don't have anything like them where I come from, and we don't have as many animals or birds either."

"Same with me," Walter added. "Why would you want to go to a zoo when you could just come up here? I would love to spend my vacation here, if I ever get the chance."

"Maybe after the war," Clarence remarked.

After crossing the moat at the East Gate of Xian and ascending the city wall to higher ground, they easily found accommodations for the night and had a light supper. The ancient fortified city gave Wei a feeling of protection, even though it would be vulnerable to any air attack.

Wei's suspicion of the army personnel moving about the area wearing the gray uniforms of the NRA was relieved when he learned they were members of the Eighth Route Army with allegiance to the CPC. The army was seemingly engaged in a united effort with the CPC to defend against the Japanese.

Later, after some lengthy conversation about their travel experience, Clarence suggested they have a late night meal, as is the Chinese custom. Wei said he would skip it, even though he had been intrigued by the sidewalk ads for the popular Shaanxi Biangbiang Noodles. They were advertised as one of the "ten strange wonders of Shaanxi." Even so, he wanted to get good night's sleep and couldn't be persuaded to change his mind.

The next morning when they met for breakfast, Walter picked up a newspaper, and they were all shocked to learn about the impending fall of Wuhan, where they had been just five days before. They had left just in the nick of time. Apparently, the city was being encircled by the Japanese, and the Chinese army had started to retreat in order to conserve their strength.

So much for Chiang's leadership, Wei thought.

Wei declined Clarence's invitation to visit the Stele with them. Wei thanked them effusively for their courtesies, and when he started to say goodbye, Clarence asked if they could pray for him. Wei was a little embarrassed by the offer, but said, "Of course. That would be nice."

"Heavenly Father, thank you for your mercy and grace. We ask for your blessing on this country and on all those who are defending it against terrible odds. Bring them peace, O Lord. And protect each of us as we go our separate ways. Guide us in the way you would have us go. Amen."

When he finished, Wei recalled the last words his father spoke to him in the morning when he left home. "My son, I hope your romantic sense of adventure and the fantasy of making a difference doesn't cloud your mind from the real world you are about to encounter. Regardless, I wish you good luck and God's speed."

Wei hoped to cover at least fifteen to twenty miles a day, depending on the weather and the terrain. Fall was rapidly approaching and it was turning colder. He had never hiked in the mountains before, but he knew the climb would become more difficult as the elevation increased. He figured getting there would take him at least twelve days.

He started up the road, and after an hour, he stopped to get his bearings. He found some shade under a tree and sat down, taking in the lay of the land around him. Spotting a straight, long tree branch that had fallen, he took out his knife and cut the sprigs growing from its side, and fashioned a walking stick.

He called it *lüyou*, meaning travel buddy, because he wanted a companion.

Wei had heard all the stories about bandits and robbers lurking near heavily traveled roads and wondered if the problem existed around Xian. When he was a boy, he and his friends studied the ancient art of Shaolin Stick Fighting as a diversion from their monotonous farming work, and the thought eased his fears a little.

Being mindful of the danger he rightly or wrongly perceived, Luyou would be there to protect him.

Wei was a long way from home and alone now in a strange place. He assessed his situation and decided on a plan.

First, he would try to find secluded campsites for the night, remain out of sight, eat moderately to extend his food supply, and rest often to conserve his energy. The food he purchased in Xian wouldn't last long, but he hadn't eaten all of his bak kwa. That would help.

Traveling on, he succeeded the first night in finding an area fairly close to the road, covered with tall grasses and other thick vegetation near a stream running with clear, cool water. After a light meal, he laid down on his camouflage color ground sheet under a blanket, and felt relatively safe in the solace he found in the beauty of the starry sky.

He would get used to sleeping out at night.

He woke up early the next morning, filled his canteen in the stream, ate a small amount, and packed up for another day on the road. After a couple of hours, he was pleasantly surprised to come upon a field of corn, pumpkins and potatoes near a small village. No one was in sight, so he helped himself to two ears of corn and a pumpkin. The raw potato would give him cramps, so he skipped that.

That night, he made a meal of the raw, sweet corn. It was delicious and nourishing. He broke open the pumpkin and removed the seeds. He spread them out on a nearby rock to dry in the morning sun.

After he packed up the next morning, he put the seeds in his pocket to snack on later.

He followed a similar routine every day; eating, resting, walking, and then repeating the cycle once or twice more while looking for a location to stop for the night. He often saw other young people on the road, going in the same direction, but he ignored them. He felt it would be better that way, and they ignored him too.

He encountered a few trucks on the road from time to time, but declined his temptation to hitch a ride, not knowing what might result if he fell into the wrong hands. The trucks appeared to be loaded going uphill and empty coming down. That caught his attention, and he guessed they were taking supplies up to Yan'an.

On the morning of the seventh day, as Wei rested on the side of the road, one of the trucks going uphill pulled over and stopped. The driver yelled to him through the open window, across the lap of his female passenger, and said, "Hey, if you want a ride, climb aboard."

The invitation looked safe enough, and too good to be true. And the attractive girl looking down at him certainly didn't dissuade him from accepting the offer.

Wei obliged, anxious to save time. He threw Luyou and his gear into the back of the truck and climbed up into the passenger's seat as the girl moved over.

Wei introduced himself to her, and she returned the favor. She said her name was Yu Mingzhu.

"Why are you on this road?" the driver asked, knowing the answer already. "Why are *you* on this road?" Wei demanded.

"Don't' be so touchy, son. My name is Wu, and I'm delivering supplies up the hill." The answer provided the relief Wei was hoping for. The girl was quiet during the interchange, and he suspected she had already gone through the same drill.

"And you're both going up there to join the communists. Am I right?"

"Right," they answered in unison.

"I pick travelers like you on almost every trip. You know, Yan'an is really becoming a bustling place. Where are you kids from?"

Wei said he was from Canton, and she said she was from Shanghai. Neither of them added any other details.

After a little while, Wei broke the silence and asked Mingzhu about her decision to go to Yan'an.

Mingzhu responded curtly, "Don't you know what the Japs have done?"

"Hey, you sound just like someone I know!" Wei whispered.

Then, she continued, "I had to leave, because I didn't think Chiang could ever get rid of those guys. The Japs were really cunning, although their victories were rather hollow. There wasn't much left for themselves or our countrymen in the wake of their terror. A pyrrhic victory I suppose."

Wei wondered if she had formed her own opinions, or if she was simply repeating what someone else had said.

"You did hear about their tactics, right?" Mingzhu asked. "After the Japs took Shanghai, they went over and attacked the Capital in Nanking. And what they did in Shanghai was nothing by comparison with what they did there. They raped and murdered thousands of people, even unarmed people, and Chiang wasn't there to defend them. He had already left for Wuhan before the attack, knowing he couldn't stop their advance. Then the coward broke the dikes on the Yellow River just to slow them down, leaving millions of people homeless or dead. Do you call that moral, or humane? Their lives were totally destroyed. That's repulsive. It looked like he was more interested in defeating the communists than the Japs. Believe me, that will backfire on him. It's no wonder people want to join the communists. I certainly do! Don't you feel the same way?"

"I don't have quite as much venom for the invaders as you do, but I know how evil they are. I'm just looking into the future, and I think Mao Zedong is the leader we need to unite our country. We're experiencing way too much division right now."

"Absolutely," Mingzhu agreed.

She's enthralling, Wei thought. *Smart, feisty, patriotic, and really determined.* They made the steady climb up the mountain, and both Mingzhu and Wei became agitated when they suddenly rounded a curve and spotted the checkpoint ahead.

The guards were at the ready, pointing their Mauser pistols at them as they approached, even though they recognized Wu from a distance. The guards inspected the truck and its cargo, and Wu quickly explained the presence of his passengers even before they could ask.

As the guards waved them on, Wu told them not to worry because sentries were stationed at every point of entry into the Yan'an area just in case the KMT were to make a move.

By the time they were waved through the last of three checkpoints, Wei and Mingzhu had finally calmed down. "What can we expect once we get to Yan'an?" Wei asked Wu, as they drove by several small villages on the way.

"I'll give you a quick overview so you won't be surprised when you get there. It's not the Shangri-La you might be expecting. Yan'an is a barren, dusty place, covered with a fine, silt-like soil, called loess. It's been deposited there by the wind over many centuries and the ground is eroded with deep gullies marking the direction of the wind.

"You'll see hundreds of caves, called *yaodongs*. The original inhabitants of the area dug them out of the cliffs for protection from the winter cold and the summer heat.

"Now, the communists use them for everything from housing and barracks to classrooms, military training, hospitals, storage, and even theaters. And believe it or not, they don't suffer much damage from the bombing. They're very sturdy."

Wei suddenly realized he hadn't completely avoided the ravages of war. "You'll also see some mud huts, wooden buildings and other structures that are still standing, along with quite a few new buildings going up, mainly for schools and universities. Believe me, a few bombs being dropped by Chiang and the Japs won't deter Chairman Mao.

"Remember, Yan'an is the base for Mao's headquarters operation, but the total area controlled by the communists is pretty large, stretching for miles around in every direction. Different kinds of activities are happening all over the place.

"You'll see lots of soldiers being trained for deployment with military units stationed in the East. However, many of those who've already finished their training are embedded in different villages all over the countryside, living with the local peasants, forming them into tactical guerilla units. They're constantly moving in and out of Japanese-controlled territory, harassing the enemy, mostly at night."

"This place doesn't sound like much to look at, but I'm really excited to get there." Mingzhu exclaimed.

"Me too," Wei agreed. "It won't be long now."

Wei had been on the road for seven days. Seven can be a lucky or unlucky number, so he hoped that number would be lucky for him.

Wu let them out and told them to go about two miles straight down the road to the center of town and ask someone for directions to the registration desk.

They thanked him for the lift and waved goodbye as he turned off on a side road.

As they starting walking, Mingzhu asked Wei what he was thinking about. "I don't know if you heard him, but Wu said that new arrivals normally become soldiers."

CHAPTER 3 ~The School

OCTOBER 2, 1938

They found the building where the registration desk was located, and Mei Zi greeted them just inside the door. He handed them some paperwork, and they looked it over as they waited in line to be called.

"Next," Mr. Mei called out.

"Is this what you need to enroll me in the Party School?" Wei asked.

"It's a routine form for all new recruits. But if you want to get into the Party School, you'll have to fill out a separate application and get it approved. If you get that far, then you'll have to pass a test and submit to an interview to see if you're qualified. Fill out these forms, and attach your sponsor's letter of recommendation."

"But I don't have a letter."

"No problem. It may to be to your advantage anyway, not to be an intellectual. Everyone seems to think he is, and finds out later that he's not as smart as he thought he was. That's a sure fire way to get into the army!

All right now, do you at least have some Communist Party identification with you?"

"No, sir."

"How about political activities?"

"I'm sorry but the answer is also no."

"So what makes you think you qualify to be admitted? I'm sorry, but chances are you'll be wearing a uniform before you know it."

"Sir, I'm young, but I've been studying communism for two years, and I've read everything I can lay my hands on. I studied at night school for peasants back home, and I think Chairman Mao is the greatest thinker of our time. If you let me to take the test, I will show you. But I had to leave my books at home so if you have any reference materials here that I can use, I would like to borrow them. I promise I'll return them right away."

"Go by the library and tell them Mr. Mei sent you. I'll show you where it is. They'll have what you need. Now, move on to the next table and get your temporary assignment. Give them your completed application, and come back and see me tomorrow. Just remember, if they let you take the Party School exam and pass it, you'll still have a period of probation."

"And if I don't make it?"

"Then you'll be relegated to some menial job around here somewhere until you prove yourself. Or, maybe, you'll be sent off to the army right away. If you want to become a cadre instead of a soldier, don't argue with them about where they send you. You have to pay your dues, you know."

Wei lost track of Mingzhu in all of his excitement, but at least he recalled wishing her well.

Owing to his background, Wei was sent to a nearby farm to stay before receiving his permanent assignment. Fortunately for him, he wasn't relegated to some straw and wood, mud-floored hut, where most of the peasant soldiers appeared to be living.

Wei's host was relatively inhospitable, but he gave Wei some dinner and showed him the bunkhouse where his sons had lived before they married. A wooden platform bed covered with a reed mat sat near the door. A lantern hung on the wall by a rusty nail.

Wei spent several hours that evening reading by the light of the lantern until the fuel was almost gone, refreshing his memory from the materials he borrowed. He felt good about his preparation.

The next morning he was first in line to see Mr. Mei.

"You are persistent aren't you, Wei?"

"Yes, sir. So can I take the exam?"

"You made it past round one, so be here at one o'clock sharp to take the exam. Be on time, or you could be on that farm for a long time."

Wei turned in his completed test papers and was again told to return the following day.

"Well, Wei, you passed the test with flying colors," Mr. Mei said, astonished.

"Told you."

"Don't get smart with me. The interview will be a lot tougher. Tomorrow morning, you'll meet with Huang Hua, our head of education. He will put you through your paces, that's for sure."

Wei's host refueled the lantern and Wei stayed up late for a second night, brushing up on the writings of Karl Marx, Friedrich Engels, Vladimir Lenin, and Joseph Stalin. For good measure, Wei memorized some quotes from Chairman Mao, including two he thought might persuade his interviewer to endorse him.

"The competition is tough," Mr. Huang said. "Wei, just so you know, we're processing over seven hundred applications every month and there aren't many slots for cadre training and education, so your chances of getting in to the Party School are still pretty slim."

"Thank you, Mr. Huang," Wei said. "And if I may begin, I respectfully offer this quote attributed to Chairman Mao from August of last year as a commentary on our situation today. 'Revolutions and revolutionary wars are inevitable in class society, and without them, it is impossible to accomplish any leap in social development and to overthrow the reactionary ruling classes, and therefore impossible for the people to win political power.'

"And also, this one from October of this year: 'The Chinese Communist Party is a party leading a great revolutionary struggle in a nation several hundred million strong, and it cannot fulfill its historic task without a large number of leading cadres who combine ability with political integrity.'"

Hua was duly impressed with Wei throughout the interview. Wei's demonstrated understanding of Chinese communism based on social situations in rural China had paved the way for his endorsement as a student in the Party School after all.

He would not be spending much time on the farm or in the army.

Wei moved his things to a semi-below-ground dormitory that housed students pursuing various other disciplines.

He began his studies in a classroom of a former Catholic church with some three hundred other students. Under Mao's presidency, the school indoctrinated its followers by reeducating them with "Mao Zedong Thought" emphasizing ethics and morality as part of a new democracy with liberal reforms.

Wei became enamored with Han Feng, who oversaw the party's internal security and intelligence gathering machinery, although Wei had some disdain for his reportedly brutal methods of dealing with perceived traitors who spoke ill of Mao. Nevertheless, Wei curried favor with Mr. Han in an attempt to self-promote his own ambition.

Feng often made reference to Wei as a shining star and a prime example of the youthful contribution to the party's future that they were looking for.

After two years of training and showing exemplary communist thought in his essays and speeches before his class, Wei was given an assignment to counsel new recruits who had been admitted to the school.

Wei never missed an address by any of the party leaders, so he could learn the best way to create loyalty and support among his own recruits.

The NRA, under Chiang Kai-shek's command, was consumed with its defense against the Japanese. Even so, they utilized a reported one-half million troops in an attempt to keep Mao bottled up in Yan'an.

All the while, the CPC enjoyed a period of relative peace in Yan'an as Mao's army personnel in the field continued to provide an additional level of support to the KMT for the anti-Japanese war effort. The "Yan'an Reds" as they were called, developed a camaraderie and feeling of achievement as they followed a particular set of rules with dos and don'ts when they interacted with the local peasants. The Reds' show of consideration for the peasants' feelings engendered support for the communists and their revolutionary cause.

During World War II, Mao Zedong undertook an effort to consolidate his power base. Wei was surprised to learn that Mao had competition for his leadership of the party, but Wei's infatuation with Mao convinced him that he should do whatever he could to support him.

A significant element of Mao's plan came to be known as the Rectification Movement, designed to purge the party of dissidents in three phases. His plan essentially put himself in charge, unrivaled.

During the first phase, Mao managed to create self-doubt and criticism among his adversaries to the degree that he was able to cement his control of the party through a committee of his choosing.

As the second phase got underway, Mao's henchmen succeeded at forcing confessions of wrong doing by his political enemies who had fallen for foreign theories. Then, he set up the Central General Study Committee to allow him to exercise all authority without elections or term limits.

Wei was in attendance at the Party School on February 1, 1942 when Mao gave a lecture before thousands of cadres. At the end of his talk, Mao declared: "Why must there be a revolutionary party? There must be a revolutionary party because our enemies still exist; and furthermore, there must not be only an ordinary revolutionary party, but a Communist revolutionary party."

The crowd applauded for ten minutes.

As Wei left the auditorium that evening, he accidently ran into his friend Mingzhu who had also been invigorated by the evening's propaganda.

"I am so happy to see you, Mingzhu. I've missed you. I can't believe it's been almost three years since we arrived. How have I managed to avoid running into you in all that time?"

"Probably because I've been living more than thirty-five miles from here, close to the Academy of the Arts. My mother owned a dance studio in Shanghai before she closed it after my father's murder, so I was assigned to the academy because of my schooling. I've been over there ever since, studying dance as a form of local culture and performing political theater art. Have you heard of our revolutionary opera?"

"No, but I am sorry to hear about your father. I don't recall your telling me that."

"Well, that's a part of war, and I can't look back."

Wei and Mingzhu married soon after their chance meeting.

Privately, Wei wished his parents could have been there to celebrate the occasion, although he didn't mention it to Mingzhu. In an earlier conversation, Wei had speculated that they surely must have perished in the extensive bombing and fires in Canton that started shortly after he left. Wei became totally consumed with his day-to-day responsibilities, and the subject never came up again until much later.

Two years later, to Wei's total delight, Mingzhu delivered a son. Little Jinli was born on January 17, 1943, in a Year of the Horse, according to the Chinese Zodiac. Wei was also born under the same sign, and he hoped that Jinli would inherit his own traits. Yongmin always said that Wei was "strong of character with aspirations."

Wei's superiors celebrated Jinli's birth with a reward for Wei's faithful service, and he and Mingzhu were reassigned to a large cave home near several officials' and officers' quarters. Their new home had two rooms, a wooden tub for bathing with a cauldron for heating well water, and it was free of the rats that were so prevalent elsewhere.

Living together was a welcome relief, since they had previously been assigned to separate dormitories and had only been allowed to be together on Saturdays.

Many of the older women who survived the long march to Yan'an became love mates to the officers, but still, the practice of relative isolation of women reduced the potential for their abuse. Nevertheless, the young female recruits fashioned themselves more as Noras, the theatrical symbol of a new China that was characterized in Ibsen's play, "A Doll's House." In it, Nora was featured as the role model of independence, freedom, and courage. It was the image of Nora that was starting to be adopted by rebellious women who bravely defied society to seek after freedom and independence from male domination, and for many of the recruits, separation from men in Yan'an suited them just fine. Revolution became their calling.

During the final phase of the rectification campaign that began a year later, Mr. Huang tapped Wei to help reeducate party members about party history and seek group retribution, the ultimate goal of rectification. Members mistakenly thought Mao would accept genuine criticism, and spoke their true feelings of anger over the hierarchy and inequality in Yan'an.

Such was not the case, and members were encouraged to admit to "errors" and "confess" wrong thought or action, and to blame others as well for the same offenses. It became a game of pointing fingers, as everyone sought to direct attention away from himself.

Fortunately for Wei, he was not responsible for judging the errors he ferreted out of the confessions. His job was simply to identify them and pass them along to Mr. Han and his abettors to mete out their discipline, or punishment. Mr. Han relished using his power to exact punishment, whether the confessions were true or not. He was especially adept at targeting members formerly associated with the KMT who were dealt with most harshly, including censorship, confinement, imprisonment, torture, forced famine, or even death. They were labeled as anti-party activists, or sympathizers of the KMT. Even their families and relatives were subject to humiliation. Only a confession of their crimes or a willingness to implicate others, regardless of the truth, could save them from persecution.

Wei became angry when he learned that many innocent people were needlessly put to death.

The democide may have been the greatest in all of history.

Wei's anger turned to weariness with the process, and he questioned if he had made the right choice in coming to Yan'an. The summer sun and the winter rages, punctuated by the occasional Japanese air raids, were beginning to wear thin, and given the devastating history of opium's addiction, he questioned the morality of Mao's consent to the growing of it to generate funds to support his war effort.

"Mingzhu, how do you feel about the process I'm engaged in now? I know I'm doing what a loyal party member should be doing, but I can't put the idea out of my mind that some individuals are being coerced into confessing to crimes they didn't commit. I've heard tales of beatings, persecution, executions, and banishment to labor camps. It just doesn't seem right to me. Doesn't everyone have a right to his own thoughts, even if he doesn't speak publically about what he's thinking? I just don't understand it. A lot of these atrocities aren't really justified."

"Regardless of your personal feelings," she responded graciously, "you just have to dedicate yourself to continue performing your duties to the best of your ability. If we believe in communism, we have to trust that our leaders are doing the right things. There will always be dissent. We have to keep our eyes on the prize of a unified country with equal opportunity for all. I want that for our son when he grows up, don't you?"

"Of course, but this isn't easy for me. Remember, I came from an area governed by the KMT, and I'm always on guard to avoid becoming a suspect myself."

"All right. But remember, you're a willing participant in a just cause, even if we agree that the cause may not justify the methods that they're using. You are the only one who can reconcile your morality with your actions. I think you can overcome your fear if you will just follow your intuition for doing good, and if necessary, pray. Wei, things will change."

Pray? Wei was surprised by that remark. Ming had never uttered that word before. But no matter, he had forgotten how anyway.

Wei excelled in his new position, and Mr. Huang took favor on him.

After World War II ended with the Japanese surrender and the repatriation effort to return their troops to Japan began, the civil war started to heat up again. After eight long years of semi-reconciliation between the CPC and KMT while they jointly battled the Japanese, their struggle for control resumed in earnest.

As Mao plotted his next moves, intelligence reports began to pour in, alerting him to Chiang's plan to oust him from his nest in the mountains.

CHAPTER 4 ~ The Struggle

MARCH 19, 1947

Before the NRA could reach Yan'an, the communists closed all their schools, including the Anti-Japanese Military and Political University and the Party School, and their leaders fled the capital.

Wei packed up his family well ahead of the anticipated attack and left the city with instructions from Mr. Huang.

They headed west to Pingliang, about three hundred miles away, in the company of the military personnel headed that way. The rural area had been liberated from the KMT by communist forces, and it was now a stronghold of the East China Field Army of the People's Liberation Army (PLA), preparing for a counter-offensive against Chiang. The PLA had been known earlier as the Red Army.

Once they reached Pingliang, Wei assumed his position as a Communist Party recruiter and work team leader for land reform in the surrounding area, the positions assigned to him by Mr. Huang.

What a welcoming, if not challenging, situation to be in, Wei thought. There, he would be free from the daily struggles and fog of war that he had faced in Yan'an. He hoped his family life would become a little more normal, even if it might become strained by the fear that war could heat up again.

As it turned out, life would be anything but normal.

As Wei became familiar with the local village peasants, his team began to educate them about their planned introduction of a land reform policy, the principal feature of the Communist Party line. The peasants affected by the new policy were eager to own their own land, and after years of waiting, it seemed to them as if it might finally be at hand.

The old twenty-five percent rent and interest reduction concept of land reform that had prevailed before the war was being replaced with land confiscation and its distribution to peasants. It was the job of Wei's team to investigate land ownership in the area and implement the new policy. The CPC's aim was to destroy the old social order of things.

First, his team had to determine the classification of the local peasants and implement a plan to return the "land-to-the-tiller," as the practice was often called. The land and other property of landlords were to be expropriated and redistributed so that each village household would have a comparable holding. People were to be categorized either as landlords, rich peasants, middle peasants, poor peasants, or laborers, to distinguish between those who rented some or all of their land, worked their own land, or simply provided labor to others.

For years, Mao had defined landlords as anyone, including their political representatives, who exploited peasants through rent collection, usurious money transactions, and power.

Rich peasants were defined as landlords who rented part or all of their land, or made loans.

Middle peasants were those who owned land, but rented out part of it without exploiting others, due to an infirmity or old age, for example.

Poor peasants were generally those who had to pay land rent or interest on loans, or hire themselves out for part of their income, or were otherwise exploited.

Workers generally owned no land and hired themselves out.

Some other work teams required people to wear armbands of different colors to distinguish one's classification from another, but Wei felt it was counter-productive and dismissed the idea as being too contentious.

Before Wei arrived in Pingliang, the land belonging to landlords had been confiscated, but rich peasants were left alone. Now, as the new policy was put in place, Wei's leadership would be tested in "settling accounts" with rich peasants who resisted the taking of their land. As for the middle peasants, they were encouraged to "voluntarily" offer their surplus land for redistribution.

Wei's experience in dealing with self-examination was helpful in hearing the complaints and charges of peasants who felt disadvantaged in some way. His calm and reasoned approach was effective in redistributing land, and he was able to avoid a lot of bloodshed by telling reluctant peasants what the results of their complaining might be, offering examples of what he'd seen in Yan'an.

Privately, Wei was somewhat ashamed about taking that approach, because he was not particularly proud of his participation in the earlier practice that led to purging suspected traitors and their probable demise. His disdain for the democide he witnessed over the previous six years was a feeling he had to keep under control at all times.

He kept urging the peasants to "go along" in order to "get along."

Regardless, he was in a constant mental battle with his actions versus his thinking, and he recalled a Bible passage he had read in school, Romans 13:1 of his American Standard Version Bible. "Let every soul be in subjection to the higher powers: for there is no power but of God; and the powers that be are ordained of God."

He had tried to dismiss his willingness to follow the orders of his superiors when he felt that their approach to their subordinates was so wrong, but he was unable to do so.

Is there really a God? Wei kept asking himself. If there is, he hadn't seen His presence in the things he'd witnessed. Why would God put people like Han Feng in charge of anything? Can murder be justified? Is Mao really an instrument of God? Is He in control of a master plan that will eventually lead to civility and peace? Can I justify my continuing involvement in the communist movement as a means to an end?

Wei had had enough of war and there were just too many questions puzzling his mind.

He had endless conversations with Mingzhu about them, but as they talked it out, they came to a mutual understanding. They agreed that in spite of any negative thinking, they would continue to support their leaders and work toward an end to hostilities. Their decision was mainly for the benefit of their son, recognizing that their contribution in that effort might nevertheless be a small one.

In the fall of that year, a new Outline Agrarian Law was promulgated.

"Here comes another change," Wei announced.

"What now?" Mingzhu asked.

"The new law will abolish the ownership rights of 'all landlords and of all ancestral halls, temples, monasteries, schools, and other organizations.'"

"So what does that mean?"

"It means that all debts are canceled, and now we have to set up an association to take all the land in the villages and apportion it and all houses, animals, and farm implements among all the peasants, regardless of who they are. Everyone will get a comparable amount of land. Of course, traitors and criminals will get nothing. It's going to be a very difficult challenge to bring all of that about, but it will be my duty to make it happen."

And, of course, he did make it happen.

After two agonizing years in Pingliang, Wei and Mingzhu were elated when the CPC finally won the civil war, and Mao Zedong proclaimed the People's Republic of China on October 1, 1949, with its capital in Beijing, formerly called Peking.

There was great fanfare and celebration in virtually every Chinese village. At last, the country was unified under one government. Wei and Mingzhu had followed their instincts, and it had started to pay off.

In April 1950, the CPC sent Wei to Kaiping in the Siyi area of the Pearl River delta, downstream from Guangzhou. The official Mandarin name of Guangzhou had replaced the English name of Canton when the PRC was formed.

At first, the earlier land use policies Wei followed in Pingliang continued in place in Kaiping. He thought about his father frequently as he evaluated the peasants in his new jurisdiction. He wondered if Yongmin was still on his farm, just eighty miles away, and if his father's work party had considered him to be a landlord, or a rich peasant, or a middle peasant. How had he been treated, and what had happened to his him and his land?

Wei feared the impact of land reform effort on his father, though he made no attempt to contact him or visit his old home.

Wei was relieved in late June, when the PRC codified its reform practice by publishing a new Land, or Agrarian Reform Law; however, this provided him with an entirely new challenge.

In the nineteenth century, the people from Siyi who left for Hong Kong, Southeast Asia, Australia, and the Americas became known as "Overseas Chinese." It started with emigration for railroad and mining jobs and continued with agricultural work and other opportunities as they opened up.

With the new law, Wei wrestled with how to deal with those Overseas Chinese who were now living abroad, but continued to rent out their land in China. In other words, should they lose their land?

The status of landlords became the main question. He had to deal with a plethora of concerns about how to evaluate the people who had left, those who returned, and how their families fitted into those situations.

It was hoped that the new law, designed to help end the feudal practices of centuries, would help to settle this particular lingering issue. It did so for a while, but Wei got caught up in interpreting the law. Many "sojourners" were still Chinese patriots, and he questioned if they really should be punished!

In and around Wei's area, discerning the identities of Overseas Chinese was extremely difficult because of unreliable records and less than truthful relatives. However, the poor peasants were not so vague in their assessment of their landlords, and they were very quick to condemn them.

The new law defined Overseas Chinese as anyone who had lived abroad for at least one year while the rest of their family stayed in China. However, anyone who had returned home more than three years before the passage of the new law was excluded from the definition.

If a family was considered to be a landlord before its member emigrated, the family would be designated as an Overseas Chinese and would lose its land, unless the family rented out a portion of it to peasants because of age or infirmity and had to do so to survive. Regardless, if their land holding exceeded 200 percent of the average in the area, they would still lose part of their land.

If they became a landlord after the member went overseas, they would lose their land, but be permitted to keep their house and some personal property.

What a mess, Wei thought, as he struggled to understand the law. It was so totally convoluted that he simply sought the most favorable outcome for the families in his area, regardless of the law's most strict interpretation.

Dealing with the Overseas Chinese who were still living in a non-Chinese country, the so-called Huaqiao people required both experience and diplomacy. Wei was adept rendering decisions that were deemed legally valid, yet compassionate toward those whose farmland was expropriated.

Wei's constituents respected him greatly for the fair way in which he managed the reforms. When Jiangmen became a city in 1951 with jurisdiction over several areas, including Kaping, he was elected to the local People's Congress, China's new parliament, and became a Deputy Commissioner of Kaping's Administrative Office.

That was the beginning of his political career.

But while his election was personally satisfying, it brought the perils of elective office with it.

After China entered the Korean War, the targets of agrarian land reform policies were expanded to include so-called "enemies of the state," including those foreigners and Christian missionaries who were deemed to be agents of the United States. War criminals, traitors, bureaucratic capitalists, and counter- revolutionaries were at the forefront of the drive.

The reforms focused on the same self-criticism and public confessions that Wei had witnessed earlier. The object was to purge the political structure of incompetent or unethical officials and create a more honest and disciplined system by eliminating the corruptive efforts of businessmen and industrialists.

The class interest of working people was extended to involve every aspect of society, including the arts and other cultural forms.

Wei was adept at maneuvering himself throughout that period by maintaining a low profile and avoiding making any statement or performing any activity that could be construed as taking an anti-communist position.

Knowing Mingzhu's strong passion in taking a stand for her beliefs, Wei also cautioned her to refrain from any form of criticism of any person or thing.

By 1953, Wei had expanded his popularity among his constituents and his superiors, and he became the Mayor of Jiangmen, with an appointment as Deputy Secretary of the CPC Jiangmen Municipal Committee.

As the country moved toward more industrialization, the centralized government adopted a collective approach toward agriculture, and Wei was once more at the forefront of yet another rural land reform policy.

Land ownership didn't change, but farmers were "encouraged" to form mutual aid teams to share their labor. Soon after, their tools and draft animals were added in to form producers' cooperatives, in which each member shared in the profits of the collective farm, divided early on by their respective land ownership and later on by the efforts of their individual labor.

As collective farming progressed, Wei wondered if his father made the transition without anger or hostility.

In 1957, when Jinli was eleven, he developed a keen interest in his family's background and history when the subject was introduced at school.

Mingzhu explained to him that her father had been killed in the war and that her mother had not been heard of since Shanghai was destroyed. Wei was tentative in his response and said he hadn't spoken to his father since he left home following a discussion of political differences.

Jinli asked if he could meet his grandparents. Wei promised to try and locate them but explained that it wouldn't be easy to track them down among the scores of peoples' communes, each with twenty thousand people controlling all of the production in their accounting unit. Wei also noted that he would have to proceed carefully to avoid any inference during his search that his father's support of the KMT might be seen as an indication of his own underlying or suppressed allegiance to it. Wei was certain that Yongmin would have never changed his political position.

Wei had ambitions to obtain an office in a larger jurisdiction, but by this time, the government was beginning to recognize the value of intellectuals, and was starting to promote more accomplished individuals to better positions. Although Wei was a team player who had never burned any bridges, he feared he would be overlooked because of his lack of a university education.

In spite of that, he was thankful for his good life and was never bitter. Mingzhu was likewise happy in her role and never complained or felt shunned, even when she was around the wives of the "get-ahead-at-any-cost" political hacks who were either incompetent, critical of their superiors, or on the take.

Mingzhu believed justice would come sooner or later, and she encouraged Wei to stay the course.

In spite of his lack of intellectual credentials, Wei was reelected in 1958, and he pressed on, maintaining a spirit of encouragement to pass along to Jinli.

Still maintaining an unwavering faith in Mao, Wei hoped for better times.

Better times were ahead, but they were interrupted that same year by Mao's attempt to hasten industrialization and crop production with his "Great Leap Forward" movement, as it came to be known. Mao's desire was to compete with the industrialized nations of the world by utilizing China's cheap labor. His plan was to become a world leader in grain production and turn scrap metal into usable steel.

The three-year effort came to an end in 1961 when unrealistic production estimates and bad farming ideas gleaned from the Soviets, coupled with a drought, resulted in less grain for the peasants. The government continued to give priority to exports and the needs of city dwellers, and it left millions of peasants to die of starvation or suicide.

At the same time, the effort to produce steel failed, because the pig iron produced on farms in backyard furnaces was of such incredibly low quality.

The movement's failure resulted in the loss of much of Mao's power base. Wei was also discouraged because of its failure, but never mentioned his personal dissatisfaction with the program. Had that become known, he would no doubt have been sent to a prison or a commune, where he would have died.

Wei was devastated when he finally got word about his parents. They had died during the famine. The news was hard to explain to Jinli, who had waited so long for an answer. Wei told him that not knowing their whereabouts had left him powerless to do anything about it. Jinli was disappointed with the effort his father had made to locate them, but he was forced to accept the outcome.

Wei and Mingzhu doted on their son, and after the famine caused so many deaths, including Wei's own parents, they hoped that Jinli's potential might someday be realized to help lift China out of its misery and despair.

When the American president Kennedy signed the Emergency Immigration Act in 1962, it authorized five thousand Chinese to enter the U.S. as refugees to escape the catastrophic economic conditions resulting from the failure of the Great Leap Forward.

When Wei heard about it, he quickly put a plan together that he hoped would draw attention to Jinli, who he believed had an extremely bright future in the CPC.

Earlier, when Jinli started school at age six, the same year the PRC was formed, he demonstrated a remarkable intellect that was evident to all his teachers, and by the time he had reached age fifteen, he had mastered both the Cantonese and Mandarin dialects of the Chinese language. He had also become proficient in English since it was taught throughout the Guangzhou area because of its proximity to British-controlled Hong Kong.

Wei's plan was for Jinli to emigrate as a refugee in compliance with the provisions of the new law, while, in reality, he would go there to study and observe capitalism at work in America. He wouldn't be a "spy" in the classic sense, nor an "agent" of the Chinese government, but he would be required to maintain copious notes on his experiences while he was in America and submit a report on those observations as Wei's requirement for his study abroad.

Wei was convinced that America was evil and that Jinli would learn the ways of the materialistic and self-indulgent Americans first hand. His report would be certain to dispel the evils of capitalism as a superior economic system that preys on the working class, and when he returned, Wei would submit it to his superiors. The government was always looking for a public relations angle, and he believed that would be a good one.

Normally, a "sojourner" in the United States would likely stay there, as many of them do. But in this instance, Wei believed that Jinli's desire to follow in his own footsteps would be sufficient to draw him back to China.

"Son, I have exciting news to share with you," Wei announced, as he described the opportunity and what he had in mind. "You've already graduated high school and started your advanced studies, but you have a chance to get a college degree in the United States. I know it will pay big dividends for you in the future. There is one condition, however. You must promise me that you will prepare a full report on what you learn and return immediately after you graduate. Can I depend on you to do those things?"

"Yes, Father. You have my promise."

Jinli had seen the devastation reeked by the Great Leap Forward, including the death of his grandparents, and when he considered the opportunity, he secretly looked forward to experiencing a different kind of life. He was full of sympathy for what his people had suffered, but now his sorrow might be replaced with happiness, even if it lasted for only a few short years.

He didn't relish the thought of what might happen at home during his absence, but at least he knew he should be safe until he got back.

Wei had secretly maintained contact with a few expatriates who moved to Taiwan after Chang Kai-shek retreated from the mainland, and he was able to make arrangements through a friend stationed there in the United States Embassy for Jinli to apply for admission to the University of Southern California in Los Angeles, California.

It was well known that USC was welcoming foreign students. Jinli's grade transcript and application were quickly processed and approved, together with an offer of a full scholarship.

Wei's surreptitious activity was never found out.

As Jinli prepared to leave, Wei handed him the diaries he had kept for almost twenty-four years. They included over twelve hundred weekly entries contained in several volumes.

"Son," he said, recalling his own bittersweet memory of leaving home at about the same age, "I want you to take these with you and read the account of my life after leaving home myself so you can appreciate the struggles your mother and I endured to be able to send you on this mission. China is on the threshold of a major new chapter in its glorious history, and now you have a chance to be a part of it."

Jinli cleared Customs and Immigration at the Los Angeles International Airport with his passport and refugee papers in hand, and headed off to the campus of the University of Southern California to start college.

CHAPTER 5 ~ The Mission

SEPTEMBER 17, 1962

Jinli stopped at the newsstand as he walked across the campus on his way to the convocation for new students and picked up a copy of the day's edition of the *Daily Trojan* newspaper, or DT, as it was called.

The editor had penned a question in big letters on the front page: "WHY ARE YOU IN COLLEGE?"

The article below began "Four years to dream … what is a dream? It is an escape from the hardness of life … College is such a dream. It is purposeful preparation of the self for an intelligible role in society, a means to judge the pressing weight of the past and its effect on the relation of your personal race to the cosmos."

Jinli read it and reread it, wondering if it was a sign meant for him. His life so far seemed to fit the parameters of the thought. The question was meaningful, even if it was presented in a rather inarticulate way. He guessed the editor was probably an engineering student.

Weeklong orientation activities called "Troy Week," were underway, including deans' meetings with new students, a luncheon, and fireside chats with other students. A "Spirit Rally" was scheduled for the next day, to be followed by campus tours. A lot of the activities appeared to be rather superfluous to him. He had already gone to a meeting with the Dean of the School of Business Administration for freshmen, and that alone made him feel like part of the college scene.

The previous week, the Chancellor had invited the ninety new foreign students to a meeting where they were to receive an orientation kit, including a handbook, a map of the campus, a schedule of classes, a football schedule, and a guide to the Southern California area.

Jinli was anxious to get settled into his room, so hadn't gone. He knew he would feel a little like a fish out of water after hearing there were only two or three other Chinese students enrolled for the fall and that they were all enrolled in the School of Pharmacy. *They were probably Chinese-American*, he thought, and assumed he wouldn't have much in common with them.

However, on the advice of his dorm counselor, he reluctantly went down to the office and picked up one of the kits.

Jinli studied his school's class bulletin, and two days later, he rushed to the registration tables in the gymnasium as soon as the doors opened in the morning, having heard that most of the popular classes would fill up quickly.

Once inside, Jinli felt a little like a monkey in a zoo, competing for the tastiest morsels. The process seemed like organized chaos, but by noon he was finished and pleased to get eighteen units of the undergraduate classes he needed. 128 units were required to graduate, and he planned to take a heavy load every semester, including summer school, and finish in three years. He saw no point in stringing it out.

Finishing early was his goal, and he wouldn't allow anything to deter him in that pursuit. It would mean concentrating on his studies and not letting himself get side tracked by extracurricular activities. He would need to apply all the discipline he learned growing up.

Now his college career was underway. He had two goals to reach before returning home: to get his degree in economics, and to compile the best report possible for his father. Jinli planned to keep a weekly journal just as his father had done, so that later on he could recall his impressions of life in America. Anecdotal evidence would be sufficient. He made his first entry at the end of orientation week, noting the attitudes and behavior of the people he encountered.

As classes began, he was a little timid, but made every effort to mingle with his fellow students. They were used to seeing foreign students around campus, and he felt welcomed. He became more confident as time passed, but shied away from getting too close to any of them. His reluctance was more the result of his cultural heritage than others' treatment of him as a newcomer.

There always seemed to be a small group of the same talkative students huddling outside his microeconomics class every morning before it began, discussing the day's assignment, or just "shooting the breeze," as they called it. Even though he generally had little to offer, he was frequently invited to sit in on their conversations. Jinli appreciated their gesture.

From what he was able to glean, they came mostly from homes with college-educated parents with decent jobs. Not surprising, he learned this was typical of a private university.

If their chatter wasn't about sports, or their next fraternity party, it was football. USC was hoping for another national championship season, and there was a buzz about it everywhere on campus.

Their inane talk didn't surprise him, though. Most of them acted as if they had been living the somewhat uncomplicated type life that Jinli had seen back home on pirated television shows like "Leave it to Beaver" and "The Adventures of Ozzie and Harriet." They had been broadcast from Hong Kong before the government jammed the transmissions and shut them down.

Jinli thought their lives must be pretty straightforward with no serious worries, much like the TV characters. *That's pretty sad,*

51

he thought to himself. *If they could walk in the shoes of my friends back home, they would have more important things to talk about.*

His economics classes presented him with a basic understanding of free market capitalism, ignoring any discussion of competing systems, just as he expected. He would have to find other sources of information to help him discredit capitalism.

He turned to the idea of getting firsthand views rather than look for textbook examples in the library, and decided to approach his friendly classmates as a starting point. He had found that people usually respond positively when you ask them for help, especially if you are a foreigner, and that offering help is a fairly common trait of many Americans, especially when it's in their interest to do so.

One morning when there was plenty of spare time before class, he approached the group and said, "Hey guys, good morning. I need a little help today."

"Glad to help. What's on your mind?" a student named Tyler asked.

Jinli jumped right into it. "What do you think about your prospects for success after graduation?"

At first, he thought Jinli was kidding. "Isn't that a rather serious question for so early in the morning? How'd you come up with that one?"

"I have to do a report for my father back home. Do you plan for your own employment, or does the government decide for you? At home, we have a central government planning process. People get jobs based on direct state assignments, but I don't know how it works here in America."

"All right, I'll take a crack at it. Jinli, here in America, sometimes it's just a matter of who you know. In my case, my dad is a banker, and I don't expect any problems in getting a good job. A lot of guys down at Lincoln Savings are SC grads. Capish?"

Jinli looked up the word up later.

Pete added, "Forget what Tyler just said. You just have to get out there, find a job and work your butt off. It's dog eats dog.

It's all about competition. Isn't that what we're learning in class? Capitalism thrives on competition."

"So that's what you would call Free Market Competition?"

"Yes, absolutely. All I know is that no one here is going to tell you where to work, certainly not our government. Let's just say you decide to go into sales and you beat the other guy to the top by selling more widgets than he does and your company's profits go up. Voila! You'd likely be laughing all the way to the bank. And the people making the widgets should do better, too. Everybody wins. 'To the victor go the spoils,' as they say."

"I think I understand. So, one guy wins, and the other one loses. Is that about it?"

"It's a little more complicated than that, but I guess you would say that the poor slob who loses probably has to find another way to make a buck."

Jinli adopted a cynical view of those classmates after that discussion, as he pondered their explanation that capitalism rewards those with initiative while those without it are left to fall by the wayside.

"But what's a 'widget'?" he asked himself.

The bell rang and they hurried to class.

Later that evening, Jinli looked up the definition of "widget." He considered Pete's example of reward based on initiative compared to the way things operate in China where the government is in charge of everything. Workers there pretty much make the same wage and no one gets a reward if sales increase, so there's no incentive to try and sell more widgets. *At least everyone has a job,* he thought.

The next day, Jinli told the guys he had been thinking about the widget example. "Pete, I'm really interested in the poor guy with no 'who you know' way to get ahead, and works for a company that fails to meet their competition and gets laid off and can't find another job. What about him?"

"Well, if he can't get another job or keeps getting laid off, he might ultimately wind up begging on the street, or turning to crime or drugs. That's a problem that our society tolerates but doesn't do much to correct. That's when our government should come to the rescue. There are a lot of social programs, but they cost a lot of money, and most of them seem to fail in the long run. We have private charities, but in the final analysis, they haven't been able to solve those problems either.

"Look, this is a free country where the rewards go to those who work for them. And if you don't want to work for them, you have the freedom to fail and suffer the consequences. Freedom is the main issue."

"So it's up to everyone to figure out for themselves how to succeed? Is that what you're saying?"

"I guess that's about it."

At least I'm getting to the truth now, as sad as it seems, Jinli thought, as he reflected on their conversation. *Pete seems to have a handle on my question, but I can't understand why all these guys think their system is so superior to ours.*

The encounter provided some ammunition for his report as well as the small, but helpful, by-product of learning some new idioms. He realized that school doesn't teach you everything because he hadn't heard any of them before. They improved his conversational skills, although he decided not to overuse them for fear of sounding too pretentious.

Two months into the semester, Jinli got his midterm grades back, and they were all A's. He reported his progress in his first letter home after arriving and hoped that his father would be pleased.

And so it went. He studied constantly and continued to get straight A's. He was always at the top of the standings in every class.

It seemed as if Jinli's challenging freshman year passed in a hurry and he was ready for a change of pace when the spring semester ended. He took a somewhat lighter class load in the summer session so he could devote more time to do research for his report. He wanted to get it finished, because he was told his classes would only get harder with each succeeding semester.

As school began in the summer of 1963, Jinli approached the Teaching Assistant in his business economics class and asked for some help. Jinli told him he wanted to find some real life examples of capitalism at work, so he could relate them to the marketing class he was taking in the fall.

"Do you know anyone in sales, or manufacturing, or business in general whom I could meet with this summer?" he asked.

"Sure, but I have a better idea for you. I'll show you a real, real-life example of how capitalism isn't working."

That's a great idea, he thought. *That's really what he wanted to learn about anyway.*

"Go do a survey of the folks in the low-income area of Watts and see how they feel about capitalism. Watts is in South Central Los Angeles, just south of the campus, not too far from here. They won't call it capitalism, but they'll tell you plenty."

"What will they call it?"

"They'll describe it differently in terms of discrimination, primarily because of their color. It's become part of their lives. You'll have to ask them what they call it.

"In fact, I'm going on a bus trip to Washington, D.C. in August to join my brothers and sisters for the 'March on Washington for Jobs and Freedom.' They're coming from everywhere, but mostly from the South. We'll be celebrating the hundredth anniversary of the signing of the Emancipation Proclamation by President Lincoln. Martin Luther King, Jr. will be there as the main speaker. There is still so much we have to do to stamp out the discrimination that still exists after all these years."

The civil rights movement in the South sure to be newsworthy around the globe, so Jinli decided it would be a good thing to feature in his report.

"Do you have discrimination in China?" the TA asked.

"Yes, some, but mostly in terms of income equality. It's been a problem forever. My father has dealt with inequality in wealth related to land ownership for most of his career. Oh, and we can add ethnicity and religion to the list as well."

"See, it's a problem everywhere, and we should work to correct it. Go talk to the folks down in Watts. You'll get an earful."

"Will it be safe for me to go down there?"

"See, you're already forming an opinion about those people. I think you'll find wonderful people down there just like you find everywhere. They just have to struggle a little more for what little they get.

Jinli would learn later that his conservatively thinking classmates, not surprisingly, labeled the TA as a "flaming liberal."

Jinli got what he needed as he rode around the area on his bicycle greeting people on the streets or in their front yards. Most of the bungalow houses were small, modest, run-down stucco structures with asphalt shingle roofs, bars on the windows, and doors for security. He became a little frightened when he saw their living conditions, but most everyone was friendly so he kept on going.

Some of the black folks he encountered seemed to be a little skeptical of him, but with a fair number of Asians also living in the area, no one really questioned his presence there. He always introduced himself as an exchange student doing research for a class paper about life in the United States and said he just had a few questions.

The folks who were willing to talk to him extensively would jump right in with examples of their problems living in both Los Angeles and wherever they came from originally. "It's pretty much the same all over," they would say. One person commented, "If you're black in Georgia, you're still black when you get to California." They had no hesitation talking about the laws and discrimination they faced on a daily basis in housing, employment, education, and politics.

Jinli hit a raw nerve when he asked them if community relations with the police created any feeling of racial injustice. Their answers were a unanimous "Yes," and he sensed that big trouble was brewing. "You come back at night. You'll see 'em in action," someone added.

He eventually hit the jackpot when he encountered a particular black man relaxing in a lounge chair on the grass of his neatly-maintained front yard. The man was an archetypal local resident of South Central, and his story provided all the details Jinli needed.

By this time, Jinli had perfected the art of asking questions designed to produce the opinions and answers he needed to support his foregone conclusions.

When asked, the man said his name was Archibald Jubilee Jackson. "My mother called me A. J. or Jubal," he said, but I likes 'Archie' better."

"So tell me about yourself, Archie."

"All right. I'll start off with my family. We moved here from Texas 'cause I needed work, and I heard lots of defense jobs here were beggin' to be filled. We wanted to settle near my new job in the Long Beach shipyards, but the law said we couldn't live in a lot of places, so we was lucky to find this place here in Watts, bad as it is."

"What do you mean?

"Well, the law said no black folks could buy houses in the area close to my job, and white folks done had all the good ones anyway. It was written on the property records, they said. Called it a deed restriction. They acted like they privileged or somethin'."

"So what happened?"

"Well my job went away after the war, and me and my wife just been doin' odd jobs ever since. Any decent jobs was goin' to white folks. My wife was able to get a job cleanin' rooms in a hotel downtown for a while but some foreigner done took that job and she got laid off. We even thought we'd pick up a couple of bucks now and then if we got a jury notice, but there's not much chance of gittin' picked if you're black."

"Didn't you keep looking for permanent jobs?"

"I guess you could say we did. For a while we had a little money and we would both take the Red Car to go lookin', but those streetcars quit runnin' last year. Makes no matter. Now we can't even afford bus fare to go lookin'. I guess we kinda trapped here, ya know? So here we is. It's hard."

"Do you have children?"

"Yes, we got two in high school now. They go to Jordan, but a lady keeps comin' by wantin' us to file a lawsuit so they can get bussed over to South Gate. I think they'd be better off over there, but that school don't want us. A couple of Jordan kids got special permits to go to there a while back, but they came back after they kept gettin' hit with eggs at school every day. It's a mess. Even Reverend King came here to help integrate our schools, but nothin' happened."

"What about your kids now?"

"Well, they still goin' to Jordan, but they 'fraid to go sometimes. If it ain't drugs or gangs tryin' to get 'em in trouble, they get stopped by the cops for somethin'. I can't be around all the time to watch out for 'em, and I'm worried."

"How do you get along? You know, money?"

"As I said, it ain't easy. We used to get some help from the government with somethin' called "Aid to Families with Dependent Children," but our caseworker says that when the kids leave school or graduate, we could lose most of what they pay us."

"So what keeps you going?"

"Simple. We go to church. The good Lord will take care of us, and we believe that new jobs trainin' program President Kennedy announced last year is an answer to our prayers. Haven't seen it yet, but I'm sure its comin'. Just like he said, we's goin' to the moon!"

Archie's story was just what Jinli had been hoping to find all along, basically an example of the failure of capitalism to provide everybody with an opportunity to achieve the so-called "American Dream."

58

Jinli's conclusion was that most of that failure is due to discrimination with roots in prejudice and bigotry and the economic policies of capitalism that lead to wealth inequality.

Interestingly, on his way back to campus, Jinli stopped to chat with a few people living not far from the university to get their opinions. He was surprised to find a strange exception to what he heard earlier.

The attitudes of disadvantaged people living close to the campus were almost universally supportive of the school, the faculty, and students, of whom they seemed to be proud. The university provided significant employment for many locals and substantial financial aid was readily available to poor families if their children qualified for admission. They had very few gripes.

The paradox puzzled him. Most of those locals were not jealous of the apparently well-to-do students and faculty at the school, even though they represented the very economic level and attitudes of society that some other people blamed for much of their misfortune. Regardless, they were proud of the university—it was their place, and they protected it.

Notwithstanding everything he heard about discrimination that day, Jinli blamed free-market competition as the root cause for the failure of capitalism to work as it was intended. Nevertheless, inequality resulting from racial discrimination would be his stalking horse.

He used several examples of inequality in his report to explain the inability of so many immigrants to enjoy the cherished "life, liberty and the pursuit of happiness" that they expected when they came to America.

Jinli's studies were seriously interrupted in the fall semester on November 22, 1963, just six days before the Thanksgiving holiday.

President Kennedy was assassinated in Dallas, Texas, and Jinli was caught up in the emotion of the moment as his fellow students mourned the president's death. He sensed he was in the United States on a truly historic day in American history.

He decided to use the occasion to add to his research, but it was hard to get any answers to his questions that weekend in view of what happened. The sadness and respect for the president he witnessed would stay with him for a long time.

The following week he researched everything he could find on Kennedy and his life. Jinli's perspective on the United States would be changed forever after he read the State of the Union Address that Kennedy gave on January 11, 1962. He began to understand why immigration numbers were increasing in the U.S., in spite of everything he heard in Watts.

Jinli continued to devote all his time to his studies, and he kept his nose to the grindstone, continuing his streak of high grades.

At the end of almost two full school years, he'd made a few friends in his dorm, and there were a couple of classmates who he might call "casual" friends, but none in particular in whom he could confide anything personal.

He frequently thought about the so-called "Four years to dream ..." article he had read in the DT on his first day of school, wondering if he was really living it. If he was, it wasn't that great.

Jinli was checking the class schedule for the next summer session posted on the bulletin board outside the Dean's office when he noticed another Chinese looking student checking the class schedule, as well. Jinli turned and faced him as he introduced himself.

"My name is Jinli Guang. And you are?"

"Tom Sheng," he replied. "Happy to meet you. You a student?"
"Yes."

"So am I. Brand new here."

They established an immediate rapport and cemented their relationship when they learned they were both planning to sign up for the same two senior level classes.

When Tom said would be a senior in the Fall, Jinli said he would be a junior. "So are you planning to graduate early?" Tom asked.

"Well I hope so. I'm trying to squeeze these classes now so I can make it in three years."

"Hey, what do you say we to go to the Trojan Grill and grab some lunch?" "Sounds good. We can talk some more over there."

Tom asked Jinli over lunch about how he got to USC. Jinli simply said that his father thought it was the right school for him.

"Big bucks, huh?"

"No, not really. I was offered a scholarship. Otherwise, I wouldn't be here.

How about you?"

"Pretty much the same story. I followed USC football ever since I was a kid I always wanted to come to school here, but my dad couldn't afford it. I made top grades at San Fernando Valley State College, and last year my dad said I should find out if there were any academic scholarships available. I interviewed with Dean Smith and told him I wanted to pursue a graduate degree. He looked at my resume and offered me a job as his assistant right then and there, along with some tuition credit. Then he said that if I kept my grades up, I could become a full-fledged TA once my graduate work started. I couldn't believe it so I said 'yes' right on the spot, and here I am."

Tom had been living at home but the commute to USC was too far, so he had moved into an off-campus apartment.

After they finished their burgers and talked a little more, out of the blue Tom asked, "Jinli, would you like to take a look at my apartment? I'm by myself right now, and if you like it, maybe we could become roommates. What do you say?"

Jinli was taken aback by Tom's rather hasty offer. After all, they had just met. But Tom was Chinese, and since they seemed to have so much in common, he was intrigued by the idea.

"That's a possibility, I suppose. Let's go see it. If it looks like it will work, I'll see if I can get out of my contract at Marks Hall."

"Hey, the building is really pretty quiet. The other apartments are rented to some pretty serious-type students. I think you'll like it."

They sound nerdy to me, Jinli thought, using another new idiom that he picked up along the way.

Jinli moved in and set up shop in Tom's two-bedroom, two-bath apartment with a small living room and kitchen, and he loved it. He had his own space and an intelligent, friendly roommate with the same cultural background and major.

"Tom, do you eat in or out?"

"Usually out, except on weekends, when I have to go home for some reason. "You know the thirty-second street market is close by. What do you say we save some money and eat in during the week? I'll bet your mother taught you how to cook."

"Yea, I can cook. She and my dad own the "Peace of Peking" restaurant near our house in Van Nuys, and I work for her once in a while."

Jinli was a neophyte, but he soon learned to cook like Tom, if you could call it that.

As summer school rolled along, Jinli felt more and more like a real college student. He adapted a great deal more to life in America since meeting Tom and he became more outgoing. The world was opening up right in front of him.

He appreciated what Tom had to offer: a friend who accepted him for who he was without being judgmental, and someone who exposed him to some real campus life.

They both had bicycles, so getting to class was easy. Jinli didn't mind the added distance to campus. He liked getting the exercise.

They got along very well, although Tom was more outgoing and worked hard at getting acquainted with other students around campus.

Jinli was still a bit of a loner, so he put in a lot of time studying in his bedroom. He felt very comfortable in his new home where it was almost as quiet as the library.

When they got together, usually around dinnertime, they often engaged in a serious discussion about a variety of subjects, but always seemed to wind up talking about competing economic systems. That was Jinli's way of extracting more information for his report. Tom was a strong believer in capitalism, rather cerebral, and the perfect subject to interview. Jinli always took the role of a detractor in order to challenge Tom's thinking, but was he was rarely able to confuse Tom with his constant reference to social issues. None of their discussions became overheated, and their animated debates were always good-natured. Tom considered Jinli to be his equal in many ways. Misguided perhaps, but a peer nonetheless.

When they got tired of debating, they usually resorted to a friendly game of Go, or Weiqi in Chinese, the name Tom liked to use since it sounded more intellectual. They were worthy opponents, but Jinli possessed a natural ability for the game. Even so, Jinli could be a gracious loser.

Saturdays provided uninterrupted time to relax. If Tom was around, they usually studied during the day and biked the short distance over to Woody's Smorgasburger for dinner. Woody's had installed a newfangled thing called a microwave oven, and they talked about buying one for their apartment. But they never did. The cost of it was way beyond their means.

They avoided the local beer joint across the street from Woody's, called "The 901," because they felt out of place among all the frat guys and sorority girls hanging around. So, after dinner, they would head over to the liquor store nearby and buy some "suds" to take back to the apartment. Jinli always opted for Tsingtao because it reminded him of home.

Fortunately, Jinli's grades never suffered from all of his new activity.

CHAPTER 6 ~ The Dream

SEPTEMBER 21, 1964

On an especially beautiful fall day that he would never forget, everything changed for Jinli. He was thinking about his "dream" as he caught a glimpse of her walking into Bovard Auditorium on that Monday morning. *What a great way to start my last year of college,* he thought.

As he sidestepped down a row near the podium, looking for an empty seat, he turned his head back in both directions, hoping to see her out of the corner of his eye. No such luck.

She was already seated and noticed him up ahead of her, but pretended not to pay attention as he looked around. He was dressed like the rest of the students, but she tagged him as a Chinese import because of his slightly darker skin.

He was fairly tall for a Chinese boy, and clean cut with an athletic build. He had shorter hair than most boys in her neighborhood back home, and it seemed to give him a more mature look.

She would learn later that his handsome good looks belied his naivety regarding girls, a characteristic that reflected his life growing up in a strange culture where sexuality was controlled, and the girls had become somewhat "androgynous."

Jinli was on track to graduate, but there had been a small glitch in his record. His counselor had advised him incorrectly when he first arrived, and he had not taken the required freshman Letters, Arts, and Sciences course titled "Man and Civilization." He was making up for it now, during his final year of all things. He couldn't quite figure out how the name of the course related to his major, so he was prepared to be bored.

The lecture hall was enormous, and he kept looking for her at every session of class.

"Tom, you have to meet my girlfriend."

"What girlfriend?"

"Just about the most beautiful creature I've ever seen, that's who."

"So introduce me."

"In due time, in due time. First, I have to meet her myself! I don't even know her name."

Where is she? he kept asking himself.

Then, a couple of days later, as he walked down the middle aisle, looking for a seat, she seemed to appear out of nowhere. He hoped he wasn't seeing an apparition.

When he reached her row, he squeezed past several students and sat down beside her in an empty seat.

Just as the professor was about to start the class, he leaned over toward her and whispered, in Mandarin, "Nihao. Wo jiao Guang Jinli."

Su Lin looked up and frowned, questioning his dialect. He had simply meant to introduce himself, but he was unaware that Chinese Americans from Chinatown in San Francisco only speak Cantonese at home.

When the lecture was over, they walked outside together. Suddenly, she stopped and turned toward him.

"Mr. Guang, let's stick to English, okay?"

"I'm sorry," he said. "I was just trying to impress you with a little formality. That was stupid of me, wasn't it?" Then, using the Western naming convention he said, "Hello. My name is Jinli Guang, and I'm a senior from Jiangmen, in China."

"And my name is Su Lin Wong, and I'm a freshman from San Francisco, in California," she said with a laugh.

"Please, call me Jinli."

"And you may call me Su Lin."

"Su Lin, it was nice meeting you. See you next time," he said, as he located his bike in the rack and hustled off to his next class.

That awkward little introduction was the beginning of a very close relationship. Little did she know then, but it was one she might later regret.

After the next class session, he waited for her outside the auditorium. "Want to talk?" he said when he spotted her coming out.

"Sure," she replied, having hoped she would see him again.

They walked together past Tommy Trojan and crossed the street to Alumni Park where they sat down on the edge of the fountain.

"I noticed the other day that your book cover has the name Keely on it," Jinli said. "Is that your real name? It's not Chinese, as far as I know."

"Of course it isn't. All my old book covers have the name on it, that's all. It's the nickname I used to use."

"Oh."

"I'm sure you don't know, but in this country it can be a lot easier for us to get along if we have a Western-sounding name. It makes introductions easier, to say nothing of putting people at ease. The racial barrier has been hard enough, and the practice of going by a different name is really helpful. It's become so commonplace that a lot of second or third generation Chinese babies are now given Western names at birth."

"So what did your parents name you?"

"Su Lin, as I told you, but I haven't used that name in years."

"Su Lin is a pretty name. Why did you want to change it?"

"When I started school, I had to walk several blocks outside of Chinatown to get there. In the beginning, my father would go with me just in case there was any trouble, and then he or my mom, but usually my dad, would collect me when my classes were over. They did the same thing for my brother later on. It was their way of protecting us."

"Go on."

"During the big waves of immigration to the U.S. during the last century, Chinese people worked as laborers in the railroad and mining industries and they were criticized for taking the white man's jobs. We were the subject of a lot of ridicule and condemnation. The situation continued, to a lesser degree, long after that, but the criticism was still there while I was growing up. You have no idea what it's like to live in a ghetto and suffer the ridicule of slurs and name-calling. I've heard every one in the book. "Chink" still offends me when I hear it, even in a war movie.

"It was especially hard when I got older. The Korean War was still going on, and my people were demeaned because of our heritage and skin color. A lot of people resented China's involvement in that war, just as they do today with our war in Vietnam. There was a lot of anti-communist sentiment. We were American citizens, but we were treated somewhat like the enemy. It was a rough time, but my father kept telling me that hardship creates opportunity. His story is a testament to that. Jinli ... I've gotten way too serious here."

"I agree, but I want to know more. But for now, let's go back to your name."

"Okay. Like most kids, I used to listen to a lot of music on the radio. Still do. Anyway, I became fascinated with a singer named Keely Smith. I'm sure you don't know who she is. I don't know why, but she sang a lot with a zany guy named Louis Prima. I loved their music. Their act was really popular in Las Vegas, and I bought all their records. She was a cute girl, and I thought she looked like some of my Chinese girlfriends, especially with her short black hair. But as it turned out, I read she was part Native American with some Cherokee blood. I also found out she had a hard family life growing up, and her family took in laundry to make ends meet. I related to her mixed heritage as someone who overcame a lot of hardship, I guess you'd say. Except for her shorter hair, I even thought I looked a little like her. So after that, I became 'Keely' Wong. You're the only person outside my family who knows that story, so please, just call me Su Lin, all right? That was then, and this is now."

"No problem. Your story is safe with me. Lunch on Friday, Su Lin Wong?"

"Lunch it is."

As she walked away, Jinli looked at her and couldn't help but compare her dress to the girls back home, where they usually wore baggy clothes with a simple fit. Their other outfits, including the so-called cadre clothing, was similar to the Mao suit but fashioned for women. The unisex appearance was popular with girls to demonstrate their ability to share work with men, and they thought and acted like revolutionaries.

In reality, the desired standard of beauty in China was almost impossible to attain, so a lot of girls were insecure about their appearance, especially if they weren't thin. If they had curves, they kept them strictly covered up. Jinli couldn't recall feminism as a character trait of any Chinese girls he knew. And then, there was a girl's demeanor. With a Chinese family's preference for boys, and a father's typical attitude toward their daughters as being inferior, it's no wonder that a girl might lack self-esteem or self-confidence. That condemnation led many girls to develop Narcissistic behaviors, looking for special treatment.

Jinli was never attracted to any combination of those characteristics: dress, lack of femininity or demanding behavior; and since arriving at USC, he had practically forgotten all about the Chinese girls back home.

Su Lin was a second generation Chinese-American, and he had never seen anyone like her. She had fairly light, flawless, porcelain-looking skin. She was soft and alluring, and reserved. She had a Nancy Kwan look about her, with her black hair pulled straight back and tied behind her neck. To Jinli, Su Lin looked every bit the part of the famous movie star. She was not as tall, but had a nice figure and wore nice, colorful, but simple clothes. Jinli was fascinated by Su Lin's refinement, and he couldn't take his eyes off her.

To Su Lin, Jinli had a shy, but sincere quality about him that interested her. He was not brash like so many of the boys she encountered back in Chinatown, and his courteous attention to her was very appealing.

She also liked his looks, and tried to subtlety indicate that to him whenever she got the chance.

They grabbed lunch at the Grill on Friday, as planned, and found a table in the corner to resume their "getting acquainted" discussions.

"Jinli, I've talked a lot about me, but I hardly know anything about you except for your name. Tell me about your family."

"There isn't much to discuss, really, but here goes. My parents and their parents grew rice on a family farm. You probably know that China has experienced famines for centuries. The last one ended about a year before I got here. We have a lot of people to feed in China, and during a famine, a lot of people die. My grandparents on my father's side died in the last one. I never got to meet them, but I've read my father's diaries. He started keeping them when he left home, just before the Japanese arrived in Canton a few years before the start of World War II. My dad joined Mao Zedong's communist government in a mountain area called Yan'an. Ever heard of it?"

"No, I don't think so."

"It was a dangerous journey, but some missionaries helped him get there safely. Anyway, he met my mother there, and that's where I was born. She was from Shanghai and escaped the Japanese herself before she joined the communists in Yan'an. They struggled through the civil war and the revolution and rejoiced when Mao proclaimed the People's Republic of China as an independent nation. My father spent many years successfully working with local peasants attempting to correct the inequities of land ownership that had left most of them stuck in a feudal system. All my dad ever wanted was a better life for the Chinese people."

Jinli was very careful not to reveal anything about his father's criticism of Mao's policies.

"Today, he's the Mayor of my hometown and a member of the Communist Municipal Committee. He is proud of his communist roots and a strong supporter of the party's leadership, without whom China would be living in its past. He has taught me the benefits of our communist system that raised our people out of their despair and provided a framework for progress. He is my biggest fan and supporter. Our constitution will be revised as we become a socialist economy. We may be struggling now about how to manage our economic development, but our future is very bright. Just wait and see."

"What a great party line, Jinli. A little impersonal, but I suspect that's because life in China is steeped in your Communist philosophy that doesn't allow for much individual identity. Is your father religious?"

"Since the Communist Party has always been hostile to religion, I'm going to guess he isn't, but I'm not entirely sure if he believes in God or not. He went to a missionary school as a boy, and I read examples in his diaries about how religious ideas affected his thinking and his life, but he doesn't belong to a church. It's not something we talk about. How about you?"

"I have no reason to doubt there's a God," she answered.

"Turnabout is fair play," Jinli said, moving the conversation along quickly, using one of the idioms he had picked up. "Tell me more about your history."

"Well, my family background is typical of immigrants who came here in search of the American dream. It has some similarity to your background, but it diverges from it in quite a few ways. But first, I'll set the stage for my story.

"To begin with, your country is ancient, and ours is new. Your ancestors struggled with many revolutions and civil wars to achieve your current form of communist government, and we suffered the same kinds of conflicts to arrive at our form of democratic government. Our countries are at opposite ends of the economic and political spectrum, but we're both striving to find what works best for each of us.

"I don't mean to insult you but we are still attracting people from all over the world who want to experience what we have to offer, including a lot of Asians. I don't see that China has an immigration problem. Do you?"

"No, not really."

"There must be a message there, and I hope that while you're here, you'll be able to find out why, and perhaps you'll be able to help reverse that trend in the future.

"Getting back to the personal side of things, your parents and my parents all came from the farm, but their paths to get to where they are today were quite different. Your parents chose the party line, quite literally, and became part of a rigid government structure that demands allegiance and adherence to what some bureaucrats think is best for them. Their personal freedoms are dictated for them. If I'm wrong please say so."

Jinli had nothing to say in return.

"In my case, my parents became entrepreneurs, building their lives around their own values and hard work to achieve what they believe is personal success derived from God's mercy and their own hard work. I don't mean to be so strident in my remarks, but that's the way I see it."

"So you really do believe in God?"

"Absolutely"

"Oh," he said sheepishly. "Fair enough. Tell me more about your parents."

"Well, my grandfather emigrated to Hawaii from China sometime in the late eighteen hundreds to work in the sugar cane fields, and later, on pineapple plantations. I'm told he met my grandmother there, but I don't really know anything about them. All I know is that Hawaii was annexed to the United States in 1898, so my father, who was born in 1920, is a U.S. citizen.

"Anyway, my father followed in his father's footsteps, and he was working on a plantation when the Japanese attacked Pearl Harbor. A strong patriotic feeling swept over the country, and he was a part of the rush to enlist. I think part of his reason was also because he hated what the Japs had done when they occupied eastern China before the war and stopped Chiang Kai-shek's effort to unite China's political parties and defeat communism. He still believes to this day that China wouldn't be a communist country if the Japs had kept their nose out of things! He's a bit of a history buff, as you can tell.

"Right after the war ended, my dad mustered out at Treasure Island in San Francisco. That means he got out of the Navy there."

"So, did he go back to Hawaii?"

"No. It was a big departure from his pre-war life on the islands, but he embraced the idea of starting a new life on the mainland. Unfortunately, he encountered a lot of bigotry and discrimination when he got here. For a long time, Americans believed that Chinese culture was disgusting and vile, and they viewed U.S. Chinatowns as depraved colonies of prostitutes, gamblers, and opium addicts. Between the eighteen seventies and World War II, lawmakers and citizens pushed those arguments just to justify excluding Chinese from mainline society, and they were forcibly segregated. It's still a bit of a problem.

"You wouldn't know it, but a popular expression in American life was, when someone described an opportunity, they would say that 'You don't have a Chinaman's chance in hell of ...' Get it?"

"Yes, I think so. I can relate to what you've told me, but I still don't understand why your government allows so much discrimination."

"Look Jinli, perhaps when you learn more about our history and the dichotomy of our democracy versus exclusion, you'll be able to appreciate what we've been through. Thankfully, we're beginning to eliminate a lot of discrimination in our society and overcome the denial of the freedoms guaranteed by our Constitution. Our system is still the envy of the world. We're proud of the gains we've made, even if you can't see it quite yet!

"My dad is a good example of our progress. In spite of what he encountered, he was not about to be held back. First, he found a place to live in Chinatown in some flophouse and then he managed to get a job as a waiter in the Tonga Room at the Fairmont Hotel on Nob Hill. It's still a popular Polynesian restaurant today. He told the guy who hired him that he was from Hawaii, and I guess my dad had the look of a South Seas native he was looking for. But before I continue, let me tell you about my mom."

"This is fascinating. Really. Please tell me more."

"Well, like you, she grew up on a farm. It was in Castroville, California, a town south of San Francisco near the coast. It's where all the artichokes come from."

"What's an artichoke?"

"It's a vegetable that's become really popular. I'll tell you more about them later. Anyway, my grandfather was a heavy drinker, so my mom's family was pretty dysfunctional.

"When my mom finished high school, she decided to run away, and she landed in San Francisco. She was really smart, but good jobs were hard to find, and she wound up doing menial-type work in restaurants and hotels. In fact, she was a housekeeper in the Fairmont Hotel where my dad worked when she met him. I think one of the reasons she was attracted to him was because she appreciated the kindness of the Chinese people in Castroville's Chinatown where my grandfather used to hang out in bars. They were always very helpful to her and my grandmother when they came to pick him up, drunk as a skunk."

"What do you mean? It sounds like maybe she isn't Chinese?"

"She isn't. She's white, or Caucasian, if you will. Her maiden name was Marlene Monroe."

"That explains it."

"Explains what?"

"The reason you're so beautiful! I've read that a lot of men think Eurasian girls are the most beautiful women in all the world," he said, and she blushed.

"Come on, Jinli. I'm not finished." "Okay, please go on."

"Well, my mom and dad had only dated for a few weeks when they decided to get married, at the courthouse, of course. They couldn't afford a church wedding. Neither one of them had any close friends, so the judge's wife stood up for them. But they were in love, and they knew they could make it together. My dad had saved some money in the service, and it wasn't long before they decided to take a chance and go out on their own. God really blessed them.

"They found a bakery for sale that had an apartment above it. The seller really liked them and stayed long enough to teach them the business and help get it going. They put in impossible hours, but that didn't prevent them from having me a short time later.

"They are wonderful people who've worked very hard so I can get the college education that I've dreamed about. I've always helped them out in the bakery and tried to hold up my end of the bargain. My dad made my dream come true for me, and here I am."

"Will I get a chance to meet them?"

"I'm not real sure about that."

"Really, why not?"

"Well, I would never do anything to disappoint them, and for one thing you represent the communists whom my dad hates so much, and what's more, I'm not real sure about you and God. That's two strikes against you. But I'll give you some time to change."

In spite of her put down, whenever Jinli thought of Su Lin, he pictured how an ideal girl should look and act, her political thinking aside.

As much as her appearance appealed to him, he was almost more fascinated by her intellect. She had command of her languages, confidence in herself, and displayed a pretty complete knowledge of almost any subject that they discussed, whether it was history, politics, or current events.

But most of all, she could articulate her position on any subject very well. He wondered how she could have become so well educated at such a young age. Maybe an American education is as special as people think.

Except for that one little incident, Su Lin was non-confrontational and appeared to have some appreciation for Jinli's communist beliefs, even though he doubted she could ever accept any of them. She had so much as said so.

How can that be? he thought. She was certainly smart enough to see there is a better way.

Jinli felt a little depressed from the "brain fatigue" caused by their discussions of communism and capitalism, but after clearing his mind, he decided to invite her to lunch again, and told her that this time he would ask Tom to join them.

Su Lin felt bad about the way she had challenged him earlier, but when he invited her to lunch, she said, "Yes, if you want to." She was relieved she hadn't turned him off for good.

"All right, then. Monday it is. We'll go to the Grill after class."

Jinli was on cloud nine. Although Su Lin had offered a rather timid response to his invitation, she was secretly just as excited, and considered that it would be their first real date, even if this "Tom" were there.

In his journal, Jinli summed up his impression of American girls as generally attractive, rather feminine and unassuming, but smart. He never mentioned Su Lin's name to avoid any probing questions by his father in the event Wei wanted to read his journals after he got home.

Jinli introduced Tom to Su Lin, and they chatted over lunch until it was time to leave for class.

Su Lin's and Tom's common restaurant experience, especially having learned to cater to demanding customers, created somewhat of a bond between them.

That night, Tom told Jinli he agreed wholeheartedly that Su Lin was really a special girl.

The association that developed was a new experience for Jinli, and he really enjoyed the three-way relationship. They sometimes referred to themselves as the "trio," and they frequently met between classes at the Grill.

Tom never attempted to step in between Jinli and Su Lin, and neither of them ever became aware of Tom's true feelings.

Then one day, Tom made a big announcement.

"Guess what just happened? My grandfather finally passed away, and I got the car he was saving for me. My folks just dropped it off. It's a fifty-seven Chevy four-door wagon, and it's in pretty good shape. I'm in hog heaven."

"Great," Jinli exclaimed. He'd never ventured very far from campus, except for his visit to Watts, so he said "Let's go somewhere!"

Tom really knew his way around LA, but to the rest of the trio, exploring the area would be a new experience. Tom was more than willing to organize their quest for adventure, and the trio took weekend sightseeing trips whenever they could.

Tom could squeeze six passengers inside the wagon on two bench seats, so once in a while he invited Isabel and the twins to join them.

Isabel Villa was a student going to school downtown at St. Vincent's College of Nursing, and she lived by herself in one of the apartments below Tom and Jin. She was from Indio, California in the Coachella Valley of California.

The twins were engineering majors at USC from Bakersfield, California. Tom referred to them as "Tweedle Dee and Tweedle Dum." They also lived downstairs.

Isabel was a little more respectful and just referred to them as the twins, although it was unanimous that the Tweedle Brothers took themselves a bit too seriously. Even so, they were a lot of fun to have around once you got them out into the fresh air.

On weekends, Tom and whoever was available would pile into the Chevy, pick up Su Lin on the way, and go looking for new places to eat. Jinli never wanted to miss a trip, so he was usually prepared to go on short notice, even if he wasn't caught up on his homework.

The Chinese kids agreed they would skip Chinatown, having had more than enough Chinese food growing up. Besides, it wasn't the real thing. Tom's Mom would definitely agree with that.

The trio became much more enamored with the places the rich, white kids were going. They tried lots of places they heard about from them, but passed on the ones that exceeded their budgets.

They went to El Cholo on Western for Mexican, Yamashiro in the Hollywood hills for Japanese and Philippe's in downtown Los Angeles for the French dip sandwiches that were invented there almost fifty years earlier.

Sometimes, on Saturdays or Sunday mornings, they would go downtown to The Pantry for a huge breakfast, or maybe it would be out to the International House of Pancakes out on Stocker at Crenshaw for an all-you-can-eat type breakfast. If the Tweedle Brothers went to the pancake house, the trio was certain the place would go broke after watching how much those farm boys downed.

Of course, Su Lin didn't go to breakfast on Sundays because of church.

The Tweedle Brothers were going home for Thanksgiving, so Tom decided to plan a special day for the rest of them. He had grown tired of Jinli's negative view of capitalism that he harped on constantly.

"Jinli, my friend," Tom said, "there is a lot more to see in Los Angeles than the disadvantaged area of South Central that seems to dominate your opinion of capitalism, so I'm going to show you a different side of the city today. I've got it all mapped out. It will be a long day, but I think our little trio will enjoy it. We'll leave early so grab some breakfast before we go. Here's the program:

"Venice Beach, famous for its promenade with its various street performers;

Beverly Hills, home to celebrities and big wigs from business;

Lunch at Pinks, famous for its creative hot dogs;

Hollywood Bowl, the famous outdoor amphitheater for musical performances;

Griffith Observatory, monument to public astronomy near the Hollywood Sign and the site of the famous James Dean fight scene in the movie *Rebel Without a Cause*;

Cinerama Dome, where we'll see the movie *It's a Mad, Mad, Mad, Mad World* on the only wide screen of its type anywhere in the world;

Dinner at Pig 'N Whistle, one of Hollywood's landmark restaurants; and finally

Dessert at C. C. Brown's, Hollywood ice cream parlor to the stars."

Tom promised they would see a movie star or two while they were in Hollywood, but they had no such luck.

At the end of the day, Tom asked Jinli, "Now do you now understand a little bit more about what living here is like? Look what we did in just one day! The people and places and things you saw today represent what's great about America: natural beauty, culture, technology, history, and people striving to make their businesses successful so they can enhance their family's future."

"All right, I guess I have to admit that my thinking was a little premature. That was an exciting experience, and I learned a lot. I'm starting to see a bigger picture now."

The adventure opened his eyes as to why Los Angeles attracts so many people. Jinli got enough of a taste of it to want more, except for one thing.

Earlier, Tom had taken Jinli and Su Lin to the Coliseum to watch the USC Trojans play football against their archrival, the UCLA Bruins. USC won 34-13. Tom loved every minute of it, but Jinli and Su Lin thought the game was just a bunch of guys running around and throwing one another down for no apparent reason.

In spite of everything Jinli saw that day, the contrast between South Central and Beverly Hills was not lost on him. He still questioned if the Civil Rights legislation signed by President Johnson the previous summer would make any difference in the long run.

As the next semester approached, Jinli got an idea. Su Lin hadn't made any close friends in her dorm, so he asked her to talk to Isabel about taking in a roommate. It was obviously unnecessary, but he pointed out that he would be upstairs with Tom, and she would be downstairs with Isabel.

Su Lin was intrigued by the idea and Isabel was more than happy to cut her rent. Su Lin was able to cancel her dorm contract, and she moved in with Isabel. Jinli's plan worked perfectly.

Now, the two lovebirds can be a little closer together, Tom thought.

On February 8, 1965, Jinli reached the final milestone in his college education: the start of his final semester. He was definitely living his dream now. He and Su Lin were living in the same apartment house, and he couldn't be happier. *Whoever said, "absence makes the heart grow fonder" was only half right,* Jinli thought. They never penned the obvious extension of that expression, so he added *"and closeness makes the heart grow even fonder."*

After Su Lin moved in, she and Jinli spent less time with Tom and more time with each other. They still enjoyed going places with Tom, but sometimes they felt like they were dating with an uninvited chaperone.

"At least he's not my father!" she confided in Jinli.

They studied often in his apartment. Su Lin's life experience offered him a different perspective on capitalism from the material he was studying in his classes, and Jinli tutored her in statistics. It seemed to be a fairly even trade-off. Jinli and Su Lin were from different cultures, but their old world heritage bound them together tightly in spite of the differences in their political and religious philosophies.

He could discuss anything with her without fear of reprisal if his opinion ran counter to hers, and that was especially comforting. They would compare notes on their respective countries' government policies and structures and respectfully agree to disagree. It was kind of like marriage should be, Jinli guessed.

As their conversations became more personal, Jinli remembered a particular exchange they had had when he questioned Su Lin about her quirky little habit. At least, it seemed quirky to him.

Su Lin sent her father a postcard every week, and once in a while she would ask Jinli to mail one for her. He thought the practice was a little amusing, but had never asked her to explain it.

"So what are those cards that you send to your father?" Jinli asked.

"Oh, they're just my way of staying in touch. He's such a wonderful father and so proud of me for getting into a big university. I just want to add a little joy to our relationship. He's a baker, as you know, and fortune cookies are a big seller for him. My cards provide him with some ideas for the sayings that go on those little slips of paper that get baked inside. I know he can get them from somewhere else, but he says he likes mine the best. Fun, don't you think?"

"I guess so. Americans do some really strange things. So how do you come up with those ideas?"

"They just come to me naturally. Some relate to my personal experiences. Some I base on the stories and movies that I like. But most of them are just contrived. I try to stay away from the Confucius stuff."

As Su Lin began to mull over her answer, she suddenly got a brainstorm.

"I enjoy thinking them up for my father. It's a diversion from my studies and gives me some satisfaction knowing that my little messages might inspire a reader or make them happy. I really love the philosophical ones in particular. Let me read the one that I just wrote. I think it's the most meaningful one I've ever thought of: The future will reveal the past."

"What does that mean?"

"It's pretty deep, so pay attention. The present is just a point in time somewhere in between your future and the past. A lot of times, what happens tomorrow is the result of an event that occurred yesterday. Or, to put it another way, an event that occurred yesterday may not manifest itself until sometime in the future. Get it? Take, for example, the birth of Christ."

"Come on," Jinli said. "Do we have to talk about your religion again? You've told me enough stories."

"Bear with me. Was Christ's birth a significant event?"

"Well, according to your Bible it was, at least to the prophets, his mother, the shepherds, and the wise men. Did I get that right?"

"Yes, very good."

"All right, now tell me how that fits in with your fortune?"

"Well, when Christ was crucified, didn't that event reveal the original purpose of his birth? To come and save us from our sins?"

"Su Lin, you know I'm not sure about God, much less Jesus' teachings that you follow. So please, can we leave religion out of our relationship."

"All right. I will for now," she said. "But believe me, there will come a day. Let's just say that my fortune cookie message is a proverb that explains what happens in the future may very well be the result of something that happened in the past. It's only when you've arrived at that future point in time that you can understand how or why it came about. Do you understand the concept?"

"Okay, I understand where you're going with that."

He was acutely aware of her strong faith and he began to examine his own belief or lack thereof. That conversation stuck with Jinli for a long time, and periodically he would rehearse it again in his mind. Could she have something he wanted? Was she so right and he so wrong?"

In spite of their differences in religion, politics, and cultural backgrounds, he fell in love with her. But soon, his commitment to return to China would overshadow everything else he had learned to appreciate while in school, including that love and the desire to stay with her in America.

Jinli wondered what was happening back at home. When he left, things were going badly, and he didn't know what his future would hold for him there when he returned. But if he could somehow overcome his father's certain objection, perhaps he could come back to America. He didn't know how or when that might happen, but he wished it could be so.

One day, shortly before their final exams, as they took a study break, Jinli asked her a question right out of the blue.

"Su Lin, tell me why I should abandon my belief in communism." probing her thoughts on capitalism once more, for the umpteenth time.

"Come on Jinli. I don't know if I can ever sway your opinion, but I'm going to keep trying. Why did you ask me that again? Do I get the feeling you're coming around to my point of view?"

"Su Lin, you do make a compelling argument, but I'm having a hard time reconciling my beliefs with those of someone I love who thinks totally differently. If I didn't have to make a choice it would be much easier."

"If you feel you have make a choice, that's wonderful, but you know you are the only one who can make that decision. I can't make it for you."

What Jinli couldn't tell her was that he was ashamed that the motive behind some of their discussions about capitalism that was simply an attempt to discredit it for his report. The word "disingenuous" came to mind. How could he tell her now that he had kind of 'used' her, even though he was beginning to see the light. Would she still love him if he told her about what he had done?

Jinli's question about abandoning communism had really excited Su Lin. She was so in love with him, and she was overwhelmed by the thought of his becoming acceptable to her parents.

Jinli was scheduled to graduate on June 10, 1965, after finishing with all A's for three straight years.

Dean Smith couldn't recall anyone else ever accomplishing that feat during his tenure. He was naturally proud of Jinli, but sorry that he wasn't going to participate in the graduation exercises. Still, he understood why with no family to attend.

Jinli had decided to tell Su Lin he was leaving. He had his tickets in hand. He dreaded what he had to do, but he had to see it through. He had procrastinated long enough. It was time. So on the morning of graduation day he told her.

His announcement came as an absolute shock. She was totally dismayed by it. He had never mentioned anything about any promise to his father.

Once she stopped crying and settled down, she was forced to accept his decision, in spite of her anguish.

She kept asking herself what she had done so wrong. It was as if she had been living a dream and had suddenly awakened. Why didn't he tell me sooner? she asked herself. It's so unfair, especially after all of our talk about the future! She had thought her influence on him might bring about a change in his political belief. Then, perhaps her parents would accept him. After that she could work on his faith. The plan she had thought about obviously wasn't the one God had for her. She was going to stay in the apartment during the summer so the two of them could be together, and she had assumed he would look for a job. Now, none of that was going to happen.

Jinli knew how stupid he had been to lead her on, knowing in the back of his mind he would have to tell her sooner or later. After all, he made a promise that he had to keep, and hoped she would come to realize that his failure to tell her earlier was not done to try and trick her.

She speculated that he just couldn't face the facts until they were staring right at him. Even so, it wasn't as if she didn't bear some responsibility herself for the way things turned out. She had told him that her parents would reject him out of hand; maybe she should never have said that.

Both of them had good reasons for their response to the situation, but now they were facing insurmountable odds as reality set in.

In spite of everything, that last day together promised to be very special, an escape from the truth set before them.

After the commencement exercises, Tom went home for the night to celebrate with his family. The twins' parents had already picked them up after their last exams to start their summer work on their almond ranch, and Isabel had taken the bus home to enjoy time with her family before the next semester was scheduled to begin. Jinli and Su Lin were left all alone.

They had gone out for breakfast and returned so Jinli could pack. After a late lunch, they took a long walk over to the campus and quietly strolled around. It was a nice, warm day with a gentle breeze that added to her complacency. Neither of them said much. There wasn't anything to say, really. The campus was empty of graduates, except for a few stragglers and the maintenance crews who were cleaning up after the morning's graduation ceremonies.

Sometimes love pulls two people together like a magnet. It had happened to them, as they recalled their first encounter. It had taken a little time for them to acknowledge their love for each other, but now it was in full bloom. They knew they couldn't stay together for now, but perhaps things might work out later on.

She wondered if she would have to go to China to be with him, or if he would return to her after fulfilling his promise to his father.

Someone said, "Love is blind." They were in murky waters now, and really couldn't see very well. They were both smart, but still young, and lacked the mature reasoning required to see the long-term picture. Their thoughts were filled with so many "what ifs."

By the time they returned to Jinli's apartment, it was late afternoon. Su Lin prepared one of his favorite dishes, and they enjoyed it by candlelight with music in the background.

Neither of them said much as they ate. When they finished, she looked directly into his eyes and asked, "Can I stay with you tonight?"

Jinli was taken aback by her question and didn't understand her intent at first. He was confused. Was she really inviting him to … have sex? They had kissed and touched each other frequently when they were alone, but she always said that she expected to remain a virgin until she got married. Could it be that she suddenly saw one last opportunity to try and keep him there? Jinli wondered how she could suddenly go against one of her strongest convictions.

As for Su Lin, what she was about to do she would leave up to God as to the consequences of her action.

He had resisted answering her question for as long as he could out of respect for her, but now his hormones were raging, and they took control. No words were necessary as they held hands and walked into his bedroom.

She pulled down the covers and crawled into his bed, motioning for him to follow. He quickly removed his clothes and slid beneath the sheets next to her. As they embraced and he kissed her tenderly, their love was consummated.

When they were finished, they lay there, exhausted, staring at the ceiling in complete silence, except for the sound of the music.

Finally, she turned to him and said, emotionally, with tears streaming down her cheeks, "Now will you stay here with me?" Regrettably, she already knew the answer.

"Su Lin, you know I can't. Is that what this was all about?" "No, no, no. Not at all, but … I was just hoping."

Jinli continued to lay there, weighing his decision. Would he go with his promise to his father, or his heart? With his decision made, he fell asleep.

Jinli had asked Tom to pick them up the next morning. He drove them to the airport and sat in the car while Su Lin went inside to see him off.

At the gate, in the midst of the crowd, embracing, ready for him to board the plane, their tears were mixed with words they could barely speak. He wished she could come with him somehow, and she wished he could stay. But both options were clearly impossible.

Little did either of them know that Jinli was leaving a lasting legacy behind that would be a constant reminder to Su Lin of her love for him.

When she got back to her apartment, there was an envelope waiting for her.

Inside was a simple note with his home address in Jiangmen, asking her to write. It was signed simply, "Love, Jinli."

CHAPTER 7 ~ The Return

JUNE 12, 1965

On the flight home, Jinli recalled how his father's diaries described the strain of his challenging life. Jinli's own experience during the previous three years in the U.S. had given him an insight into a totally different kind of living.

Wei was a loyal communist who had moved up in government ranks because of his dedication to the party and the unwavering support of his superiors, regardless of his true feelings about the fairness of their policies and their treatment of ordinary Chinese citizens.

Jinli wondered if his father's puppet-like life was worth sacrificing any part of his morality in order to succeed. Was he truly free in any respect to make personal decisions about anything, or was his life gamed by the system?

On the other hand, Jinli had observed that success in America is more likely the result of hard work, risk taking, and a belief in oneself. Many Americans would argue that one's ability to succeed is a blessing from God, but Jinli decided to consider that proposition at another time.

Which was the better path to success? The obvious answer for Jinli was that it boiled down to the inherent ideology of communism compared to capitalism. Jinli hoped that after Wei read his report that he would never be asked that question. Even if Jinli were never put on the spot, he would continue to struggle with the question, and it would haunt him for years to come.

Jinli walked through the front door, less than forty-eight hours after his graduation, fulfilling his promise to return.

"Huānyíng huí jiā," Wei said, welcoming him home. "I am happy to see you," he added in English, with a face lacking expression.

"I am happy to see you as well."

Before Wei could ask, Jinli anticipated his next question and said, "Here is my report, as you requested."

After dinner, they sat down to review the report in detail.

"Tell me, Son, before we begin, do you now view communism with disdain? Did they warp your mind? I'm sure they tried. I want you to tell me the truth, because I need to have total confidence in what your report says before I pass it along. If you were soft on the issue, we will both be in trouble. I don't have to tell you what happens to people who question our party's principals and policies. Did you read my diaries? If you did, I'm sure you know what I'm talking about."

"Yes Father, I read them completely. Just read the report. I stand behind every bit of it."

Jinli had taken a philosophical approach, describing the appearance, attitudes, opinions, morals and behavior of the people he encountered, as well as the little freedom they described, or denied. It stated that in capitalist America, its people suffer from the same class struggles that Marx wrote about: the conflict between workers and the ruling class.

Repeating words he'd heard his father use before, he noted the "materialistic and self-indulgent" behavior of the privileged class of students and faculty in the midst of an urban slum, where there appeared to be few visible signs of support from the government or anyone else.

He surmised that well-educated, rich, and influential members of American society succeed because they own all the businesses and the means of industrial production, the same kind of situation in China that brought about Mao's revolution.

"So, I did correctly describe the capitalist evil you would find, did I not?" Wei asked.

"Well, I wouldn't call it evil, exactly …"

"Well I would," Wei shouted, red faced.

"Father, please let me explain in detail what I meant by my answer. Their government stimulates the growth of private businesses by the laws it enacts. However, at the same time, the laboring class appears to be underpaid, assuming they have jobs. If they don't have jobs or can't find work, they resort to living partially or totally on welfare program benefits. Many of them resort to dealing drugs, prostitution, burglary, or begging to support their families.

"The open attitude of condemnation toward the lower class by many white upper and middle classes was apparent from my conversations, while the same folks criticized their own government for not helping them more. The system of big business is hypocritical: take advantage of the poor, while pretending to be their defenders."

"That's what I told you, Jinli. Right?" Wei insisted. "Please continue."

"I observed that after more than one hundred sixty-five years of experimenting with capitalism, the United States' current form of it has not yet been able to guarantee economic equality for every citizen. Two laws were passed during my sophomore year, proving my thesis: "The Civil Rights Act outlawed discrimination based on race, color, religion, sex, or national origin, and in August of the same year, the Economic Opportunity Act that was signed into law by President Johnson as part of his "War on Poverty." Both were aimed at "correcting" past sins.

"My conclusion is that Los Angeles is a microcosm of big city America and that, contrary to the economic opportunity that is so highly publicized, Americans are allowed to fail miserably.

"I supported my conclusions with anecdotal evidence that describes unsafe streets, poor schools, police discrimination, high unemployment, residential discrimination, sub-standard housing, and other limiting factors in the area near the school I attended.

"Finally, as to your question about evil, as just one example, I did opine that the morals and depravity depicted in some blockbuster movies reflect a somewhat corrupt society."

Jinli finished his report with a question stated in bold, capital letters.

"IF CAPITALISM IS SO GREAT, WHY DOES THE UNITED STATES HAVE SO MANY PROBLEMS?"

Fearing some form of reprisal, Jinli hadn't offered any comment about how capitalism really works in a free society. His report was a just a treatise on its ills, rather than the wonderful economic benefits of capitalism that so many people enjoy as a reward for their hard work. Naturally, he failed to mention the attraction of the U.S. to so many would-be immigrants seeking a better life.

Wei's plan for Jinli going to California had produced a sparkling analysis of the America's ills and a rationale for why capitalism would never overcome communism as the leading economic system in the world!

The report presented a vivid condemnation of capitalism, and as Wei circulated the report, it made its way up to the office of the Secretary of the Guangdong Provincial Committee of the CPC. The Party Chief loved it and referred it to the Communist Youth League of China, who published it in their official newspaper, the China Youth Daily, where it became "suggested" reading for all members, ages fourteen to twenty-eight.

The Watts Riots that occurred on August 11, 1965, shortly after the report was published, provided additional evidence that capitalism had failed to correct the disparity between black and white in America, and Jinli was continually praised for his insightful analysis.

In recognition of his contribution to education, he was hired as a research assistant in the Department of Commerce of Guangdong Province in early 1966 and assigned to its main office in Guangzhou. Shortly thereafter, he joined the Communist Party and the CYL. "Smart move," Wei chuckled to himself, having studied the background and success of men in high places.

Just as Jinli began his job, the government announced the latest of its five-year plans of social and economic development initiatives fashioned by the CPC, the third since 1953. It included the goal of increasing agricultural production to the levels that existed prior to the Great Leap Forward. The emphasis was placed on solving problems associated with providing food and the other basic needs of their burgeoning population, and Jinli was excited to get an opportunity to participate in the effort.

"Jinli, I am happy for you," Wei said, "although I will be sad to be living apart from you. Nevertheless, this is a unique opportunity for you to prove yourself, and you will have the advantage of being at the forefront of creating a new economic model."

"Father, this job fits well with everything I learned from you about land reform and farming. I am in your debt."

"Enough of that, my son. Just go and make your mother and me proud."

Wei didn't tell Jinli that he hadn't run for reelection and was pursuing other appointed government positions.

A year after Jinli returned, Mao Zedong regained the leadership of the CPC after being forced to step aside earlier following the economic failure of his Great Leap Forward.

Jinli's report fit only too nicely into Mao's new plan, better known as the Cultural Revolution. The primary goal of his latest revolutionary thinking was to preserve fundamental communist ideology and purge any hidden capitalist and traditional aspects of society. Then, his "Mao Zedong Thought" would prevail, and peasants would become the revolutionary class exemplified by his life-long struggle.

To quote the party's Central Committee: ". . . our objective is to struggle against and crush those people in authority who are taking the capitalist road, to criticize and repudiate the reactionary bourgeois academic 'authorities' and the ideology of the bourgeoisie and all other exploiting classes and to transform education, literature and art, and all other parts of the superstructure that do not correspond to the socialist economic base, so as to facilitate the consolidation and development of the socialist system."

Jinli suffered through the difficult first year of the revolution, protecting his image of loyalty against the zealot's constant challenge. The leftists, under the banner of the Red Guards, a mass paramilitary movement, were hell bent on leading the revolutionary cause. They were a bunch of insurgent adolescents out to destroy all of the "old ways" of customs, culture, habits, and ideas, attacking every vestige of the bourgeoisie, including every western or imperialistic reference to their former society. Their numbers grew quickly as their message got out.

Jinli was in constant fear that he would be caught up in the hysteria of "their" revolutionary ideas, but he remained steadfast.

Unfortunately, the revolution delayed economic progress under Mao's plan due to frequent interruptions in transportation by the Red Guards who appropriated trains and trucks to transport themselves around the country. Inexperienced revolutionary committees took over the direction of factories and caused output to fall under their poor management, and finally, the political activity of students and workers closed the universities.

Even street names were changed to revolutionary words and slogans, to the dismay of the post office. It's no wonder that Jinli never received Su Lin's letters.

In addition, the Red Guards were intent on attacking anyone sympathetic to those who might lean toward capitalism, the so-called "Capitalist Roaders." To them, even the mention of the word "capitalism" in polite conversation would arouse suspicion. Jinli avoided as much social interaction as possible, but if confronted, he was able to successfully elude any discussion that could be construed as a personal criticism of Mao's plans.

Like most men, Jinli donned a green Zhongshan, or Mao suit. It was the Chinese tunic style worn by the revolutionaries, and he wore it in order to better fit in with his contemporaries.

Public opinion deriding the Red Guards was eventually reversed by 1970, and a more normal social order with political stability was gradually restored. Even though Jinli was constantly tested throughout the next few years, he somehow managed to escape the continuing purge of government officials by staunchly defending his support for Mao and his plans.

Jinli had learned a great deal from his father's experience about how to walk the straight and narrow. However, he began to lose confidence in the future because of the dogma that had enveloped the country.

When the universities reopened, Jinli enrolled in Sun Yat-sen University in Guangzhou to pursue a postgraduate degree in economic research. With that decision, he was promoted to Director of Research in the Department of Commerce where he worked.

He met Yuan Shuchun there in 1973. She was from the ranks of the urban youth in the big city of Tianjin, where employment was in short supply. Consequently, she had been "sent down" to perform manual labor on a farm during the rustification movement, another directive derived from Mao's focus on teaching the value of peasantry.

They fell in love and quickly married without family members in attendance, since Wei had not yet been able to meet her and bless their marriage. In Shuchun's case, her parents were still on the farm as "sent downs" themselves, and she told Jinli she wanted to leave that life behind forever.

Shuchun's exemplary scores on the university entrance exams and the recommendation of her work unit had earned her a spot in a two-year nursing school that had reopened in Guangzhou near Jinli's university. Nursing had become her passion when she had witnessed the lack of adequate medical care in the villages surrounding her farm. No emphasis was placed on monitoring a patient's condition or nutritional management, and she was appalled at the number of infant deaths, notwithstanding the horrific degree of female infanticide in particular.

Shuchun's life's work would be to change the perception of nursing and elevate its social standing. Unfortunately, she herself would fall victim to the failure of the hospital system to provide proper patient care, as her first and only pregnancy ended in a stillborn baby boy in 1974.

"Jinli," she cried, as tears streamed down her face. "I have failed you."

"No you haven't, my little Popo. We will just have to live with it as our lot in life." Popo was the term of endearment that he used only for her when they were alone.

"I will always love you," he said as she looked into his eyes and put her head on his shoulder. "Believe me, there will be better times ahead," he continued, and comforted her with both hands.

Mao Zedong died in 1976, and things began to change with a great deal of unrest and jockeying for political leadership as the Cultural Revolution ended. By then, Jinli and Wei had feigned estrangement, since they decided it best not to remain in contact during the revolution. Had one of them been singled out for harsh treatment, or worse, because of some lunatic's charges, the other would have been implicated by virtue of their relationship.

Jinli finally decided it was time, and took Shuchun to meet his parents, who greeted her warmly as they shook hands as she bowed slightly. Upon learning that she was a nursing graduate, Wei produced a wide smile of admiration.

Jinli and his father met infrequently after that, but spoke often by phone.

The voice on the last call Jinli received from Wei's number in 1977 was not from Wei, but from his caretaker. Jinli was devastated to learn both of his parents had been hospitalized with the bird flu, as it reached a pandemic level in several parts of the country. The virus in Jiangmen was thought to have emanated from a visitor who arrived from Shanghai, where several deaths had already resulted from the disease.

Jinli was tied up in very important meetings, so he told the caretaker that Shuchun would make the trip immediately. She made her way to Jiangmen, but it took her two days, as she was frequently stopped and required to produce her nursing identification to avoid the martial law travel restrictions that were in effect because of the pandemic.

When she arrived at the hospital, she learned that it was too late. His parents had already passed. Shuchun fell to her knees and cried loudly in the entrance area when she received the news.

Wei and Mingzhou had left a note with the hospital staff for Jinli and Shuchun, together with a small package. The note read:

> *Our bodies will have been cremated together*
> *by the time you arrive, as the thought of being*
> *stolen by grave robbers is horrifying. We will*
> *not give them the satisfaction.*

Corpses were being sold to the government for cremation rather than burial, to make room for farming and development. The note continued:

> *Jinli, please cherish this small gift that my father stuffed into the bottom of my school bag many years ago as I headed off to Yan'an. May it comfort you as it has me over the years.*

Shuchun returned to Guangzhou. There was nothing left to be done in Jiangmen.

"They had been cremated by the time you arrived?" Jinli exclaimed. "Yes, to avoid grave robbers."

"How disgusting!"

They mourned the deaths together as he read Wei's note and carefully unwrapped the package. Inside was a copy of the New Testament of a Christian Bible with an inscription inside the cover that read:

> *Wei my Son, may you and your sons go in peace, and may God protect you and them forever. Chen Yongmin*

"What are you thinking, Jinli?" Shuchun asked.

"Well, he did survive the war, didn't he?"

Jinli's parents had passed away long before he would reach the potential that Wei had predicted for him so many years earlier.

Although Deng Xiaoping never held the top spot, he was considered the paramount leader and assumed control of the CPC in 1978. The Central Committee concluded that Mao's stranglehold on a centrally planned economy did not work, and they decided to gradually move towards a socialist market economy. Part of their program became the imposition of the one-child policy, aimed at curbing population growth. It was a sad reminder to Shuchun, as she recalled how they had tried and tried, but had given up after several miscarriages.

As Jinli continued to publish his research papers on competing economic systems, his name caught the attention of high-ranking policymakers in the new regime. With his firsthand knowledge of capitalism, he was identified as a thoughtful economic planner, and his reputation spread quickly, followed by his first foray into politics.

He held his first office in 1981 as an appointed deputy party chief of Shantou, a prefecture-level city of five million people, and one of the original treaty ports for Western trade. Shantou is located on the Southeast coast of Guangdong Province, where several million Overseas Chinese with roots in the area lived previously. Jinli's knowledge of sojourners, gleaned from the many discussions he had with his father, was invaluable in his new position.

Shortly after they moved to Shantou, Shuchun got involved in the new Shantou University.

"Jinli, this is a dream come true, a real answer to my prayers," she said. "I was asked to assist in developing the curriculum for their new clinical medicine degree." He was taken aback by her "prayer" remark, but let it pass.

"Popo, I am happy that you are happy. We will be happy together." Shuchun continued to remain behind the scenes as Jinli's career progressed, but she took up a number of social causes relating to care for the poor, and contributed to nursing development at every turn.

A year later, Jinli was named Chair of the Guangdong Economic Commission. From the very beginning of Jinli's career into politics, he was elevated with each passing election cycle. His appointments placed him as Communist Party Chief in successively larger spheres of political influence, mixed with government administrative positions in jurisdictions of economic importance and population growth. As China's economy exploded, he continued to march upward through the ranks of party and government leadership.

Jinli carefully navigated his way through several economic and social changes that were punctuated by events that occurred while he was Governor and Party Chief in Guangdong Province. Unfortunately, the Tiananmen incident of 2001 became a major social issue, as the government showed its power to suppress free speech. The protesters called for government accountability, freedom of the press, freedom of speech, and the restoration of workers' control over industry. Again, Jinli showed his deftness by avoiding the sympathetic demonstrations held in Guangzhou, the largest city in Guangdong Province, and virtually every other big city.

The incident was a reminder of the old ways, but the government's response did not stop China's march forward nor did it impede Jinli's career advancement.

Despite that turbulent event and the lengthy negotiations in which he assisted as a visiting professor of international trade from Sun Yat-sen University, his alma mater, China was finally admitted into the World Trade Organization. The U.S. was supportive of the addition of China to the ranks of the WTO, as it could no longer ignore the doubling of imports from China over the previous five years. Membership in the WTO put China on the world stage and positioned it for spectacular growth.

Each move exposed Jinli to additional responsibility and a wider audience, especially among top officials. Finally, in 2003, he was elected to the Standing Committee of Guangdong Province while continuing to serve as its Governor.

The National People's Congress appointed Ma Xing as China's Premier in 2013. Jinli's reputation as a policymaker was unparalleled and at the next meeting of the National People's Congress, he was made first vice premier for finance and economic development.

As such, he became China's principal spokesman on all economic affairs. Concurrently with that appointment, he became a member of the Politburo Standing Committee of the CPC, its highest ruling body with only seven leaders who oversee the party.

Shuchun could not have been more proud of him, but when she spoke to him privately, she asked, "Jinli, now you have reached the top of your profession.

But has it been worth it to stick by your communist beliefs, given your knowledge of other systems? You have to admit that our spectacular economic growth has come at the expense of the freedoms of our people. So are we missing something?"

"Popo, their freedoms have not been suppressed. In capitalistic nations, freedoms are spelled out. In our constitution we use the term 'rights and responsibilities.' It's really the same thing, except that our people have a duty to the state to get an education, safeguard the unity of the country, not divulge state secrets, perform military service, and pay taxes. Our people have more rights than ever before, including the right to vote, the right to an education, the right of opinion and expression, the right to worship or not, the right to own property and the right to public assistance based on age, illness or disability, just to name a few.

"The problem I see is that our constitutional provisions regarding freedom aren't really enforced and, in fact, many of them are repressed. The Internet has changed everything and brought the ever-increasing practice of surveilling our ordinary citizens. I am not in favor of this activity, but there are two sides to every story. I will keep an eye on it, but that issue is not in my jurisdiction."

"I knew you would see it my way," she said. "You always do the right thing. I'm just sorry your parents aren't around to see everything that is happening."

Jinli relocated his offices to the Zhongnanhai, an imperial garden in central Beijing, similar to the White House.

From there, he continued his efforts to transform China's economy into a more capitalistic model without compromising his unwavering adherence to communism as the core foundation of its political structure.

His star had approached its zenith.

PART TWO

The Future

CHAPTER 8 ~ The Transition

FEBRUARY 1, 2016

Michael Simon burst onto the national scene as a candidate for President of the United States, bringing many of the same ideas that got him elected previously as Governor of Ohio for two consecutive terms.

Prior to entering politics, Simon had served in the U.S. Navy, retiring after twenty years of distinguished service as the captain of the nuclear-powered aircraft carrier *USS Harry S. Truman*. Simon relished the motto of the Truman, "The buck stops here," which was attributed to the former President. Simon often praised Truman as the kind of decision maker he strove to emulate.

In his speeches, Simon took a reasoned approach in addressing the nation's security issues and protection of individual rights, and he demonstrated a thorough understanding the role of government in helping those in need.

"Isn't our national defense and the general welfare of our people the cornerstones of our constitution's mandate?" Simon would ask. He had his detractors, of course, but who could argue with the powers granted to the federal government by the constitution regarding national defense and the general welfare of the citizenry?

And he would add, "Shouldn't our federal government's role be limited to those two basic responsibilities?"

He repeated the same two questions over and over again, and no one could present a compelling argument against his position. To be sure, that concept was used by big government ideologues to justify every cockamamie plan they could come up with. Most of those plans carried an unjustifiable cost, regard less of public benefit.

Simon argued successfully against such pork-barrel ideas in Ohio. He was a strict conformist to the original intent of words of the United States Constitution, and his spending measures embraced that intent.

Simon had been chairman of the National Governors Association as a result of his accomplishments in Ohio, where a substantial reduction in unemployment and a balanced budget had put him in the national spotlight. His record was the envy of virtually every governor.

Of particular note, however, was his advocacy for school vouchers and charter schools. He achieved major education reform in Ohio with a program of scholarships and tax credits after a protracted battle with teachers' union members, and the polls indicated that his approach was rapidly gaining support in many other parts of the country. Quite naturally, Simon had his opponents, but he never let the critics get the upper hand.

He kept preaching that there should be a school choice program in all fifty states. Gone would be standardized testing and federally mandated performance goals, which would be replaced with a simple requirement to teach his so-called five Rs: Reading, 'Riting and 'Rithmetic, plus Respect and Responsibility. The last two would be added to the conventional ideas of literacy and numeracy in education to help create a better environment for teaching and a better-educated citizenry. Teachers would no longer have to teach to the test.

As his national campaign moved along, Simon never allowed himself or his handlers to criticize his rivals or mention them by name. He was determined to remain a small target. The hired guns, with their lengthy campaign experience, recommended the creation of negative ads against his opponents, but he would have none of it.

He continued to maintain the neutral path, out of the fray, and he stayed the course. Simon argued with his staff that emphasizing his record of accomplishment and establishing his vision for the future would see him through to the very end. He was confident of that, although his campaign manager continued to disagree with his position on several other smaller matters.

Nevertheless, Simon kept the manager on board, acknowledging that good people can agree to disagree.

His demonstrated success as a Governor, combined with his good looks and positive debating style, eventually won over even his harshest critics. He seemed to have the magical, visionary leadership ability of Kennedy and the hopeful appeal of Reagan. It was nearly impossible to compete with that combination.

Simon liked to refer to himself as the only so-called self-proclaimed conservative independent in the field, even thought the title smacked of being an oxymoron. Still, Simon was thought to be a moderate. He was known as a consensus builder. Even the press and his opponents acknowledged that.

Simon's win in the Iowa caucus on February 1, 2016, got him off to a good start as the voting season began in earnest. After his victory, his momentum started to build. He hoped to capitalize on that success in the next three primaries and caucuses in February and go into Super Tuesday's fourteen state contests with a substantial lead.

By the time the last primary was held in early June, Simon had a sufficient number of delegate votes to secure the nomination.

Austin Cook was an investigative reporter for Online-Truth-in-Politics, a new web-based newspaper and blog site featuring happenings in and around the District of Columbia, and he was assigned to cover the Simon candidacy.

Cook had made the transition from traditional journalism to the web. His methods were indisputable and his results were unquestionable. He had the inquiring mind of a scientist and played "what if" to a ridiculous degree. He saw alternatives, choices and possibilities that were way beyond the bounds of natural curiosity. Fortunately, he never gave in to paranoia.

He told himself he simply wanted to learn the truth and would not stop until he found it. His aptitude for politics had earned him a Pulitzer at a pretty young age, but he dismissed the accolades as journalistic self-indulgence.

Austin disdained all the flim-flam talk he heard around the beltway. In spite of Simon's announced positions and ideas on how to fix the nation's problems, it sounded to Austin like the same old political swagger: long on problem identification and short on solutions.

He committed to his followers that he would shadow Simon's every move, attend every press conference, and ask hardball questions. He was determined to challenge the candidate in every one of his articles, blogs, and tweets to live up to his promises.

In short, he was on a mission to hold the candidate accountable to the truth.

Once the convention got underway in Cleveland in July, the groundswell for Simon's nomination began to build.

After the perfunctory business matters of the convention were out of the way, and the keynote address had been given, Simon announced that James Charlton would be his choice for Vice President. Charlton was an ex-Army Ranger officer and a congressman from Texas whose patriotism and devotion to duty were unquestioned.

Simon said that he and Charlton would offer the nation a team of experienced leaders with a thorough understanding of the nation's military and security needs. Simon chuckled as told the delegates that if they selected his ticket, they would get a "twofer," one now and one for later at no additional cost! The remark was a little arrogant perhaps, but it reflected his confidence in his choice of a running mate. After all, fourteen of forty-seven vice presidents have become president.

As the convention votes were tallied from the alphabetical roll call of the states, the secretary of the convention paused. Just before the vote total reached the number needed to select a nominee, as is the custom, each of the remaining states listed ahead of Ohio passed on its vote until the secretary called on the chairman of the delegation from Ohio.

Their chairman began in a loud voice, "As Ohio goes, so goes the nation. The election results in Ohio have decided all but two elections since 1904, and it will be the same this year. Our nominees' name will be added to the list of the most presidents from any one state, the state that features the Buckeyes, the Bengals, the Browns, the Cavaliers, the Indians, and the Reds."

Then, she hesitated, before raising her voice again above the roar of the crowd, and announced, "The great state of Ohio requests a suspension of the rules and proudly casts all of its votes for Michael Simon and James Charlton, and we move for their unanimous selection by acclamation as our party's nominees, respectively, for president and vice president of these great United States of America."

As the cheers went up, the convention secretary's words were drowned out as she said, proudly, "Having heard no objection, Michael Simon is hereby declared our party's nominee for President of the United States, and James Charlton our party's nominee for Vice President of The United States."

The crowd shouted its approval, and the cheering and hand clapping lasted until well past the moment that the last red, white, and blue balloon hit the convention floor.

"To my fellow citizens of this great nation: With profound gratitude and a humble heart, I accept your nomination for the presidency of the United States. To the next Vice President of the United States, Jim Charlton, I say thank you. I thank you for your service to our country, and I look forward to serving with you. Ladies and Gentlemen, this vessel we call home has been listing to port for far too long, and together, we will right the ship.

"To my loving and supporting wife, Suzanne, and your soon-to-be-first lady, and our three wonderful children, I say thank you, and I love you. You are the inspiration that keeps me going every day, and will forever and ever.

"I stand here tonight and offer to you the only promise I can make. I will do my very best to honor you and serve you in the only way I know how: with honesty, integrity, and a sincere desire to make this country a better place for you and your children and your grandchildren."

Simon's authenticity was there for all to see, and the standing ovation continued until he finally asked them to please be seated. Then he continued.

"If elected, my initial focus will be on the creation of jobs and an improvement of the economy. I will bring that about by becoming energy independent, stopping illegal immigration, increasing exports, and revising our tax code. The size of government is too big. We will reduce its size and eliminate its regulatory burden on business. We will cure our government's addiction to spending.

"That is not to say that welfare will take second place. I believe that growth in jobs and the resulting increase in the standard of living, particularly for those on the lowest rungs of society, can relieve—if not eventually eliminate—the ills of unemployment. We must reduce the dependence of our citizens on entitlement programs, such as unemployment benefits and food stamps. I will evaluate every entitlement program including the Aid to Families with Dependent Children that does little beyond encouraging women to have more children. The goal will be to improve effectiveness wherever we can and eliminate the plague of waste, fraud, and abuse.

"I will pursue new ways to provide jobs for the chronically unemployed through a revision of unemployment insurance benefit qualifications and by providing substantial federal tax credits to employers for job training and hiring. They can do the job better than the government can.

"In other words, able-bodied people will need to work in order to continue receiving benefits after an initial short period devoted to a job search following a job loss. They will have an opportunity to learn skills on the job in the private market situations that fit their aptitude and potential for growth. This will create a public-private partnership to provide job training and employment, much like the Works Progress Administration did in the thirties. That program created millions of jobs and wonderful public works projects as a result.

"Although we are not in an economic recession, we need to rehabilitate healthy people who suffer from hopelessness and have given up on society. I aim to correct that with dignified employment opportunities.

"I plan to move quickly to bring those responsible for immigration and border control, homeland security, and energy together in an effort to address the need for better protection of our the country. Our nation should be better prepared to resist domestic and foreign attacks of every kind, including coercion and extortion. Over the years, our country dropped its guard, and I am determined to flex our country's muscle once again.

"I acknowledge there are a multitude of foreign affairs challenges facing our country. They are no less important than the domestic concerns I outlined, but I am reluctant to address them directly until I am thoroughly briefed after taking office. I will not be drawn into a contest of theoretical propositions. In the interim, I refer you to the current administration and the United Nations for answers regarding any international concerns you may have.

"Regardless, I am committed to rebuilding our country's military and returning to the number one position of leadership in the world by controlling the sea lanes and the air space above friendly countries.

"I know these plans are ambitious, and that I will have to be a quick learner if elected to satisfy those of you who vote for me. However, I assure you that I am up to the task.

"Thank you, and may God continue to bless you and this great nation, the United States of America."

Simon loved to talk with bullet points, figuratively speaking, to emphasize concepts that were easy to recall. Before he had even wrapped up his nomination speech his team was ready and way out in front with a number of strong television ads. In each one, Simon looked directly into the camera, essentially speaking face to face with his audience, and proclaimed, "It's really quite simple: A vote for Simon and Charlton is a vote for this alliteration:

- Strong defense
- Social safety nets
- Smaller government
- Spending control
- Simple tax structures, and
- Separation of church and state

The word "alliteration" sounded like it came from some intellectual, but Simon refused to dumb down his choice of words, just to avoid being labeled as condescending.

He said journalists would just have to deal with it!

> Austin Cook @ OTP Jul 21 Simon – That
> was a real mouthful. But can he put his words
> into action? Or is he just pandering to voters?
> We'll see. View on Twitter.

Simon and Charlton ran on a platform that stressed the idea that strength can be gained by understanding diversity and creating a revolution of thought among the citizenry. Simon believed that the greater good would be achieved if different ideologies were embraced and a consensus reached after considering every competing idea before taking action.

Simon's campaign buttons shouted, "WE WANT YOU!" Some pundits thought it was corny, but it was highly effective. He said he wanted to attract the most capable people in the entirety of the cultural and political universe, and then build support by advancing the most promising ideas coming from his followers. As he explained, "No matter how new or different an idea might be, if I see merit in a thoughtful proposal, I won't be above trying it."

After suffering through a period of arrogance that bubbled up in the current administration, the country seemed ready for a different approach to problem solving, and Simon's willingness to embrace new ideas filled the bill to a tee. It was a refreshing concept that really seemed to resonate with voters, according to the pollsters.

Simon's pledge to incorporate solidarity within in his administration started with the announcement that he would appoint a Hispanic, a woman, a black, and an Asian to Cabinet posts— if elected, of course.

As his final push began, Simon took the unprecedented step of pre-announcing the names of five of his intended Cabinet appointees, each of whom had committed to Simon should he be elected. That particular group all related to highly important voter concerns. He believed his strategy had the potential to pay off big.

First, Simon's goal of becoming energy independent led him to select Russ McKinnie as his Secretary of Energy. McKinnie was a veteran and retired petroleum executive from one of the nation's largest domestic oil producers. His accurate assessments of the market were often quoted in industry magazines, and he had appeared on nearly every business television show over the years. As the current president and CEO of the American Petroleum

Institute, the only trade organization representing both the oil and natural gas industries, he seemed to be the natural choice.

Next, since closing the border was another of Simon's highest priorities, he planned to focus more attention on the problem by removing the activities of Customs and Border Protection and those of Immigration and Customs Enforcement from the purview of the Department of Homeland Security, and elevate the combined operations under a new Cabinet level position to be designated as the Department of Customs, Immigration, and Border Protection. Dan Rodriquez would be at the helm. He was a seasoned, high-level immigration officer with twenty-five years of field experience and was very familiar with the turmoil at the border caused by conflicting instructions given to CBP and ICE personnel. The organizational change would produce a more coordinated effort to stop the entry of illegal individuals, including terrorists, and the smuggling of weapons and drugs into the country at the border.

Simon's choice to lead Homeland Security was Tomas Retsuc. Retsuc was a Polish immigrant and Silicon Valley technology whiz who developed several applications to combat cyber crime, including a number of anti-virus products that won worldwide acclaim. He had consulted for senior officials at the National Security Agency and had led many conferences on the role of technology in supporting intra- and inter-agency efforts in support of the mission of the Federal Emergency Management Agency. Retsuc had recently turned his attention to cutting-edge retinal and iris- scanning technologies, for use in recognition applications.

Commerce would go to Jack Donnelly. Donnelly was a former chairman and CEO of a Fortune 100 food and beverage company with both domestic and international operations. He was well known around Washington because he had testified often before several congressional committees on trade issues, oftentimes together with the U.S. Trade Representative.

Fearing the growing imbalance of trade with China and the size of the U.S. debt they hold, Simon chose Dr. Winston Lee, a

Chinese-American, to be Secretary of the Treasury. Dr. Lee was a professor of international economics at Georgetown University, where he had gained fame for his treatise on currency manipulation. Simon had it on good authority that Lee's name had been submitted as a candidate for the Nobel Prize in Economic Sciences, even though the nominations were strictly confidential. That information, although not verified, had been considered by the president to be a strong endorsement of Lee's qualification for the job. Lee was somewhat short on government experience, although he had done considerable staff work for the Council of Economic Advisers and the United States International Trade Commission. He was sure to be confirmed.

Simon's choices met with resounding support from Wall Street and his advocacy groups everywhere. Contributions took off, and the money rolled into his campaign.

The non-partisan Commission on Presidential Debates announced their quadrennial television debates with a great deal of fanfare, highlighting the independent nature of their selections. Although the nation's two main political parties comprised the Commission, they still managed to select left-leaning moderators and interviewers with a liberal bias. There was nothing new in that. Regardless, Simon was prepared for every twist and turn in the debates.

As the interviewers addressed the candidates over the course of three nights in October, Simon maintained a respectful posture throughout the evenings: he never criticized his opponents' statements, or the accuracy of their facts. He stuck to his talking points and refused to be sidetracked by "what if" and "assuming that" type questions.

The final debate was typical of the earlier ones. He continued the dual theme of constitutional mandates, to provide for a common defense and the general welfare of the country. He always reminded his audiences that those two responsibilities were mentioned in the Preamble to the United States Constitution and again in Article 1, Section 8, the so-called Taxing and Spending Clause of the Constitution.

He pointed out that, over the years, many Constitutional responsibilities had unfortunately been expanded or interpreted to fit current circumstances and he pledged to work to avoid that in the future.

Simon's rhetoric was designed to remind the nation of what their next president's job is supposed to be all about, and his ability to perform that job.

With every answer to a question or challenge by his opponent, Simon had the facts on his side. Moreover, whenever he was asked about a troubling issue facing the nation, he turned his answer into a discussion about his approach to problem solving. He stressed the importance of minimizing the role of attorneys and influence peddlers on his decision-making, and his disdain for political correctness.

The next questioner turned to another subject after the huge sound of approval from the audience following that statement by Simon. He clearly struck a nerve with them.

The final question came from a veteran newscaster. She asked Simon about his thoughts on international diplomacy as a solution to throttling back aggression in the nuclear age. In response, Simon thanked her for the question and said that it was as good a time as any to announce his choice to head up the State Department.

He said he had selected Glenn Boyd, a clear leader in international matters, and former Ambassador to the United Nations under the current president's predecessor. Boyd had worked in several previous administrations and was a frequent critic of the approach the country was currently taking to resolve international disputes.

Asked about his choice, Simon said that he and Boyd shared the same philosophy in approaching international conflicts, and he articulated his approach to diplomacy, stressing leadership, resolve, and cooperation among friendly nations. He emphasized his belief that the American democratic process as the envy of men and women everywhere, and one that will ultimately provide the framework for world peace.

However, he also stressed that in most negotiations, nothing should be off the table, including military action as a last resort, and that "A red line is a red line!"

In his concluding remarks, Simon returned to the basic promises he had put forth during his campaign for his party's nomination, stating that he would, to the best of his ability: uphold and defend the Constitution and enforce the laws of the nation, but work with Congress to enact changes that he feels are necessary; review all standing Executive Orders and rescind those that are not in keeping with the authority of the office; protect the rights and dignity of all persons, including illegal immigrants, the ill, the indigent, and the incarcerated, to the extent provided by law; and correct the economic, social and racial problems that divide our country.

As usual, he was totally prepared, and according to the pundits, he won every debate.

> Austin Cook @ OTP Oct 19 Simon – There
> is a lot of hope in these tea leaves, but I'm
> still reserving judgment. View on Twitter.

The current president had completed two terms and was desperately attempting to salvage his reputation as a lame duck president by rallying his supporters to continue his party's dominance, as the date for the election approached.

The press relied on historical statistics, not wanting to take a chance, and opined that the nominee of the incumbent party would likely win a close race, even in the face of so many polls that favored Simon.

Simon chalked it all up to conventional politics.

It was really no surprise that Simon's fresh approach to problem solving and taking action resonated with the electorate. His plan worked. The Hispanic, black and Asian minority voters turned out en masse on November 8, 2016, and helped sweep Simon into office by a considerable margin of victory. Clearly, the electorate was disenchanted with the current administration and wanted fresh new faces and ideas.

Simon's acceptance speech was classic Simon. He would normally have delivered his victory speech at the Ohio Statehouse, but he opted to give it from the deck of the USS *Dwight D. Eisenhower* in Norfolk, Virginia, where she was being prepared for deployment. The USS *Harry S. Truman*, the *Eisenhower's* sister ship, was his first choice but it was at sea.

He thanked God, his family, his supporters, and the voters for placing such enormous trust in him. His speech was a short five minutes, and he promised not to let them down.

He thanked the military for their continuing service to the country and said he was honored to be their Commander-in-Chief.

As he and Jim waved to the crowd, a joint military band played "Hail to the Chief."

Then, it was time for Simon and Charlton to deliver, and prove his critics wrong.

> Austin Cook @ OTP Nov 9 Simon – …
> and they're off and running with Simon in
> the lead and Charlton close behind. View on
> Twitter.

It didn't take long before those who distrust government to advance another conspiracy theory. One almost always follows a presidential election.

This one popped up on the Internet and suggested that Simon was hoodwinking the public while secretly moving toward a police state, a sort of twenty-first century Illuminati. Austin was always on the lookout for evidence to support every cockamamie idea, but he never fell into the trap of encouraging his followers to consider the theories that abound on the Internet. Nevertheless, he promised his followers that he would consider the latest one and be on the lookout for any evidence of its veracity.

Highest on the theorist's list of possible concerns was Simon's goal of stopping illegal immigration. Certainly closing the Mexican border had been discussed ad nauseam, but the idea had consistently failed. Simon had always acknowledged that when he had hammered home his call to close the border.

Was there anything new in that proposal? Austin wondered. No. But the theory suggested that Simon was part of an elaborate scheme that would completely isolate the country by stopping all immigration, and then establish an economic and military might to contend for some leadership role in a new world order.

It didn't make sense, but the same critics of the Trilateral Commission had been around since the seventies and continued to fear some combined government of global proportion.

He quickly dismissed the latest theory as more poppycock.

Austin allowed himself few distractions, but on Wednesday nights he hosted a poker game at his place. He liked to get one or two tables of seven, but never more than eight. It was first come, first serve.

Austin was the only journalist among the players and according to him, the only normal person. The other regular players included his close friends Ben Elliott, the Chief of Staff for Senator Stephen Mickiewicz from the State of Washington; Lucho Santiago, a Chilean restaurateur popular with the D.C. crowd; and Billy Eddie Phillippi, a lobbyist for the beer and wine industry. Since Billy Eddie was owner and distributor of a craft beer called Billy's Beltway Beer, he always provided a generous supply for their gatherings, along with some pretty decent wine.

Most of the "irregulars," as Austin called them, were either federal appointees from one department or another, or "beltway bandits," the leeches who compete for government contracts.

Before each game got underway, Austin always posed some challenging question or two about controversial political issues in the news. Everyone knew that Austin would treat anything he heard with the utmost confidentiality and never reveal his source, so most everyone was comfortable discussing his views with him.

The bandits were always a talkative bunch, but the appointees were a little more guarded. A little booze always solved that problem. If someone purposely offered a "politically correct" answer to one of Austin's questions just to be on the safe side, Austin would chide him into coming up with a better response. Frequently, the conversations would strike a chord with Austin and provide him with an idea to follow up on the next day.

In the games themselves, Austin applied his customary analytical skills that made him so successful at his trade, and he usually won most of the money. His poker buddies always met at Austin's place even if he couldn't make it. They were more than happy when that occurred, thinking they might recoup some of their losses. On those rare days, Billie Eddie was more than willing to fill in as the host.

The election had Austin's mind spinning. What was really behind the new President's thinking? Simon was upsetting the proverbial apple carts of professional politicians and hacks. His approach was electrifying, but was it rational? Could he move quickly and get his administration in place as he promised without making enormous mistakes? Austin decided to take a poll of his buddies.

On Wednesday night after the election, so many guys called Austin for a seat that they decided to set up three tables—a first. They couldn't stop talking about the election results as they played, dissecting the votes and offering their personal perspectives on why certain candidates won or lost.

Senator Mickiewicz's contest was too close to call, and the race was still undecided when they sat down to play. Ben thought he might lose his job if the senator were defeated, so he decided to go home early and watch the returns on television.

The players discussed the Cabinet names Simon had announced before the election. They wondered if a cohesive group would emerge from Simon's quest for diversity. His platform was so bold that getting everyone on board with his big issues was sure to be a daunting task. For sure, they knew Simon would have to take his case to them individually before their confirmation hearings.

Simon's challenges would take some real poker skill. You better know if your opponent is bluffing, they reasoned. Or be good at bluffing yourself, like the old cowboy said!

They were generally happy with Simon's picks, but wondered if he could get Senate confirmations for all of them and run the table. If he could, that would erase all of their doubts. If not, well …

Before everyone left, Austin announced that he expected the events after the election would be pretty time consuming for all of them, and he recommended they meet monthly for a while. They all agreed.

"Jim," the president-elect said, "Thanksgiving is tomorrow, so I appreciate your making time in your schedule to discuss the transition. I hope we can make it as seamless as possible so I can praise our lame-duck president for his cooperation."

"We'll see about that."

"To begin, Brian McNeill has agreed to join us as my Chief of Staff. I think you know him."

"Yes, sir. I talked to him several times at the convention. Good man."

Brian McNeill had been Simon's Lieutenant Governor in Ohio, and before that, a CIA officer with a posting in Iraq. Prior to joining the CIA, he was Colonel in the Army. A military background seemed to be the order of the day. The president always called Brian by his nickname, Mac.

"Mac will take a big burden off us as we get organized. He is highly disciplined, and he will keep us focused on the big picture and on message. By the way, that will apply to everyone in the White House."

"Totally agree," Jim concurred.

"He can help us identify the best qualified nominees for the remaining jobs we have to fill, including the White House staff, and manage their day-to-day interface with all those damned bureaucracies we have to deal with. I don't want any vestige of the current administration to taint our organization, and it will be his job to make sure that doesn't happen. Mac will help defend our policies and interact with Congress on our behalf. In effect, he will be our public face in a lot of areas."

"That's a bit of a relief, Mr. President. I'm comfortable being in the limelight, but I would be more than happy to deflect any attention that comes my way over to him so I can concentrate on my job."

"Jim, I was advised that the General Services Administration will make five million dollars available to help us with the transition. Can we save any money in that budget?"

"Yes sir, I think we can."

"Great. I think so, too. That will send a positive signal to the country if we can pull it off.

"All right, let's review today's task. I've already noted my ideas on several key positions, and I'll get that list to you as soon as possible. If you will provide me with your recommendations, as well, I'll review them and get back to you so we can finalize the names. Then you and I can get busy contacting them about their agreement to serve.

"I've already announced a few Cabinet names so we can finish up that list right now. So far, we have Glenn Boyd for State, Dan Rodriquez to run our new Immigration post, Tomas Retsuc for Homeland, Russ McKinnie for Energy, Jack Donnelly for Commerce, and Dr. Winston Lee for Treasury. Let's push for

122

immediate confirmation of those six appointees so they can start work ASAP after my inauguration. I've already asked the Office of Personnel Management for warp speed on vetting their names.

"Jim, I really pray those choices will withstand the rigorous test of the process. One false step and our creditability would be over in a heartbeat.

"That leaves the Attorney General and the Secretaries of Agriculture, Defense, Education, Labor, Health and Human Services, Housing and Urban Development, Transportation, and Veterans Affairs."

"That's still a tall order."

"Right, especially since my soon-to-be predecessor elevated several more positions to Cabinet level, requiring Senate confirmation of course: namely, the Director of the Office of the Budget, the Ambassador to the United Nations, the Administrator of the Environmental Protection Agency, the Trade Representative, the Chair of the Council of Economic Advisors, and the Administrator of the Small Business Administration."

"Unbelievable."

"And, of course, he left his National Security Advisor out of the mix. I guess he planned to keep national security within his own purview, away from the prying eyes of Congress."

"We'll have to see about that!"

"Oh, scratch trade off the list. I forgot to tell you that Aimee Remington sent me her acceptance for the job an hour ago. She'll make a great Ambassador, and she's fluent in French. That's the second most useful language in business today, you know. Smart as a whip and tough as nails, but awfully charming. Nothing gets by her!

"Now we have to get busy. We only have a few weeks to make our remaining Cabinet selections.

"After reviewing the number of people we have to consider, there's no doubt the system is totally inefficient and too unworkable. Although I am in favor of reorganizing and reducing the size of the Cabinet at some point, we'll have to deal with that problem later."

By the time Inauguration Day arrived, the president-elect and his aides had scoured the stacks of resumés from a boatload of job seekers. It was a daunting task, with almost a thousand positions to fill that require the Senate's Advice and Consent. Some candidates were well known to Simon or Charlton, and the rest of them came from the names submitted by the Office of Presidential Personnel in the White House.

Simon and Charlton extended offers to everyone on their "A" list for the highest-ranking positions requiring Senate confirmation, including the remaining Cabinet jobs, and almost immediately received a unanimous willingness to serve.

Simon submitted those names to the Office of Personnel Management, as well with a request for expedited full background checks by the FBI, together with simultaneous IRS reviews and clearance of any tax issues that might come up during the confirmation process.

Too many times before, names had been challenged over a nominee's failure to list what they considered "insignificant" issues, such as an inaccurate resume, or failure to properly report income, or failure to pay taxes on wages of household employees. Regardless, there are no insignificant character issues as far as the federal government is concerned.

Jim assured the president that his choices were "squeaky clean."

"No stone unturned, right Jim?"

"Right, Mr. President."

In addition to major positions, there were another six thousand or so that had to be filled that didn't require Senate confirmation.

For Simon, the process was way too lengthy, with so many positions that would end up being filled by people lacking substantial political or government experience. But he was undeterred by that fact and worked hard to find good people and accelerate the process.

In typical Simon style, by Inauguration Day, the selection process had been completed, and his administration was ready to roll. Now the burden shifted to the Senate.

No one, especially those in the press, had ever witnessed that kind of efficiency in government, and they were rightfully impressed.

Simon's inauguration on January 20, 2017, the day prescribed by law, was a smashing success. He opted to downplay the extravagance shown in so many earlier events and ordered a straightforward "plain vanilla" approach.

The president insisted that the entire cost of the Inauguration be funded by private donations, including police, fire, and the other ancillary services required of the surrounding states and cities. Reducing the administrative cost of government was clearly on the table for all to see.

It was a typical cold January day, but the crowd was overwhelmingly enthusiastic, even though the fancy evening balls had been eliminated and replaced with afternoon receptions.

In the front of the gallery, space was reserved for campaign supporters and regional government officials from all fifty states and all national political parties. The Chairman of the Joint Chiefs and other military leaders, along with the Supreme Court Judges and members of Congress, were seated behind them. That had never been done before. Clearly, Simon's emphasis was on the people.

With his wife holding his grandmother's Bible, Michael Simon placed his left hand on it, raised his right hand, and took the Oath of Office with resolute delivery in his responses to the required questions from the Chief Justice.

Simon's Inauguration Speech that followed was simple, short, and forthright. He thanked God and his family for their support during an exhausting campaign, and also his supporters, who had worked so tirelessly for his election. The composition of the Supreme Court was definitely on his mind as he looked out over the crowd.

A seat on the bench was likely to occur during his first term, and he knew he would face a difficult battle gaining approval of his first nominee for justice. All presidents do. Everything is politics, he kept reminding himself.

He had a clear mandate from the electorate to stop the haggling that had dominated the previous Congress, and he presented a clear message regarding the goals he laid out for his administration and his resolve to accomplish them. Having already presented a critique of the nation and his plans for the future over the course of the election, he announced his decision to skip the annual State of the Union message, normally scheduled for February in inauguration years, and use the time to continue organizing his administration.

> Austin Cook @ OTP Jan 20 Simon – Very impressive. A little military like, but still impressive. Will see how it goes from here.
> View on Twitter.

The president and first lady, Suzanne, and the vice president and his wife, Susan, made the rounds of every reception, shaking hands and posing for pictures until early evening.

The next morning, they were in their offices bright and early, ready to hit the ground running.

CHAPTER 9 ~ The Suspicion

JANUARY 21, 2017

The president and the vice president went on national television the day after being sworn in to make their first joint announcement. Simon said he or members of his Cabinet would hold a press conference as each new major development unfolded, and that Brianna Norman, his new White House Press Secretary, would continue to hold daily White House press briefings, as had become the custom since the days of President Franklin Roosevelt. Then, in a moment of jest, he kindly asked the press to take it easy on the newcomer, just for a little while.

The request drew several polite chuckles from those in attendance.

If the press held off, it still wouldn't provide much of a vacation for Brianna, but if she handled things just right, it might buy her some time before the real shelling started. Fortunately for her, the White House press corps is generally pretty quiet during the traditional ninety-day "honeymoon period" after an Inauguration Day.

Simon's idea was to keep Norman from having to skirt the press corps' probing questions with clever answers before his policies were firmly in place. Waiting to inform the press about news until conditions were more favorable to the president had been a tactic used by his predecessor, and it had backfired.

Simon was determined to get out in front and not to lead from behind.

In their reports to the public via their newswire releases, blogs, tweets, etcetera, the members of the press signaled their willingness to comply with his request, up to a point, of course. They knew they would have plenty of time to dig in later.

The country's new leaders would lead, but the press would press.

> Austin Cook @ OTP Jan 21 Simon – That was some kind of a request! We'll have to see who plays nice. View on Twitter.

As they walked back to their offices, the president turned to Jim and said, "If we are forthright and honest about important issues and take an approach that creates trust right away, we should succeed before things get out of hand. Hopefully, our frequent announcements will create more transparency than the public is used to seeing. Just so you know, I plan to begin right away by addressing issues that involve the border, China, drilling, and education."

Simon always organized subjects alphabetically in his mind. It was a tool he used to help his recall.

The confirmation hearings went well at an accelerated pace. The Senate committees quickly approved all but one of Simon's Cabinet nominees, and their names were sent on to the full Senate. They were all approved by unanimously by a roll call vote.

However, in the instance of Donnelly, a couple of newly-elected Senate committee members from the minority party seized upon his apparent lack of government experience. They puffed themselves up while asking a continuous stream of softball questions, taking every bit of their allotted time to extend the vote.

The rest of the committee actually enjoyed the idea of the little circus: their party was in the majority now and had waited long enough to have a little fun at the expense of the opposition. They relished the exchanges; the nominee acquitted himself very well and turned the table on their questioners with his astute answers, making them look like, well, monkeys.

The junior senators had a lot to learn about Senate decorum, and after the new Majority Leader spoke to them privately, the newbies fell into line and the nominees' names were approved the next day. The full senate voted quickly on Donnelly, and he was confirmed.

Austin was particularly interested in the background of two of the newly-confirmed Cabinet members: Rodriquez at Immigration and Lee at Treasury. Austin had seen presidents get into trouble with confirmation of minority nominees before, and he was surprised at how easily the Hispanic American and Chinese American nominees were confirmed.

Rodriquez was born in Texas to parents who came from Mexico. His story resonated with millions of immigrants—legal and non-legal. The public accepted him at face value, in spite of the charge by his detractors that he was nominated solely because of his ethnicity. His background investigation was clear, so Austin focused on Lee, who he wasn't so sure about.

Lee had done staff work for several government agencies prior to joining the faculty at Georgetown, but he wasn't a political animal. Even so, he learned his way around D.C., quietly making insightful recommendations to congressional committees on a wide-ranging list of monetary issues.

He was a go-to guy around the hill.

Austin respected Lee's stellar career in academics, but still questioned the somewhat narrow scope of his government experience. After all, the position of Treasury Secretary requires thinking at the highest level and an absolute commitment to the policies of the president. Austin thought Lee might be a little too much "middle of the road" in his statements—not too liberal, not too conservative. That said, Simon had handpicked him and put his full faith and trust in his ability to do the job.

But to Austin, there was still the question of his heritage.

Austin got one of his hunches and decided to dig a little deeper. Good old Senator Mickiewicz chaired the Senate Finance Committee, and Austin's poker buddy, Ben, had been involved in the confirmation proceedings.

"Hey, Ben."

"How's it going, Austin? Still digging up dirt?"

"Naw, the confirmations are done," Ben said smiling. But the senator did compliment me on my work during the vetting process. No raise, though. You know that OPM is something else. Nothing but questions on top of questions. I thought they would never stop coming."

"Are you alone?"

"Yes, why?"

"I've been thinking. When they did the background check on Lee, how far back into his record did their investigation go?"

"What do you mean?"

"I mean, did they absolutely confirm that he is a United States citizen?"

"Come on, Dude. His birth certificate shows he was born in Los Angeles. We have a copy of it in our file. Why would you want to know more than that?"

"Well, he has a Chinese father and a white mother, doesn't he?"

"Yeah, so what? I'm not sure what you're getting at. Are you challenging the competence of the OPM or the FBI? You don't think they did their job, right?"

"No. It's just that I read an article about him that mentioned he was adopted. It's probably not a big deal, but it just piqued my curiosity. I've just been thinking about his ancestry and wondering if your guys went back beyond his adoption date and interviewed his birth parents."

"That's probably not part of their normal protocol," said Ben, admonishing his friend.

"I have an idea, so let me think on that and I'll get back to you," Austin said.

"Okay. Your ideas usually pay off so let me know if I can help."

The president's first press conference was scheduled for February first, a date less than three weeks into the new term. Simon began by thanking the Senate for their quick and decisive votes to confirm his Cabinet appointees. Then, he launched right into his agenda.

"As you know, one of my highest priorities is the challenge of becoming energy independent. We have relied on foreign oil imports for far too long, and I'm determined to free us up from the stranglehold being imposed by the Organization of Petroleum Exporting Countries, and others.

"I am pleased to announce that I signed an Executive Order this morning that is designed to unleash the economic power of our nation's resources. The Department of the Interior, and by implication the Bureau of Land Management, have been directed to accelerate the approval of permit applications for drilling oil and gas on federal lands, and the Federal Energy Regulatory Commission is directed to do the same for all pending pipeline projects. There is a heavy backload of applications, and this directive will substantially reduce the waiting time for permits. The new target for a permit approval will be ninety days, considerably longer than the approval times currently being experienced on private land, but shorter than before. That timing should provide an adequate safeguard for the public. Interstate pipeline applications will take a little longer because of environmental considerations, but the process will be streamlined.

"Once we are able to satisfy our domestic needs, we will promote exporting oil and gas to friendly countries to improve our balance of trade. I am consulting with our neighbors to the north and the south to discuss their interest in creating an OPEC-like organization, tentatively called the Canadian American Mexican Exporting Countries, or 'CAMEX.'

"Reciprocity among our three nations would permit cross-development of their offshore drilling projects, and no other countries would be permitted to participate in them. By working together we can satisfy our individual internal needs and stabilize the price of exported crude. There is strength in numbers.

"To assist with this plan, I've asked Chairman Bragg Donaldson from our Export-Import Bank to explore an expansion of their loan guarantee programs to assist our commercial banks in making loans for CAMEX drilling projects and buyers of their exports.

"We already dispatched our ambassadors to meet with the presidents of Canada and Mexico and present the details of this proposal, and we've received a positive response from both of them.

"Further, the Department of Energy and the Environment Protection Agency will be directed to maximize their assistance in developing clean coal technologies by working with, and not against, the efforts of the coal industry. Regulations must be scaled back to permit the implementation of performance standards for coal-fueled power plants over time, consistent with the industry's ability to allocate financial resources to convert to the new technologies. In other words, the coal industry has a bright future, and I am committed to preserving its importance as a significant contributor to our energy needs while we develop economically feasible alternative energy solutions.

"On another issue, members of my Cabinet will meet as soon as possible to discuss their individual roles in implementing these new policies. In particular, several departments have overlapping responsibilities, and building a consensus will be their first order of business. Fiefdoms, or arrogant protection of individual domains, cannot be tolerated, because interagency cooperation will be paramount as we tackle our nation's most immediate problems— national security, in particular. We have a big job ahead of us, and we will all be united."

Finally, he reminded his audience that every action he was taking was consistent with his oath and the law.

"Now, I will take one or two questions. Yes, Leonard."

"Leonard Murdock, Reuters. Mr. President, are you abandoning the emphasis on alternative energy, and what do you expect to gain by turning on the spigot and cozying up to our neighbors?"

"On the contrary, alternative energy is the future, because we believe that fossil fuels are a finite source. Yes, we keep finding new sources in our three countries, but we will have to develop other alternatives over the longer term. I support any financially feasible alternative, but until we find them in substantial quantities, oil, gas and coal will dominate our supply. As to your last question, we already import oil from both Canada and Mexico, so it makes sense to 'cozy up' with them, don't you think? Next question. Yes, Austin."

"Austin Cook, OTP. Mr. President, are you signaling that jealousies are already creeping into your Cabinet as your secretaries jockey for position?"

"Austin, I'm aware of your musings and aphorisms and 'Sometimes, methinks thou doth protesteth too much,' but I do understand why you asked the question. Competition and discontent have infected other Cabinets, so I'm just heading off any possibility that friction might develop before it gains a head of steam. The public needs to know that we will be a united bunch."

"Yes sir, thank you for the clarification."

"No more questions please. Thank you for attending."

> Austin Cook @ OTP Feb 1 Simon – I like the sound of CAMEX. Simon says, OPEC, you better watch out! Here we come. View on Twitter.

"Good morning and welcome to all incoming Mister and Madam Secretaries," Simon said as he began the meeting. "This is truly an historic occasion. Our party now controls the presidency and both houses of Congress. That hasn't happened in quite a while. Our election carries with it a significant responsibility, and you are all expected to serve with honor and distinction.

You've all heard my rhetoric over the past several months, and I think you know where I stand on virtually every major issue confronting us.

"Thank you for your input and agreement to support the executive order that I just signed on energy. Please understand that yesterday's announcement was designed to show that we are not waiting for the grass to grow under our feet. It was a one-off. I won't lean on you in the future for your immediate input on every issue I propose, as I did on that one, unless time is of the essence.

"But, I repeat what I've said before: Although we face challenges in many areas, certain of those stand out where I feel we need to take immediate action. These include our budget deficit, the economy, and unemployment, with particular emphasis on immigration, national security, and trade, not necessarily in that order. They all play into each other, so the solution to any one problem is dependent on the understanding of each of the others. As a result, we need to develop a broad framework of ideas that we can agree on.

"As I've said before, international issues, especially those related to instability around the world, are no less important, but are extremely complex and cannot be resolved quickly. So, let's start by addressing what we can change now. Military issues will be the subject of another meeting.

"For today, your assignment is to learn everything you can about your individual department's structure, personnel, culture, and any plans that are already being implemented. Then, evaluate those items with respect to where we should be headed, and come back to me with your recommended changes that we can implement now, within ninety days, and within one year.

"Longer-term comprehensive planning for a number of objectives will be discussed for your individual input and consensus of the entire Cabinet at a future date.

"Tomorrow, I will be announcing a few ideas that I have discussed with some of you individually. You will no doubt be questioned in detail about our policies in those areas. Stick to the basics until the reaction dies down and we can get feedback and read the pulse of the press. Then we'll move forward, quickly. Understood?"

There was solid agreement with Simon's statements, as the members whispered to one another in hushed tones.

"Mr. President," said Secretary Retsuc. "Will you please explain why you felt the need to mention fiefdoms in your address yesterday?"

"It must be my military background coming out. I've seen too many instances where the men and women under my command were not in sync regarding our mission. Teamwork is essential, and I wanted to convey the importance of that message to everyone listening, even the press. The press is prone to reacting negatively to every bit of scuttlebutt they hear, and I wanted them to know that we will present a unified position on every issue.

"Now, if any of you ever disagree with any policy we announce, you need to come see me right away, and we'll work it out. I'm willing to listen to any criticism or recommendation. I can be persuaded to change course when necessary. Agreed?"

"Agreed," they responded unanimously.

"You are all excused, except for Secretary Boyd."

"Thanks for staying, Glenn. I want to talk to you about closing our southern border with Mexico. No one should be able to enter our country without proper credentials. The problem has gotten worse, because we haven't been able to find an adequate solution on our side of the border, and I want to try a different approach."

"Mr. President, I'm all ears."

"As I'm sure you know, the Merida Initiative, the agreement signed by the U.S. and Mexico, acknowledges the need to disrupt organized crime groups and stop drugs coming into the United States. Merida also has a stated goal of creating a 'twenty-first century border.' The billions of dollars we've given to Mexico to help in that effort has failed, in spite of our improved cross-border inspections. With a two-thousand-mile border spanning four states, the problem of illegal immigrants entering our country with impunity has become a monumental political issue. We've ignored enforcing our own immigration laws, and the corruption of Mexican border officials compromises their obligations under Merida."

"What is your idea, Mr. President?"

"I want you to go and meet with President Corvera and present a solution that involves more cooperation by his government in exchange for more assistance from us. I think their government has as much to gain as we do by controlling the drug trade. Stopping drugs from coming in, once and for all, would remove the cartel's incentive to keep operating. I'm proposing to increase our foreign aid to Mexico through the Merida Initiative with the specific purpose of funding increased border control on the Mexican side. They would station their designated military or police units as border guards along their side of the border within a specified distance, say ten or twenty miles. Let's call it a 'security zone.' They would wear special uniforms and be paid enough to attract their finest personnel, and we would train their units.

"We would match that effort with similar type personnel located within a similar zone on our side. All immigration laws of the United States would be strictly enforced, and anyone who attempts to cross over the border illegally would be subject to a program of DNA testing, fingerprinting, and iris recognition before being turned back. That would apply to whomever they catch, as well as whomever we stop."

"That's a rather inventive idea, Mr. President. I don't have to think about it. Count me in."

"Well, Glenn, it's a start. We'll still have to deal with the illegal immigrants who are here, and Congress will take up that matter early this session. I'm going to give them a head start with another Executive Order. It's certain to raise the ire of a lot of people, but it will send a clear message that we mean business.

"I am stopping all undocumented individuals from transferring money back to Mexico from the U.S., including those who were allowed to stay as a result of any previous presidential action, especially those taken by my predecessor. The enforcement of the plan will require more government oversight than we exercise now, but the need for it won't last forever.

"I expect many illegals will return to Mexico if they can't send money back home. Glenn, the amount of money that is being transferred by illegals is staggering. It is approaching twenty-five billion a year. That comes right out of our economy. That will pay for a lot of border guards!"

> The White House Office of the Press Secretary
> For Immediate Release:
>
> February 3, 2017
>
> Today, the President dispatched Secretary Boyd to Mexico City to discuss issues of mutual interest with Mexican officials.

At the conclusion of Brianna's February eighth briefing, when the Q and A began, the room exploded with raised hands. It didn't seem like they were "taking it easy" to her.

The initial questions centered around the Executive Order on Energy and the restriction on money transfers. She handled all of them deftly with clear, informed answers, just as Simon had intended.

The final question concerned Boyd's trip to Mexico City.

"I know you have a lot of questions about his trip," she said, "but until the talks conclude, we will have no comment. I don't have to tell you that the president is concerned about the border issue, but unless we can open a meaningful dialogue with President Corvera, we have nothing to discuss. We don't want to speculate about any agreement at this point, so I have to respectfully decline to answer your questions at this time. I will add, however, that President Simon believes that any change in our immigration policies must begin with a solution to the crisis on the border."

"All right," she said, as the raised hands continued. "One more question."

"Austin Cook, OTP, Ms. Norman," he said, jumping to his feet and waving his hand in the air. "Can you tell us if the talks extend beyond the border crossing issue itself? Will there be any discussion about the North American Free Trade Agreement, or our Maquiladoras manufacturing operations in Mexico? We all know that Mexico is our third largest trading partner, and any change in those agreements would be critical! And what about CAMEX?"

Brianna held her composure as she framed a response in her mind. She had seen Cook in action and was still trying to determine if he was friend or foe.

"Mr. Cook, as I tried to emphasize earlier, for your benefit, the details of the discussions will not be announced until Secretary Boyd returns. Until then, I have nothing to add."

> Austin Cook @ OTP Feb 8 Simon – It's still clear as mud. Is Boyd is up to the task? Doesn't he have a Latina daughter-in-law? Y'all better start learning Spanish. View on Twitter.

"Good morning, ladies and gentlemen," the president said, as he began his second press conference. "Thank you all for coming. I haven't spoken to you in over two weeks, so basically I want to hear from you today. However, before we begin, I want to make an announcement about an important issue regarding foreign relations and our economy. I am pleased to announce that I have invited Premier Ma Xing of the People's Republic of China to visit us here in Washington to discuss trade matters, and we're waiting for his response. I've asked our Treasury Secretary, Dr. Winston Lee, to take the lead in developing an agenda that will include a number of issues to be discussed, especially our trade deficit, and we are hopeful that we can announce a date for the premier's visit in the near future. Now I will open it up for questions ... Austin."

"Austin Cook, OTP. Mr. President, aren't you moving a little too fast? And do you feel you have a mandate to take immediate steps on all the issues you've announced when you have only been in office for a few weeks? And, with regard to the border issue, did you consult with your Cabinet on such an important matter before moving ahead? What if you take too many giant steps and one of them backfires?"

"Austin, never let it be said that you fail to miss an opportunity to ask compound questions." He paused for the press corps' laughter. "Let me see if I can make some sense of this for you. You and others have been critical of the snail's pace in Washington and the lack of progress—a result of the polarization that has gripped our government. Well, I intend to move decisively within the boundaries of the law to address the voter concerns that decided my election. So no, I don't think I'm moving too fast for my own good, or yours.

"As to the border issue, to my knowledge, no one has really addressed this from the standpoint of the Mexican government. If you've heard something I've missed, let my office know. My plan may be radical, and if it's a bad idea, at least it's a new idea. Nothing has worked so far, so I'm willing to stick my neck out to try something that might. Next question ... Jane."

"Jane Appleby, CNN. Mr. President, none of the issues you've included in your recent remarks involve the conflicts in the Middle East. Can you tell us why you have avoided discussing that international concern, to say nothing of Russia and the Ukraine, or North and South Korea? Don't you consider them equally important as the issues you discussed today?"

"They are equally important. However, as I've stated previously, if we are not strong at home because our national defense suffers from our inability to maintain our armed forces in the face of mounting debt, and our budget is out of balance because of the cost of the entitlements guaranteed to all of our citizens and residents, then we will be weak abroad. As to my remarks today, and earlier, our approach to problem solving will put us on the road to a stable economy with sustained economic growth. Our position in the world depends on getting our house in order, and we are starting to do just that.

"I hope that answers your question."

"Yes, thank you, Mr. President."

"All right, I have time for just one more question … Kate."

"Kate Summerville, CBS. Mr. President, are you planning to adopt a White House dog, and if so, what kind and what will its name be? Perhaps you might consider a Chihuahua. It would provide you and the first lady with excellent protection should your Secret Service detail fall down on the job!"

"Finally, we have a serious question," he said, and again, the press corps burst into laughter. "Well, Kate, Mrs. Simon and I haven't had a dog in a long time, and you raise a good question. I'm going to appoint you as my authorized puppy pollster to collect some public opinion on the kind and name for a new White House dog. Report back to me with your results. I'll go by whatever you recommend.

"Thank you all for attending."

Austin Cook @ OTP Feb 22 Simon – Canada, Mexico, China. Who's next? The president is off and running. Will he stumble at the gate or break down at the turn? Only time will tell. View on Twitter.

Austin thought about Secretary Lee all the way home from the press conference. He hadn't been able to find anyone who had witnessed Lee's negotiating style or ability, and the outcome of the Chinese talks might depend on that. The Chinese are seasoned international negotiators, and Lee was still wet behind the ears, he reasoned. Lee lacked direct experience in government, and Austin wondered if he'd even found the bathroom in his new office yet!

Wasn't Simon crazy to throw Lee into the deep end within just a few months of the inauguration? The premier will eat him alive, Austin thought, and began to formulate one of his famous what-if scenarios.

Austin got home, poured himself a Billy's beer, and continued thinking.

What if Lee's birth certificate was modified somehow and he really wasn't a citizen at all? Documents can be forged. And if he wasn't a citizen, he could never become president since the Secretary of the Treasury is fifth in the line of succession.

And what if his birth parents came out of the woodwork seeking some notoriety, or to put the muscle on their boy to keep quiet? Anything like that would really be embarrassing for the president, and it would go over like a lead balloon if it came out just before the big meeting with the premier. It might not be the end of the world, but it could cause a stink of biblical proportions!

Austin simply needed to be satisfied that all the facts were investigated. Austin knew he had to do something. The OPM obviously hadn't thought of those possibilities, but Austin had.

He placed a call to Ben.

"Hey, Ben, it's Austin. I'm calling to follow up on my hunch. It's probably nothing, but I want to cover all the bases. I have a favor to ask."

"Shoot."

"You remember our talk about Lee's vetting?"

"Yes."

"Well, listen to this. Lee's adoption record was sealed. That means Winston's original birth certificate can't be seen by anyone unless they can show good cause, like Winston himself if he wanted to know who his real parents are. He would have to request access to the adoption record and get it unsealed to get that information, and it would take a court order to do that. So, can you quietly get a court order from a friendly judge in California to unseal the adoption record? I want to see what his original birth certificate shows."

"Are you sure that's absolutely necessary?"

"I wouldn't ask if I didn't think it is critical. We can't ask Lee or his parents to do it. What would we say? Oh, we're just curious to know who your son's real parents are. Think about it. We couldn't justify a request like that, could we?"

"Well, no … Oh boy. I'd be way out on a limb trying to get a court order, but I'll do it. Let me find out how, and I'll call you back when I have an answer. You owe me, you know."

"Yes, and I promise not to bad mouth the senator, so you can keep your job."

Two weeks later, Brianna Norman began her daily briefing with another important announcement.

"Ladies and Gentlemen. You will recall that a few weeks ago, the president announced that he had extended an invitation to the Premier of the People's Republic of China to meet with him here in Washington to discuss trade and other issues of mutual interest. The Premier declined the invitation, but has offered to send his First Vice Premier, Guang Jinli, in his place. Mr. Guang will already be here in the U.S. on the May dates the president had suggested as possibilities. The president felt the premier's response was reasonable and accepted the offer.

"The president will kick off Mr. Guang's official visit with a White House Reception to welcome him on May fifteenth, followed by an official dinner to acknowledge the respect we hold for his high office.

"China represents the world's biggest holder of U.S. debt, so the event will be an important first step in the president's international diplomacy efforts.

"It will also provide an opportunity for a few members of Congress and some Wall Streeters to hob nob with an old client. You will recall that China gained access to bid on purchasing our treasuries directly from the previous administration, and Wall Street has requested that the president reverse that decision, because it took business away from them. The affair will be followed by two days of meetings involving our respective trade negotiators. As we indicated previously, Secretary Lee will lead our team, and he will be assisted by our Trade Representative and the Secretary of Commerce."

> Austin Cook @ OTP Mar 1 Simon – This should be great fun. A Kung Fu Broadsword vs. a U.S. Navy Cutlass Sword. Lee better be up to the task. View on Twitter.

CHAPTER 10 ~ The Intelligence

MARCH 2, 2017

The president asked Mac to join him in the Oval Office.

"Mac, I want to know everything about this Guang fella that China is sending over. I want to get inside his head and find out what makes him tick. We don't have much intel on him, but you're perfectly positioned to get the answers I need. He's coming in ten weeks, so you don't have forever."

"Got it."

"And nothing gets leaked to the press about whatever you dig up."

"Yes, Sir."

Mac went right to work. His first instinct was to call Bo Dugan in Los Angeles. Mac had worked with him in the CIA before Bo got tired of the life and left its service.

Bo grew up in Los Angeles and knew the territory. Now he was running around Hollywood as a PI chasing celebrity cheats. It wasn't as glamorous as it sounded, but the pay was good for a carefree gig, and it was fun, to boot.

"What do you need, Mac?" Bo asked.

Go to the local FBI office. I'll have an encrypted cell phone ready for you, and the line will be secure. I'll call you back on that phone."

Bo didn't ask questions. He drove to the Los Angeles Division office in West LA, where the phone was waiting for him.

"This is hush hush, straight from the top," Mac said when he called. "I mean the very top, so you'll have to keep your trap shut."

"As usual. So what's the job?"

"Simon says he wants the skinny on a Chinese kid that went to USC back in the sixties. The job is right up your alley."

"It sounds challenging, but as dull as Arthritis. Who knows? I guess I'll find out."

"The name is Guang Jinli, and Simon wants to know everything you can find out about him, anything at all. We have his birth date as January seventeen, nineteen forty-three. We know he was a foreign student at USC back in the sixties. He's a high-ranking Chinese official now, and his wife is an advocate for China's medical profession."

"That's not much more than his name, rank and serial number, as they say. He sounds like a pretty stable guy, but I guess the big man wants to know more."

"Absolutely. We don't have a lot of detail, so try to find any of his friends from his school years if you can, and talk to them if they're still on this side of the grass. Find out where he hung out, what they discussed, any organizations he belonged to—you know the sort of thing."

"Okay, I'm on it."

"Call me back as soon as you find something."

Bo went home and visited every USC website he could find.

Great! His target was coming to Los Angeles to speak at the next graduation and receive an honorary degree. *Gee, Mac could have told me that*, he thought.

146

There was a brief bio on the Marshall School of Business website but it was mostly pabulum. Not much there.

Guang Jinli graduated from the University of Southern California in 1965 with a bachelor's degree in business and is known as the principal author of Chinese trade policies. Lives in Beijing, married, no children, member of the Communist Party.

Duh!

Looks like I have to start at the very beginning, he thought. First, he decided to explore Jinli's student life.

The following Monday morning, Bo paid a visit to the USC Admissions Office. They told him that, except for names and years of graduates, any other student records going back that far might have been kept on microfilm and stored in the library.

Might have been! he thought.

At the library, Bo asked to see the record of one Guang Jinli or Jinli Guang, who graduated in 1965.

The so-called other student records for the years in question couldn't be located. *No doubt purged by some foreign operative,* Bo thought.

A library counselor told Bo that, even if they found what he was looking for, the Family Educational Rights and Privacy Act would prevent him from looking at the records without proper permission.

Would permission from the president of the United States be sufficient? he quipped to himself under his breath.

He decided to move on. If he needed those records, he could get a court order, but it was way too soon to resort to that.

Mac had learned a long time ago that names can be very confusing and in this instance, he had said there just might be two Guangs since Chinese names are so similar, or their target might have gone by another name or used middle names or partial names, or used the Chinese convention of last name followed by a first name, so Bo should be careful not to overlook anything that looked interesting.

Next, Bo asked if they had copies of their old school annuals. He was directed to the stacks where he found the El Rodeos, or "El Rods," as they are called, for the years 1962 to 1965. He leafed through the pages, looking for Jinli's name and pictures. Mac had sent him a current picture of Jinli that was age-regressed by the FBI's Forensic Lab to match it to his school picture, just in case he found the right one.

Nothing popped out at him; however, to Bo's surprise, the 1965 El Rod showed the name Guang Jinli with no related page numbers for any pictures or affiliations. As a double check, Bo studied the annual again, spending almost an hour. Nothing. No luck. He had run into another dead end.

The next morning, Bo embarked on a search through all of the school's online records. That produced an unbelievable number of articles and pictures from the years in question. The university had embarked on a program, together with the library, called the USC Archives. They digitized every edition of DT and all the El Rods published since 1912.

Of course, athletics were in the spotlight all over the place, given USC's athletic heritage and the fact that the football team had won the National Championship in 1962.

Guang Jinli seemed to be invisible.

Wait a minute, he thought. Bo went back through the archives again. He focused on graduation day, June 10, 1965. It was referenced in the DT as the last regular school day edition before the summer that year. Then he started looking backwards from that issue until he found something.

"Here we go," Bo said out loud.

There was a picture of two students walking across the campus with the caption: "Foreign students prepare to graduate and return home." Somehow he had missed it earlier. The picture was obviously a candid shot. One student appeared to be Asian, and the other was definitely from the Middle East. There were no names or other identification. The article just said that an increased number of foreign students were expected in the fall, and it provided some stats on foreign student attendance in previous years, including countries, majors—that sort of thing. The picture was nice, but not particularly helpful.

Nevertheless, he snapped a picture of the photo in the article with his cell phone.

He thought he found pay dirt when he saw a reference to an International Students Association in an archived edition of the DT, but there was nothing there. Jinli was not a member.

He called Mac that afternoon.

"Mac, this assignment is a lot tougher that I thought it would be. I'm not making much headway, but I'm trying. I think I may have one lousy picture of Jinli, but nothing else so far."

"Bo, if this wasn't "top secret," so to speak, I'd say forget it, but you have to keep going."

"All right. I have another idea or two. I'll get back to you," he said. *I always have more ideas,* he thought. *That's why I get paid. If I ever get paid.*

Bo parked near the campus and walked over to the Marshall School of Business. It paid off.

The sign on the door said, "Dean Peter Smith." As Bo entered his office, he smiled at the nice lady sitting behind a desk and complimented her on her hair.

"Well, darlin', thank you very kindly," she replied.

By her accent, Bo assumed she was from the south. And he was sure she wasn't accustomed to a smooth pick-up line like his, especially as he thought she might be at least seventy-five!

Faculty members were rushing through her office with their heads buried in their paperwork. And students were pleading with her for things she had no authority to provide.

Bo handed her his card and told her he planned to write an article on the outstanding success of the business school. His card read Bo Dugan and underneath, Freelance Writer.

"So you're a PI, huh? What can I do for you, Mr. Eye?"

He gave a hearty laugh and said he was hoping to interview some of the important people coming to graduation, and asked her if she had a list of invitees. She was more than happy to oblige and pulled it out of a desk drawer. The list of showed the names of current and retired professors at USC, as well as business leaders who had attended USC, together with detailed contact information. She said Dean Smith had asked the provost to invite other prominent businessmen and civic leaders from all around the Southland as well.

"The idea is to showcase the quality of our school leadership over the years and impress our graduation speaker, Vice Premier Guang Jinli."

"Interesting. How was he selected to be this year's speaker?"

"The USC Alumni Club of Beijing recommended his name to us. Before that, we weren't even aware that he had attended school here. Dean Smith seized the opportunity and invited him. It's quite a coup, wouldn't you say?"

"Yes I would say so."

"Were any of the retired professors on the list teaching here when the vice premier was in school?"

"Yes. I got positive response cards from three of them, two from the sixties." "Can I get a copy of those cards?"

"Sure can," she said, and returned shortly with them in hand.

Bo looked at them and smiled. Now he was getting somewhere! One of the names was a Professor Sheng Tom, obviously Chinese or Asian. Professor Tom had been there from 1965 to 2010.

If he is Chinese, the he surely must have known all the Chinese students, Bo reasoned.

Bo phoned Professor Sheng, and they arranged to meet.

"Should I address you as Mr. Sheng or Mr. Tom? I'm trying to invoke some understanding of the Chinese language," Bo asked, as Tom came to the door. "And I'm not sure which is correct."

"Either is correct. Just call me Tom."

"Tom, as I mentioned on the phone, I'm doing an article about the USC business school in connection with Vice Premier Guang's visit." It was a hunch, but Bo continued, "How well did you know the vice premier?"

"Know him? We were good friends back in the day. I just returned my invitation to graduation. I want to hear what he has to say, and I hope I get a chance to say hello."

"So, how did you get to know him?"

"I transferred in from San Fernando Valley State College during my senior year as a business major. I got my master's degree and eventually became a full professor. I taught there until I retired.

"Jinli was a favorite student of all the professors, and there was no question about his potential for success in business or economics. Unfortunately, he returned to China after he graduated, and I lost track of him."

"That still doesn't answer my question about how you became so close to him."

"Well, I met him in an upper division economics class. He was simply brilliant and graduated in three years. I was looking for a roommate, and he moved in."

"So, what were your conversations like?"

"We spent a lot of time talking about sex, religion and politics."

"Isn't that supposed to be taboo?"

"Well, we didn't stick to the accepted behavior. We talked about everything. Remember, we were just coming out of the sixties. There were no taboos."

"What can you tell me about his views on government and politics? He was a communist, right? Who did he associate with? Did he appreciate our way of life here? That sort of thing. I want to get a slant on how he saw the world."

"Okay, I'll start with religion. I'll let you know about sex in a couple of minutes. The subject of religion is an easy one. I'll tell you what he told me. In the fifties, religions were essentially banished in China. Members of organized religions had to register with the government and repent. The state constitution only protected patriotic believers; if you were a Christian, as an example, the CPC was the god of the Christian God. The CPC became the all-encompassing religion of China. Jinli's father didn't practice his faith before the crackdown, so he escaped the harsh treatment of believers. I don't think Jinli was instructed in religious matters, so he was immune from any punishment as well. That's about all he said about religion.

"I can tell you this much about his political views. He was an unabashed member of the Communist Party and defended Maoism to the fullest. Mao embraced the revolutionary struggle of the vast majority of people against the exploited classes and their state structures. Jinli had witnessed firsthand the horrible failure of his Great Leap Forward and the results of land redistribution and rural collectivism. At that point, I think Jinli began to question the idea of central control, but he steadfastly defended communism in our discussions.

"Talk about an ideologue! I can tell you that he focused his studies on the comparative economic ideologies of communism versus capitalism, trying to rationalize what he had seen happening in China versus what he was witnessing in this country. He was a hard nut to crack, but I sensed he was open to new ideas. More on that later."

"What about the sex part."

"Patience, patience. I'll get to that."

"So, who did he hang around with?"

"Jinli was somewhat of a loner in the beginning when we first became roommates. Then near the end of that semester, he met a girl from San Francisco, and things changed."

"What was the girlfriend's name?" "Su Lin Wong."

"I guess we're getting to the sex part now." "Yes we are."

"So, tell me about Su Lin?"

"Well, they met in a Liberal Arts class, but learned they were both majoring in business. He was studying economics, and she was concentrating on statistics. After her first semester, she moved into our same apartment complex. Her roommate was a girl named Isabel Villa, who was attending the St. Vincent's College of Nursing in downtown Los Angeles. I think she was the only Hispanic girl the apartment owner ever accepted. We also had a couple of kids from Bakersfield living there, as well. We got to know one another pretty well, and I think Jinli really got a taste of the benefits of having a friend with no ulterior motives."

"You must have gotten close to him personally I would think,"

"We had a lot of conversations, but little discussion about his life in China. Once I stopped asking questions, my non-inquisitive nature began to resonate with him. In other words, if you didn't want to talk about his personal life, he would open up to you, you know, with things that interested him, like current events and other things in the news. But one thing was for sure: he wanted to know everything about capitalism. He seemed to be infatuated with how Americans live. I remember that well."

"So what about the sex part? You still haven't talked about that."

"Bo, there's only so much study time in a day. And at that age, hormones are awake around the clock. When Su Lin's roommate or I was in class or gone for a long weekend, I'm pretty sure they were together in her room or his. Doesn't that give you a clue? Bo, my boy! You figure it out! But that's only a guess on my part.

"They were really in love. But the romance came to an abrupt halt. He graduated at the end of the spring semester, leaving her heartbroken. At one point, she confided in me that she had hoped to go to China with him, but her parents would have disowned her for falling in love with a communist. Chinese are very honoring of their parents, so she relented and didn't press the issue that I know of.

"She disappeared a couple of months later. I came home one day and she had moved out, and I never knew why. She was pretty upset after he left, and I could certainly understand that.

153

"I don't know if you're interested, but let me tell you about something else before you leave. Su Lin followed a curious practice, or hobby, if you will. She had a very strong bond with her father, and once in a while she would ask one of us to mail a postcard for her if she couldn't get to the mailbox in time for a pick-up. She mailed the cards like clockwork, and I never knew why. I still remember the name on them. They were addressed to her dad, Mr. Jimmy Wong, care of Wong's Bakery at a P.O. Box in San Francisco. Every card had a little one-line note on the back, and she signed them—Su Lin, forever. Nothing else. She obviously loved her father very much."

"I don't suppose you recall what one of them said, do you?"

"Yes, I do, as a matter of fact, but they were all different of course. I found one that she must have planned to mail but didn't, so I kept it as remembrance of her. I guess I had learned to love her a little bit, too. She was one of the sweetest girls I ever met. Let me get it for you."

Bo studied the note. "Love is like a flower that never loses its fragrance." It was signed—Su Lin, forever.

"You'll notice there was no return address on it, just like the others."

"Where is she now?"

"As I said, she just disappeared. She didn't leave me a note or even a forwarding address. She didn't leave one with our landlord either. And, to the best of my knowledge, she didn't come back to school that fall, so I have no idea."

Bo called Mac to give him an update.

"I found a good friend of Jinli's, and I think I'm on to something. Jinli had a girlfriend, and I'm going to try and find her."

"Good idea. If you can find her, she may have more to say about the vice premier than he did. We need to find out everything we can. She's worth pursuing; we can't afford to fail the president. Go ahead and do a write-up on this guy Tom anyway, and tell me everything he said."

Bo submitted it right away, including the picture from the *Daily Trojan.*

"Austin, you're a stinking troublemaker," Ben said. "The senator doesn't want to be connected to any failure to do a thorough job of vetting, so he approved your request, provided you never disclose how you got whatever information comes out of this. If there is something screwy about the birth and it's ever revealed, the senator will be as surprised as anyone. Understood?"

"Done deal. Now, here's what I need to have you do. Once you get the court order, arrange to have a Secret Service agent in Sacramento take one of those little portable color scanner/printers with them to the Department of Health, Office of Vital Records and execute on the order. I'm guessing that somewhere in their file will be a notation of any previous inquiries after the original filing date, so make sure to scan those dates if there are any. That's important, because I need to know if anyone has beaten me to the punch. Then, the agent needs to scan and print a copy of the original birth certificate, put the original back in the file, and put the copy in a sealed envelope marked CONFIDENTIAL. Then, have the envelope sent to the senator's office to your attention."

"Put my name on it! Are you crazy? I'd be toast if I'm found out."

"Trust me. It will be okay. Then, make a copy of the birth certificate that was in the Secretary's confirmation file, and put the whole thing in another envelope and me bring it to me personally. Repeat, personally."

"I think I understand, but this may take a little time to accomplish, so be prepared. We have to be very careful and find the right judge that won't ask too many questions. That might blow the whole thing."

"Calm down. I know what I'm doing. But remember, not a word to anyone about why or what you're doing, other than to the senator of course. Please don't ever mention my name to anyone. Remember, 'Loose Lips Sink Ships.'"

"Yea, yea."

Bo's next stop was St. Vincent's. He went to the office of the school administrator and asked if they had any record of an Isabel Villa.

"Ms. Villa! She was our long-time head of nursing, but she's retired now," came the answer.

"I have a friend who knew her from way back, and I'm trying to reach her for him. Do you have an address or phone number for her?" Bo asked.

She located the information and wrote it down on the back of her business card for him.

He thanked her and said goodbye. *Pay dirt again! Boy, am I good, or what?* Bo thought.

He plugged the address into his cell phone, and it displayed the location and the route to take. *We can't do anything without our cell phones these days,* Bo thought.

He arrived at his destination, an old three-story brick apartment house on South Carondelet Street, not far from St. Vincent's. Ms. Villa answered the door.

He gave her his famous card and said he was doing a story on minorities in the sixties. He said her name had been given to him as an example of success in the Hispanic community and asked if she would talk to him.

She invited him in, and, looking around the room, it appeared to him as if she didn't have many visitors. The place was neat, and not overly furnished. She had stacks of papers and periodicals piled up next to a desk.

"I still keep up with medical advances, you know," said Isabel. "It takes a lot of reading. My eyesight isn't what it used to be, but cataract surgery sure helped. Both eyes. So, tell me about your story."

Bo explained that he had met a fellow named Tom who said he lived in the same apartment with her years before.

"It seems to me that it must have been somewhat unusual for minorities to live together in those days," Bo said, "and I thought that might be an interesting angle for my story."

"Please, call me Isabel," she said. "It was pretty simple. One person meets another, and pretty soon it just happens. Tom and Jinli were both Chinese and roommates upstairs, while the two white boys who were twin brothers lived downstairs. I was by myself when a Chinese girl named Su Lin came to see me and asked if I needed a roommate. As it turned out, I think Jinli put her up to it. She seemed like a nice girl, and I needed to cut my rent, so she moved in. It was a good arrangement. We were all hard-working students, but we had fun and became good friends."

"So you had three Chinese, one Hispanic and two white kids living there. I suppose that wouldn't be unusual today, but I suppose it might have been in those days."

"Yes, I guess so."

"Do you know that Jinli is a big muckety-muck in China now, and he will be here in a few months to give a speech?"

"Yes, Bo, I read the newspapers."

"Do you think you'll try to see him while he's here?"

"No. I stay at home pretty much these days. My wonderful husband passed last year, and my kids are up north. Don't see much of them, or my grandkids. They're too busy with sports."

"How well did you know the other kids in the apartment house?"

"I knew them well. We used to meet, usually on weekends, and go for a hamburger. Things like that."

"Were there any conflicts at all?"

"No, my parents were not as comfortable with the arrangement as I was, but I was fine with it."

"Specifically, what did you know about the Chinese kids?"

"Well, we didn't talk about their backgrounds, if that's what you mean. I suppose the Chinese kids were close, since they had so much in common."

"You know that Jinli and Su Lin were an item, as they used to say, right? That's what Tom said."

"Yes, I heard that. How close were they?"

Seeming a little more relaxed now, Isabel said, "Well, it's been a lot of years now, so I guess I can tell you a little story. But we have to talk off the record. Isn't that what they say in journalism?"

"Yes."

"Okay. Jinli and Su Lin were from similar cultures, but were worlds apart in terms of social thinking and politics. Regardless, they were madly in love. And love is the same the world over. I had several boyfriends growing up; I know.

"Well, Jinli left right after he graduated, and she was torn apart. She couldn't sleep for days. Then, about a week after he left, she came to me and confided that she had missed her period. I don't think she had any other close friends at school, so I was the only girl she could talk to. And she certainly didn't want to tell her mother. She didn't know what to do, but she figured I was in nursing and could help her. I told her to wait one more month, and then we'd see. A month went by, and she missed another one. She was so distraught.

"I gave her some choices: she could get an abortion, keep the baby or put it up for adoption. She seemed more concerned about disgracing her family than anything else. Her father had told her to be careful. 'Boys only want one thing,' he had said. 'But how can you love someone and not make love?' she'd asked. I certainly wasn't a mother with sage advice, but I had several brothers and sisters. I saw a lot and learned a lot from my own mother, who was so wise. She always handled things compassionately.

"I asked Su Lin if an abortion was in the cards for her. She said her Christian faith would never permit her to do that, and I was relieved since that was the way I was brought up, too. So I asked her if she could care for the baby. She said she didn't think so without family help, and that wasn't in the cards.

"So that left adoption as the only remaining choice, and the best one in my opinion. I told her there was a place nearby that would help her called St. Anne's Maternity Home. They had doctors and nursing students who donate delivery services. I had even volunteered myself on occasion, so I knew the process well.

"I managed to get her the prenatal care she needed, and I arranged for her to live at St. Anne's before the baby's delivery. I checked on her periodically to make sure everything was going well, and always checked on her just prior to weekends, when I went home to visit my parents."

"Wow, that is quite a story," Bo said. "Don't worry. I would never reveal my source if I were asked. Not in a million years. So, what happened after that?"

"Well, the next time I went to St. Anne's to check on her, she had left. She did leave a kind note with the nursing staff thanking them, and me."

"So, what do you think happened to the baby?"

"I don't know but, St. Anne's had a wonderful relationship with Holy Family Adoption, so I'm pretty sure it was adopted by one of their applicants soon after it was born."

"Can you call St. Anne's and Holy Adoption and find out if Su Lin left a forwarding address with either of them?"

"I'll see what I can find out and let you know tomorrow."

"Thanks. I'll call you on Monday, if that's okay."

Isabel had some news for Bo, but not what he was looking for.

St. Anne's couldn't come up with anything and Holy Adoption told her their records were likely destroyed after five years because they couldn't find anything in their files either.

Bo thanked Isabel for her help and ended the call.

The next day, a dozen roses arrived on her doorstep.

"Mac, I've got hot news," Bo said excitedly.

"Jinli's girlfriend, Su Lin, was pregnant when he left, but he couldn't have known. It looks like she may have given the baby up for adoption. I'll run up to San Francisco in a few days when I finish the job I put on hold to help you. Su Lin grew up there, and I'll try to locate her family. Hopefully, they will know where she is. And maybe they'll know something about the baby, too."

"Let me summarize for the record: Jinli graduates and returns to China not knowing that his girlfriend was pregnant when he left. Is that about it?"

"Yes, essentially."

"Bo, the president may appreciate knowing about the baby, but I know he abhors blackmail. He says it isn't honorable, so keep it quiet until I get some directions from him. Okay? Just treat the baby news as 'inside knowledge' for now. Find the girlfriend. But if you can't, you can't."

"Mac, are you sure this is worth all the effort?"

"I just take orders, Bo. It's not my job to ask why."

Bo did a little homework before leaving for San Francisco. Tom had said that Su Lin always used a P.O. Box number for the cards she sent to her father. Personal security is one of the reasons why people kept boxes, because gangs, including remnants of the Tongs, roamed the streets of old Chinatown, making it too risky to entrust mail delivery to the mailman. They were frequently held up for the money, or whatever else they might be carrying.

There was only one U.S. Post Office in Chinatown, but trying to convince someone there that he needed to know the street address of a box holder would be futile. Besides, he didn't even know if the P.O. Box even existed after fifty years!

Chinatown only consisted of twenty-four square blocks, but there were hundreds of small businesses. Bo knew his job would be difficult, but not impossible. With no street address, he would just have to resort to the old "shoe leather" approach. But he was on a roll, and he was determined to find Jimmy Wong, certain he would know how to reach his daughter,

Bo hopped on an early flight and emerged from a cab at nine a.m. on the edge of Chinatown and began combing the streets, looking for the name "Wong" on every building and sign. "So, how many Wongs can there be in San Francisco?" he whispered to himself. "Thousands, I suppose. But how many Wongs does it take to make a Wight? I must be going a little batty. All right, now, pull yourself together and find the wight Wong."

First, he knew Jimmy Wong was a baker, so the little notes that Su Lin sent to her father were likely intended for the little printed slips in her father's fortune cookies.

Bo typed "fortune cookies" into Google on his cell phone and got more information than he needed. *No wonder they call it a smart phone,* he thought. It said that the honor of inventing the cookies had gone to a Chinese immigrant in Los Angeles in 1918. A different search produced a list of Chinatown bakeries, but none with the name Wong popped up. Bo headed for the first one on the list, the Golden Gate Fortune Cookie Factory, because they advertised themselves as the biggest cookie supplier in San Francisco. In his exuberance to get there, he overlooked the fact that the Golden Gate operation opened in 1962, presumably much later than Jimmy Wong's bakery had opened.

With some probing, Bo narrowed his search and finally walked into the last bakery on his list, Chinese City Noodles. Bo was losing heart, but when he questioned the friendly proprietor, he said he had bought the business from a Mr. Wong just a month earlier, and had changed the name. He said Wong had moved to Oakland.

"Nothing beats a good old-fashioned shoe leather investigation," Bo remarked to himself.

After getting Wong's new address, Bo headed over to Oakland the next morning. *Hot damn! I'm getting close*, he thought.

"Hello," he said as the door opened. "My name is Bo Dugan and I'm trying to locate Su Lin Wong for a friend of mine. Does she live here?"

After explaining that the gentlemen who bought his store had given him his address, Wong said, "Well you are at the right place. I'm Jimmy Wong Junior, and Su Lin was my older sister. But, she doesn't live here anymore."

"Do you know where I can reach her?"

"Sorry, I don't. She went away to college down in Los Angeles after high school. My dad used to talk to her by phone off and on, but he lost track of her. He thought she moved, but she never sent him a forwarding address. He tried writing, but his letters all came back marked 'Addressee moved and filed no change-of-address order.'"

"How did he take it?"

"As you might guess. My parents were devastated and never really got over it. They just couldn't understand what happened. I suppose they would have pursued the matter, but they were chained to the bakery and could never get away to go down there. You do realize she dishonored my parents by the way she left with no explanation, right?"

"Right."

"Even so, I've always been ashamed that I didn't try to find her myself, but I was too young and had my own problems. I was too selfish to worry about her. My mom died several years ago, and my father passed away soon after that, heartbroken. That's when I took over the business. I'm glad you showed up here. After all these years, I've had a change of heart, so I hope you can find her. Can you?"

"Maybe. I have an idea. What about the cards Su Lin used to send to your father?"

"How do you know about them?"

"No matter, but they may provide a clue as to her whereabouts, if she's still alive!"

"She made them for my dad for as far back as I can remember, and continued sending them every week after she left for college.

They stopped for about a year after she disappeared, but started coming again, except that instead of every week, they arrived monthly."

"So, how did your father react when they started coming again?"

"He was encouraged, but nothing else changed. There was never a return address. Nevertheless, he joyfully put them in his cookies. I think it was a small indication of his forgiveness and love for her. After my folks both passed, and I took over the business, the cards kept coming, and I used them just like my father did."

"Are they still coming?"

"Yes, believe it or not. The new owner started forwarding them to me." "And?"

"I just received another one. Let me get it for you. I haven't tossed it out yet."

"Yet?"

"We always tossed them after we used them. Otherwise, we wouldn't have room enough to keep them all. There would have been hundreds of them accumulating over a span of fifty years."

"Didn't your dad look at the postmarks?"

"Maybe. But after a while, he didn't care anymore. She didn't try to call or write, except for the postcards, and there was absolutely no indication she was ever coming back."

Jimmy Jr. returned with the card and handed it to Bo. The note read, *"Love is all around, even when you can't see it. Su Lin, forever."* The postmark was stamped Washington, D.C., with no return address.

"Thanks for your help, Jimmy."

"You're welcome. I'll be anxious to learn what you find out."

Bo had been careful not to tell him why Su Lin had disappeared, but he knew it was because of her love affair.

He thanked Jimmy and said goodbye. Then, he headed to the Oakland airport to fly home.

Bo was closing in on his target, and he called Mac with an update before he boarded the plane. He didn't know what Mac might be able to find out, but thought he was in the best position to locate her with all the resources at his disposal.

"Mac," he said, "Wong is one of the ten most common Chinese surnames, so don't forget that it might be included in some tricky name combination. There must be a zillion Wongs out there, but hopefully there aren't that many in the D.C. area. Call me if your learn anything. I'll be anxious to hear back."

Three days later, Mac sent him a text message. It read, "Looks like your job is done. I'll take it from here".

Bo didn't think he'd finished the job, but the boss is the boss.

CHAPTER 11 ~ The Interview

MARCH 27, 2017

Reluctant to ask why he was "done," Bo waited a few days before calling Mac.

"So, what did you find out? I have to find out if my work paid off."

"You're so lucky, Bo. Believe it or not, she was right under our nose. It wasn't easy finding her with so many people named Wong, but we think we have the right one. Several people named Wong live in the area, but we focused on an S. L. Wong listed in our government employee database. She has also used the alias Sue Lyn Wong, according to her employment application. She retired from the Department of Commerce, but now she's consulting to their Bureau of Labor Statistics where she used to work as an analyst. She must be a pretty smart cookie.

"We're sending someone over there tomorrow to talk to her. I'll let you know what we find out if it isn't deemed to be confidential. Take your bill to the FBI office and hand deliver it to the chief, personally. Don't answer any questions, but keep the phone for now in case we have more work for you to do."

Mac called the director of the FBI and said, "The president wants you to contact a woman named Sue Lyn Wong and find out what she knows about a vice premier of the People's Republic of China named Guang Jinli. He wants to find out anything she can tell us about his political thoughts, personal habits, interests ... those sorts of things. She met Guang as a foreign student during her college years in the late sixties, and now she lives nearby in Bethesda."

"Mac, isn't that a stretch? That's fifty years ago."

"I know, I know, but I have my orders. Mr. Guang is coming to Washington soon, so you'll have to get right on it. I'll text you with what we believe is her current address. To the best of our knowledge, she has never been married, so she may live alone. Her parents are deceased, and she has one brother living in California."

The director called in his Assistant Director for Intelligence, Bob Fishback, who recommended they send Special Agent Cole Stickman from their Maryland office to interview her.

Cole was known to take an "original" approach to his investigative work, but he had a unique ability to get at the truth. Neither Fishback nor Stickman were told who had made the request, although the confidentiality of the matter was understood, as it is in all FBI assignments.

After Cole was given his marching orders, he left to pay Sue Lyn a visit. She was living in a seventeen-story apartment house in an upscale part of Bethesda, Maryland. Cole thought it was a little too rich for a federal employee, but wages in the D.C. area had soared over the past era of big government, so it did make some sense.

Cole left his unmarked car in guest parking and walked to the building. In the foyer, he showed his badge to Bill, the security guard at the front desk, and said he was there to see Ms. Wong.

Bill was a retired United States Capitol Police officer and well trained in VIP protection. With so many government personnel living in the building he was the perfect man for the job.

Without taking his eyes off Cole, he buzzed Ms. Wong and told her that an FBI agent named Stickman was there to see her. Cole could hear her voice over the intercom.

"What about?"

"Tell her it's a confidential matter affecting her boss," Cole whispered, loud enough for her to hear.

"All right, send him up."

When she answered the door, Cole introduced himself and flipped open his ID wallet. Stickman was one of these guys who could put a snake on defense with his bad-guy persona.

She reluctantly asked him to come in and sit down, even though she was taken by surprise by his tough demeanor. She was careful to sit between him and the door. Perhaps she watched too much television. She had attended classes on self-defense that had been offered in D.C. for single women, so she felt she should be safe with him, even if she was wrong about him and had to run away. She knew her reflexes were not what they used to be, but she still went to the gym three times a week and was pretty quick on her feet. But who was kidding whom? Stickman was much younger and was no doubt well trained in martial arts himself.

Then Cole put on his Cheshire cat smile. He said he just had a few questions. She had never had anything like this happen to her before. She was a quiet lady, just going to work and doing her job. She'd never done anything wrong.

So, what is this all about, she thought.

"Before I begin," Cole said, "please confirm that you were born in San Francisco to Jimmy and Marlene Wong and attended the University of Southern California in nineteen sixty-five. Is that correct?"

Sue Lyn was puzzled, but she saw no harm in answering, as her parents were both gone and the school was certain to have a record of her enrollment there.

"That is essentially correct."

Not wanting to dig too deeply just yet, Stickman didn't pursue the "essentially" qualifier. Her answer was satisfactory, so he continued.

"And you work at the Bureau of Labor Statistics?"

"Yes, I consult to them," she answered, wondering where the conversation was headed.

"Ma'am, we're led to believe that someone in the Bureau may have compromised some of the important data that you prepare." Cole had concocted a plausible storyline for his visit.

"What data? Are you accusing me of something?" Without stopping, Cole picked up the pace.

"You know that the Jobs Report is kept confidential until it's released to the public, just like all other government economic reports. Correct?"

"Correct, but I've never committed any wrongdoing. I am very careful regarding my emails and never bring anything home with me. I'm stunned! If you have any information to support your claim that I'm involved in something, I want to see it right now."

Now he really had her going.

"This is just a preliminary visit, ma'am. We're not suggesting anything right now; we just want to know if you suspect anyone in your office of wrongdoing, or have ever witnessed any unusual activity."

"No, never," she retorted.

"Please keep the nature of our conversation to yourself, and we'll get back to you."

Cole stood up and started moving toward the door. Sue Lyn stood up quickly and moved back out of the way, as he said, "Thank you, and good afternoon. We'll be in touch."

Compromised government reports? she thought. *That's preposterous!* She was certain they had the wrong person.

Stickman was so proud of his playacting. He could have taken a different tack with and perhaps gotten the real information that he was seeking in just one visit, but he just couldn't help himself.

Stickman relished these kinds of assignments and thought he just might become a permanent member of his local Community Playhouse when he retired, playing the part of a CIA or foreign agent—of course, preferably in one of his own productions. He was proud of the ruse he had devised in this instance and thought he may use the same sham in some future story he might write.

Cole called Fishback immediately and confirmed that he had talked to the right person, but needed a second visit to fully explore what she knows.

There was no need for another visit, but Stickman wanted to carry out his pretense a little longer, just for fun.

Fishback passed on the information to the Director, who got in touch with Mac, who immediately called the president and requested a quick meeting.

"Mr. President, we've been able to generate a little information about Mr. Guang, although it's somewhat sketchy at this point," Mac said.

"I'm due in a meeting shortly, but I'll take just a minute to listen."

"Mr. President, let me cut to the chase. Sir, Mr. Guang graduated from college here in the U.S. in nineteen sixty-five and returned to China right after that. We located a girl he was seeing when he left school, who we believe is the mother of his child. She is now seventy-one and a retired federal employee living in Bethesda. She goes by the name of Sue Lyn Wong. We didn't want to alarm her too much, so we conducted a preliminary interview designed to put her on notice and make her think.

"The agent assigned to her has requested a second visit to finish his interrogation. If we can gain her confidence, we believe we will get some insight to Guang's character that might give you a leg up in your meetings with him, although we haven't developed any information on the child yet. The stage is set for another visit, if you just say the word. We're letting her think for a few days. Do I have your permission to press the issue?"

"Yes, of course. The lady might have known him better than anyone, so go ahead. Lovers have been known to say things to one another that they wouldn't tell anyone else. I think knowing everything about a potential adversary is the secret to a successful negotiation, so the more I can find out about the vice premier, the better. Do you think she's had any contact with him since their college days? That's important to find out."

"There is no evidence of that yet, but we'll check it out."

"Oh, and one more thing, Mac. Forget about the child. I don't see how that information is useful. Besides, I'm not in favor of using coercion just to get information for information's sake, unless there's a security issue involved. Don't mention the child to your investigators unless they uncover something. Just use your discretion."

"Understood. I thought that's what you'd say. We'll get right on it."

Cole asked for permission to take Emma Legrand with him on the next visit, and reminded Fishback that women always appear to be more comfortable when questioned by another woman. Fishback said that even though Legrand was known for being a smooth interrogator, he'd also heard she could be a little chatty around the office. She'd never snitched on Cole regarding his extracurricular acting pursuits or the weird people he hung out with, so Cole vouched for her integrity. Fishback approved Cole's request.

When they returned to Sue Lyn's apartment, Cole introduced Emma to Sue Lyn as his trusted associate. Sue Lyn invited them in immediately, having a good feeling about Emma.

Sue Lyn offered them tea, and they sat in the living room while she went into the kitchen to make it. When she returned, the two agents were standing in the middle of the floor. Sue Lyn was pretty sure they had been snooping around, but had no idea what they might be looking for.

In fact, while she was out of the room, the agents *had* taken a quick look around. There was not much to see, really. A few books were neatly lined up on a bookshelf, a few Chinese newspapers were scattered on top of the coffee table along with the day's Post, and a few pictures hung on the wall. They found nothing much of interest, except for the Post.

It was the previous day's issue, folded over to the third page to an article about the president's agenda, with a story on his upcoming meeting in Washington with the vice premier of China. Sue Lyn had obviously read it carefully.

Cole began the questioning. This time, he came across with the charm of a James Bond.

"I'll come right to the point, Ms. Wong. It's come to our attention that many of China's purchases of U.S. Treasuries in the open market have coincided somewhat with the release of our Jobs Reports. In fact, those purchases seem to decrease when employment increases, sending rates higher, and their purchases decrease, sending rates lower, when the employment report is negative. Do you have any answers for that?"

"No, absolutely not."

"Well, is it possible that you have been sympathetic to the PRC because of your past relationship with the vice premier, and that you're just trying to favor him in a small way, hoping he will find out what you're doing?"

"That's absolutely preposterous!"

"Well you did—or do—know him, isn't that correct?"

She could see that they had done their homework and probably knew the answers to all their questions, even the bogus ones. Stopping to ask for an attorney would just delay the inevitable. Besides, she wanted to keep the details of her relationship with Jinli private at all cost, if she could.

After a pause, she replied.

"I did know him when we were in school together, but that was a long time ago, and we haven't spoken or had any other contact since then."

"You do know that the vice premier is the top man for financial affairs in China, yes?"

"Yes."

"And you know his success depends on his ability to efficiently direct their monetary operations, right?"

"Right again."

"So, you maintain that the coincidences I described are just that? Coincidences?"

"Yes, absolutely."

The line of questioning was so off-the-wall that Sue Lyn suspected there was something else they really wanted to know, and guessed they were just bluffing. What were they really after?

"All right. Now, let's talk about the vice premier himself," Emma said, taking over the questioning. "And please, call me Emma."

"And call me Sue Lyn."

"All right, Sue Lyn. We understand that you had a close relationship with him. What can you tell us about that?"

She decided to continue cooperating for a little longer; maybe that would get rid of them.

"Well, we knew each other fairly well. We were in some of the same classes for just one year. There weren't many Chinese students there at the time, so we were naturally friendly toward one another."

Be careful, she told herself.

"There isn't much to say, really. He was very smart, and very curious about how capitalism works in this country. He understood our concept of reward for investment and hard work, but couldn't get away from the idea that a government based on central control would be better at caring for its people and more responsive to their needs.

"He was forward thinking, but maintained his ideological stance. Remember, he was already schooled in communism when he arrived here. However, the more we studied and discussed economic and political issues in class, the more I think he began to consider the merits of our system and embrace our ideas. That notwithstanding, he was sure we had too much freedom for our own good."

"That's an interesting perspective, I would say," noted Emma.

"I do think, however, that he went back to China believing that some elements of capitalism might benefit his country. With some more time here, he might very well have come completely over to our side, so to speak. I think that his allegiance to his family and his country might have been broken if I could have just—" She stopped short, realizing she was babbling.

"Yes, please continue," said Emma.

"Oh, nothing," Sue Lyn said cautiously.

"If you could just have done what?" pried Emma.

"Had more influence on him before he left, I started to say."

"What influence?" Emma asked smartly.

Feeling the pressure, Sue Lyn took a deep breath. Then she replied, "Maybe I could have convinced him to stay in America and enjoy all the freedom that we have under our system. Unfortunately, his family roots ran too deep."

"I see," Cole said, granting her a short reprieve before moving on. "What about his interests, habits, hobbies, and that sort of thing?"

Now the questions were getting personal. Why? Had they learned something about her secret that she kept for so many years? Who was behind this inquisition?

"I don't know much about that," she answered, "but I can tell you one thing. He was very competitive and loved to win at a board game called Go."

"Go? Never heard of it," Cole said quizzically. "Can you think of anything else about him? Just give me two words to describe him."

Sue Lyn thought for a moment and said, "Inquisitive and competitive." She might have used the word "sensitive," but that might have imparted a personal view that could be misinterpreted.

"I think we're just about finished here," Emma chimed in. "One more question. Do you have any interest in contacting him while he's here? You know, for old times' sake, as they say?"

"No, not at all. We weren't that close. And anyway, we haven't had any contact since he left school."

Switching gears to change the subject, she added, "I am happy to hear he's going to Los Angeles to receive an honorary degree before coming here. I think it's wonderful for someone to be recognized for his or her accomplishments. And he has made a significant impact on trade policies around the world from what I read."

Sue Lyn quit talking. She knew she had said more than enough, and was satisfied she hadn't revealed anything personal about their relationship, just enough to hopefully come across as sincere and believable.

As they prepared to leave, Emma turned and said, "Sue Lyn, I noticed your pictures on the wall. Is that one of the vice premier taken when you two were in school together?" she asked.

Sue Lyn quickly gathered herself together and answered rather forcefully, "No. You're probably looking at the picture of my brother on the right. Handsome, don't you think? Everyone used to say he looked like my father, who is in the middle picture with my mother. It was taken in front of his store when it first opened. Do you see the resemblance?"

"Maybe. Who is the young man on the left?"

"Oh, that's my cousin. It was taken at his graduation." "Your cousin?"

"Yes, my father's brother's son." *Whew! That was fast thinking,* Sue Lyn thought.

Cole and Emma said they had no more questions and thanked her for her cooperation as they left.

Sue Lyn knew the Feds were good at their job and anything tying her to Jinli now wouldn't be too smart. Luckily, the photographs had been reproduced in a sepia tone that made the years between Jinli and her father seem to disappear. Her artistic bent had paid off.

What was I thinking? Sue Lyn questioned herself. *Why didn't I put the stupid pictures in the bedroom, rather than the living room for every prying eye to see? I do think Jinli does seem to resemble my dad in his younger years, though.*

The picture on the right side was a picture of Jinli. She had snapped it at the airport in 1965 just before he boarded the plane. She kept it as a constant reminder of the way he looked at her with those adoring eyes. She had hoped that their parting might not be forever, but after several years with no contact, she dismissed the idea of ever seeing him again.

The picture in the middle was of her parents, and the picture on the left was of Winston, her love child, who was now a brilliant, accomplished economist and academic, fifth in line to succeed to the presidency! She had taken it with a telephoto lens as she stood up quickly from her sitting position, unnoticed in the back of the gallery during the Ph.D. hooding ceremony when he got his doctorate from Georgetown.

Sue Lyn loved the pictures of the three men in her life.

But she still couldn't figure out why the agents paid her two visits. Who sent them, and why?

Recently, Sue Lyn had read that Jinli would be accompanied on his White House visit by his wife, Shuchun. She thought that Jinli must be quite happy. In spite of that bit of information, Sue Lyn thought that if she could just exchange a glance with him, her long-held curiosity of his affection for her might be satisfied.

After they left the apartment, Cole and Emma compared notes as the drove away.

"That was interesting," Emma said. "Did Fishback mention her deceased parents or a younger brother to you?"

"That is a check."

"But I never heard anything about an uncle or cousin. You know, she might be lying about who's in that picture on the right. Or, maybe the one on the left, as well."

"You don't think she told us everything, do you?" Cole said.

"Well, I think she's pretty clean. I know we're supposed to be talking about her memory of Guang, but there is something about that one picture in particular that really bothers me. I just can't put my finger on it. Just for kicks, I'm going to locate a current headshot of Guang from somewhere and getting a picture of her brother's driver's license should be easy. The boys down at the lab can age regress them for me. Then I'll compare them with her pictures. You do know I have a photographic memory. It's a simple process of elimination. See which one is the brother, assuming one of them is, and violá. I'll have my man. The next interview would really be fun."

"So what? If there is no match, then why press the issue? Hey, we got some of the stuff Fishback wanted, so forget that angle. Emma, I know you're a Special Agent with advanced training in intelligence, but the picture is meaningless."

"But Cole, funny clues raise my suspicion."

"I said forget it, Emma, it's just a waste of your time."

"Sorry, I was just curious, that's all," she remarked, resigned to Cole's rebuke.

"Let's move on."

"But do you make anything of all the newspapers and her nervous behavior just before we left? When it came to the question of any contact, she might well have been bluffing. I got a sense that she fears something. I just know there's something there. I can just feel it."

"Emma, you're paranoid."

They agreed to ask Fishback if they could keep an eye on her.

"One of them may try to reach the other during his visit," said Emma. "That would really be interesting, and if it happens and we get the drop on it, Fishback might recommend us for a commendation."

"Come on, Emma. Mr. Guang is married?"

"Yes, he is, and you obviously don't know much about love, do you?"

Cole didn't respond, and asked Emma if she would write up the report since he had to get to rehearsal that evening. He had just been chosen to play the part of Petruchio in "The Taming of the Shrew"; a role that he felt fit him to a tee.

Emma readily agreed to do it, and Cole left for the theater, knowing that his performance would be a grand one, just as good as the one he had put on for Emma in Sue Lyn's apartment.

"Mr. President, let me sum up the FBI's report for you," Mac said.

"You can read their full report at your leisure; however, I think the essence of their findings will provide you with some of what you want to know."

He began to read from his notes. "Sue Lyn was rather philo-sophical about her relationship with the vice premier. She said he was forward thinking, but totally ideological. He felt a central government is more responsive to their people than ours is. He felt we have too much freedom, but acknowledged there are some benefits to capitalism. He was smart and curious about how capitalism works, and she thought he could have been co-opted if she had had enough time with him to convince him to stay. She described him as very inquisitive and competitive."

"Thanks for the summary, Mac. That gives me an idea, but I'll wait to digest the whole report before I cast it in concrete."

CHAPTER 12 ~ The Exposé

APRIL 12, 2017

Ben called Austin with good news. "I just got my hands on what you've been waiting for. I know we're not playing poker tonight, but I'm coming right over to drop it off."

When Austin opened the door, he said, "You made such a big deal about this, I thought I'd better hand it to you personally."

"Come on, Ben, those were your instructions. Personally. Remember?"

"I know, but I need to know if I, your faithful lackey, got what you wanted." Austin was not amused.

Austin opened the envelope and peeked at the other envelope inside. It was marked, CONFIDENTIAL. DELIVER TO THE OFFICE OF SENATOR MICKIEWICZ C/O BENTON ELLIOTT.

"Perfect. And remember, do not speak a word of this to anyone."

"Of course. Are you kidding? How many times do you have to tell me? And please, don't get me involved in any more of your skullduggery, okay?"

"Okay, but tell me one thing before you go. How did the senator get the court order?"

"It turned out to be harder than he thought. He looked at the roster of judges in California, and there was a friendly name he remembered from law school. He called him ostensibly to reminisce as old friends, but eventually had to lean on his Senate position to make the request. The judge thought it was strange since the senator is a third party with no direct interest in the matter, being neither one of the birth or adoptive parents. Without going into any detail, the senator was forced to say that it was a matter of special interest to the government. His friend was reluctant at first, but finally signed the order 'for old times' sake," he said.

Austin thanked Ben profusely and complimented the senator on his assistance, ushering Ben out the door to send him on his way. He wanted to savor the moment alone.

Austin hesitated before opening the envelope. He felt a kind of reluctant anticipation, likening it to an oxymoron. You're wildly excited about something but you delay enjoying it until the last moment. *It's a strange feeling*, he thought, and figured a sex therapist might be able to shed some light on it.

He hoped the original birth certificate would satisfy his curiosity.

Austin racked his brain thinking of several possibilities. First, would there even be a baby's name? A lot of children leave the hospital without one. And would the mother use hers or the father's last name? What if there was no father's name at all? Perhaps the mother might not know who the father was. Or perhaps the father denied paternity. If the father fit the latter possibility, the mother might not want to use his name. But, on the other hand, if she knew who he was and loved him, regardless of whether he came forth or not, she might want to reflect his love for her by using his name. There were endless possibilities.

The ultimate possibility would be if someone had been able to pull a shenanigan and doctor up a false certificate to conceal the fact that the baby wasn't even born in the United States! Austin had considered that one earlier.

He had waited long enough.

He sat down at his table and spread out the contents.

First, there was the amended copy of Winston Lee's birth certificate that had been filed in Los Angeles County.

Then, he opened the confidential envelope with Ben's name on it. There was the court order signed by some obscure Superior Court judge. Attached to the order was the printed picture of the original birth certificate.

You could plainly see that it bore a multicolored embossed government seal impressed into the paper. If it was a fake it was a really, really good one! From its appearance, you wouldn't know that the amended birth certificate wasn't the original. The only difference was that the adoptee parents' names were apparently substituted for the birth parents' names, with a new name for the child.

It showed that Winston Lee had been born on February 3, 1966 in Los Angeles, California to a David and Grace Lee. Austin's most important question was answered: the baby was born in California and Winston was a U.S. citizen. Austin stood and shouted "Hallelujah"!

The original birth certificate looked essentially the same as the new one except that the child's surname was Wong, with the first and middle names of Jinli and Guang. No father's name was provided, but the mother's name, S. L. Wong, was typed in below a signature that was impossible to read. Austin noticed the difference because the signature didn't appear to use initials.

That raised the next question. Are Winston's birth parents still living? And if so, where are they? That question was unanswered.

Suddenly, Austin almost fell out of his chair as he looked back at the child's name on the original birth certificate.

Austin had been so intent on the citizenship question that he skipped right over the names: this baby's original name was Jinli Guang Wong, and Guang Jinli is the name of the vice premier who is on his way to Washington! In his haste, he overlooked the obvious. To him, all Chinese names looked about the same.

The vice premier? Good grief! There's been no public notice that he or Winston has acknowledged their relationship. Hmmm ... I'm guessing the vice premier must have had a little affair and doesn't know he has a son. If I'm correct, shouldn't he have known there might be consequences? The vice premier will be here in just a few days so I really have to move on this. This could be my biggest story ever, Austin thought.

Austin's hunch had paid off, but in an unexpected way. The facts might have been clear to anyone looking at a copy of the original birth certificate, if they had half a brain, but it didn't appear the adoption file had been seen by anyone else.

Now Austin knew who the birth father was and where he is, but he hadn't learned anything about the mother, except that the name she gave her baby was no coincidence. She simply combined his name with hers, and made no attempt to conceal the father's identity. Austin's conclusion was that she really must have loved him enough to honor him in that way.

Austin decided his interest in her would have to wait. The big story was simply the relationship between the son and the father. That story alone was too big for him to get bogged down with too much detail. "There's nothing to be gained by swatting at flies," an old boss of his always told him. "Focus on the big picture," he had said.

The next morning, he rethought his strategy. His journalistic instinct told him that to pursue a story without all the facts would be a travesty. What if the reports of the time about Bonnie Parker as a cigar smoking, machine gun-toting moll had not been true? As a matter of fact, they weren't true. A good investigative reporter might have checked that out before the story got out of hand. Not that she was a damsel in distress, mind you!

Austin decided to look for the mother and get the entire story before printing it.

He only had the name of S. L. Wong to go by. Without access to government databases to quickly do the job for him, he would have to resort to the new old-fashioned way, by searching the Internet himself.

After trying the search sites offering to locate people for a fee, he gave up. Without more information than just a name, it was going to be impossible. There was no guarantee of success anyway, and he didn't even know what state she might be living in. Besides, those sites were probably a ruse just to make money.

He had to put on his thinking cap. Who maintains data on people? Credit card companies, phone companies, banks, and the government of course, via the records maintained by Social Security, the Census Bureau and the NSA. There were so many possibilities; he hardly knew where to start looking.

First he tried the Census Bureau web site, only to learn that their record of names is restricted for seventy-two years before genealogists can get hold it, and the baby's mother would be about seventy by now. Bummer.

Then, he turned to his next best idea where he figured he might have a shot. He used to date a girl named Linda Snuggs over at the Social Security Administration, in the benefits section. Ah yes, Linda—another one who wanted to get married. Oh well. Maybe Linda can find S. L. Wong if old S. L. is collecting Social Security. It was certainly worth a try.

He gave Linda a call. "Linda, this is Austin. How have you been?"

"Good," she replied, sounding annoyed. "I got married recently, so if you're …"

He cut her off mid-sentence. "Not to worry. I just need a favor. Can we meet?"

"I'll get back to you in ten."

Austin met her at eleven that morning at an old pizza place they had once frequented. It was close to her office, and she could walk there and get back quickly.

It was one of those hole-in-the-wall places on M Street that should be featured on one of those faddish TV cooking shows. The owner was Michael (Mikey) Angelo Gagliano, a descendent of Nicolo Gagliano I, a famous Italian violin-maker from the 1700s. It had wallpaper with pictures of violins.

It had been there for at least fifty years or more, and looked like it. It was mid-block, brick building with a green and white awning out front. In an hour people would be lined up down the street to get in. The White House was a really good customer, but their tips were lousy.

Linda waited for Austin outside, and they walked in together.

"Hey, love birds. How've you been? Long time, no see," Mikey said loudly from behind the counter.

This wasn't such a good choice, Linda thought to herself. "Good, good," she replied, smiling. "Mikey, I'm on a short break so I'll just grab a table and Austin can give you my take-out order."

"Molto bene," Mikey replied. "Molto bene." Austin ordered one small pepperoni pizza for Linda.

Linda and Austin had dated on and off for a few years, but she finally gave up on ever getting a ring. She had really wanted a family. They had talked marriage many times, but Austin always just said he would let her know when he was ready. "Ready" never arrived, and Linda turned elsewhere.

Austin picked up the order and sat down with her.

"I have to make it quick Austin, so what do you need? I hope this isn't something to do with the president. I follow your tweets. You've really been hard on him."

"No," he said in a quiet voice. "I just need the address of someone. I'm sure you've never met her or ever heard of her. It's for a story I'm researching. It's a lady by the name of S. L. Wong."

"I think I can do it. At least, I'll try, but this is a one off for old times' sake. When I say 'one time' I mean it, Austin. Okay?"

"Okay. For sure."

"I'll call you this afternoon. Our computer systems are probably the best of any agency. If that person is out there, I'll find her."

Austin jumped up and gave her a peck on the cheek. "Thanks. You always did come through for me. And congratulations to you and what's his name. I owe you one," he yelled to her over his shoulder as he went through the door.

With that he departed, never to see her again.

"Did you find anything?" Austin said when she called him back, without so much as a hello.

"Oh Austin, once again you hit pay dirt! I have to say, you haven't lost your touch. You are the luckiest guy I know, or knew, as the case may be. There are thousands of Wongs but only one S. L. Wong. I'll text the address. Please delete it right away."

Austin googled the address and up popped a map. Now he really had it going. *She's not far away,* he thought. He doubted she would be working on the weekend, so Saturday should be a red-letter day. This was too easy, but as he always said, "all problems are easy when solved!"

It was a short drive, and when he arrived he was surprised to see her apartment building. He was aware that salaries of government employees had risen under the past administration, but this was a really first-class facility. It was certainly a step above the trap where he lived!

The guard left his desk and disappeared around the corner, heading to the men's room, just as Austin entered the lobby. Seeing no one around, he stepped behind the desk and buzzed the name "Wong" on the directory.

"May I help you, Bill?" the voice said. "This isn't Bill."

"Where's Bill?"

"He'll be back shortly. My name is Austin Cook. I am a journalist with OTP. Perhaps you've heard of us?"

"Yes, go ahead."

"May I speak with you privately?"

"What about?"

"I uncovered some information that may be of interest to you, and before it's published, I thought you might like to comment."

"Look, Mr. Cook, this is an invasion of privacy. I don't want to speak to you."

"Please listen," Austin said in a soothing voice. "I understand your reaction. Someone approaches you out of the blue and says they have information to share. Look, this really isn't the best way to have a conversation. May I please come up? I think it will be worth your while."

This was the second stranger in less than three weeks with a request to "talk." Something was going on, but she still hadn't figured it out. First, the FBI wanted to know what she knew about Jinli, and now a stranger approaches with important information. What important information? She considered his request. If she turned him down, she might regret it.

"Come on up."

Sue Lyn answered the door. Austin presented his card to her, and she seemed relieved that he was telling the truth. She had heard of him and had actually read a couple of his posts. That familiarity satisfied her, so she asked him to come in and sit down.

"I take it you want to talk politics, Mr. Cook," she said. "I'm not really into that, even though I work for the government. But how can I help you?"

"I'm not interested in your help, Ms. Wong. I just want you to be aware that there is information about your past that has come to my attention."

"Such as?"

"Such as your relationship with the vice premier of China, who will be here in the city in about three weeks."

Sue Lyn was being asked about Jinli again. What could anyone possibly know?

186

"I don't know how to break this to you so I'm not going to beat around the bush. I'm aware that you have a son, and that his father is the vice premier."

"Aiyah," Sue Lyn exclaimed, horrified. *How did he find out about that?*

She had been so very careful ever since his birth to maintain her anonymity. She was ashamed, knowing she had committed a terrible sin in the eyes of her Lord, and had not honored her mother and her father.

"Please forgive me for being so abrupt," Austin said as he reached for her hand to comfort her.

Feeling a little more comfortable with him now, she asked, "May I call you Austin?"

"Thank you Ms. Wong. Yes, of course. And how shall I address you?"

"I go by the name Sue Lyn now," she replied, feeling totally disarmed. Then she proceeded to tell him about her relationship with Jinli at USC; her trial of saying goodbye to him before she found out she was pregnant, of giving birth, and then putting the baby up for adoption without telling her parents.

Austin had been correct. He chalked it up to another lucky guess, or maybe it was just instinct.

Then she started to cry, taking him by surprise.

"I'm so sorry that my news is disheartening," he said.

"That's all right," she replied, as Austin consoled her. "It had to come out sometime, but I'm surprised that I'm still so emotional about it after all these years. I know that God has forgiven me and that he only wants the best for Winston and me. His adoptive parents are wonderful people and they gave him a strong name that I've come to love, just as I love him. I am so grateful for them."

Then Sue Lyn told him the rest of her story.

"It was plain and simple. I found out where my baby was taken by his new parents, so I moved to D.C. to be close to him in case he needed me. Besides, jobs were plentiful here, and I just needed to get away from California. As it has turned out, he's had a good life without me in the picture and that's a good thing. He certainly doesn't need the complication of having two mothers.

"You might ask how I could just walk away from my family in San Francisco. They might not have known about my baby, but my feelings for him prevailed over every other thought. I just had to be near to him. It was hard at first, but grew easier as the years went by, especially after I learned my parents had passed away.

"I still take the San Francisco Chronicle and always look at the obits. I'm always relieved my brother's name has never appeared. I was never really that close to him, but I hope he will forgive me. Perhaps I was too hard on myself, but I never second-guessed my decision."

"I'm beginning to understand," Austin said, "but how did you know where your baby had been taken?"

"Well, I had opted for an adoption when I went to St. Anne's Maternity Hospital, and they sent a lady from Holy Family Adoption Services to explain the process to me. I told her that I wanted my baby to go to a family with at least one Chinese parent. As luck would have it, she had a couple on her list from Fairfax, Virginia who desperately wanted a Chinese baby. He was Chinese and she was white, and the man desperately wanted a boy. That's the Chinese preference, you know.

"The woman had followed her father to China as a Christian missionary, where she met her husband while working with Chinese Outreach Ministries and their Far East Broadcasting Company, sending Christian radio broadcasts into China. I knew they would not let my baby forget his heritage.

"Eileen Stansfield, the Holy Family lady, was kind enough to give me their address, although I don't think she was authorized to do that. The information she passed along allowed me to move close to Winston's parents and watch him as he grew up.

"I've always thanked God for how she helped me. David and Grace Lee have been wonderful parents. David is now the lead pastor at the Chinese Community Church here in D.C., which Winston has attended for several years. The church holds services in Mandarin, Cantonese and in English. I believe Winston usually attends the service held in Mandarin. He has never forgotten his heritage. What a blessing that is!"

Sue Lyn went on to explain that, as Winston grew up, she had marveled at how he showed the intellect and abilities of his father. She said she frequently read the local news section of the Washington Post for Arlington, Virginia where Winston's parents lived, and the paper was always including stories about his high school's athletic success and its academic standings. It was a terrific school, and Winston's picture was always in the newspaper for one thing or another. He was the captain of his debate team, which took top honors in the state. And in his senior year, the paper featured a story about Winston when he received his Eagle Scout certification. David offered the invocation at the ceremony, and afterwards, Winston's Scoutmaster read several letters of congratulations, including one from Virginia's then Governor.

"Well, after high school, Winston attended Georgetown where he ultimately graduated with his doctorate. In fact, I was in the audience and took a picture of him in his cap and gown when they announced his name as a magna cum laude recipient. Do you want to see it?"

"Absolutely."

"And I also have a picture of Jinli that I took shortly before he left for China."

She retrieved a scrapbook from her bedroom that contained all the articles she kept on Winston.

As Austin perused the book, Sue Lyn said, "He looks a great deal like his father. And I can tell you that from watching him on TV, he has some of the same mannerisms that his father has. Do you know how proud it makes a mother, Austin, to see her son on the world stage? My little boy!"

"No, I can't possibly feel the depth of that pride."

"I'm sure I'm boring you, so maybe we should stop right here."

"You're not boring me in the least, so please go on. But you still haven't shown me those pictures."

She retrieved the pictures from the cabinet drawer into which she had put them away. She explained how she had fooled the FBI agents who had come to visit into thinking that the photographs of Jinli and Winston were of her brother and cousin.

The FBI? Austin thought. *Who sent them to pay her a visit?*

As she showed him the pictures, he said, "Very impressive. And you're right, there is a striking resemblance between father and son."

"Well, if you've been tracking as much politics as I think you have, you know a lot more about Winston than I've told you, so I'll stop right now."

"You may be right," he admitted. "I've looked into his past, but nothing to do with his character. I was concerned the president may have made a bad choice for other reasons, but now I'm convinced that he was the right choice, especially now that I know something about his mother and his parents. Sue Lyn … did you ever marry?"

"No, I guess I never recovered from my experience in college, as strange as that may seem. Although I've had many opportunities to date over the years, I held out hope for the first couple of years that Jinli would come back to me. I tried to connect with him after he left, but he disappeared from my life, until now.

"Jinli did leave a note when he left and asked me to write. So while I was waiting for the baby's birth, I sent him a letter expressing my love and asked him to come back. There was no response so I thought the letter might have been lost. I wrote to him a few weeks later with the same result. Perhaps he might have written back if he knew I was pregnant, because I never mentioned it in my letters.

"I knew he loved me, but the distance and circumstances were just too much, and it wasn't part of God's plan for us, I guess. So I stopped writing."

190

"Did you continue hoping he would return?"

"No, not really," she said. "My faith would never let me question God. There can be joy in disappointment. You never forget your first love, and in my case, my only love, except for Winston, of course. He provides me with all the contentment I need. I know that Jinli is married now. From the pictures in the papers, they look very happy. That also gives me some satisfaction.

"You know, Austin, when Winston was appointed to the Treasury post, I recognized that as a validation of his contribution to the study of economic theory. Winston has often remarked in his speeches that his ultimate goal is to serve his country in some policy-making way. Jinli's father, Wei Guang, also felt that his son would someday make a similar contribution to his country, and next week Jinli will have the privilege of doing just that. Incredibly, Jinli and Winston will be meeting each other for the first time to fulfill each of their destinies. That will be a truly remarkable event."

"Sue Lyn, does anyone else know what you've shared with me?"

"No."

"All right, I'll sit on the story for now, but I have a duty as a journalist to report the facts of any important story that I uncover, for the good of the public. I plan to tell the president about Winston if I get the opportunity."

"The president? ... And just what will he do with that information?"

"I don't know, but I think I know him well enough that he will want to honor your wishes, whatever they are. Beyond that, we'll just have to see."

"Austin, I've waited a lifetime for this moment. I haven't interfered with Winston for the reasons I've explained. But secretly I've hoped that one day he might meet his father. If I had tried earlier to contact him or let him know who his birth father is by some other means, it might have angered him for some reason. With no way to contact his father, he would only have gotten one side of the story. Now he may be able to hear both sides. I know Winston will appreciate his father's sensibilities after meeting him. Jinli is such a wonderful, caring man.

"Please, please help me find the best way to let Winston know who he's meeting with. Will you do that for me? I've come to terms with myself over my mistake; however, Winston had no role in that. But look how Winston has turned out. As a mature, well-educated leader with a family himself, he deserves to know who his real father is and not miss this chance to talk to him. This may be his only opportunity. I think I can trust you, Austin, but if you can't help me, I may have to handle it myself somehow. But that doesn't mean I want a public display. I want to maintain my privacy and anonymity, if I can."

"I can't promise anything, Sue Lyn. It will depend on the president. But I will do my best. When I know more, I'll come back to see you."

"All right. I thank you for coming and allowing me to finally get this out in the open, so to speak. Believe me, it's a Godsend after all these years. And, by the way, you still haven't told me how you discovered who Winston's birth parents are and then find me?"

"Sue Lyn, it's just in my nature to be inquisitive. That's my job. I'll fill you in later after I meet with the president and see how he wants to proceed."

CHAPTER 13 ~ The Cover

APRIL 17, 2017

"Ben, I have to meet with you face to face," Austin said. "How about Lucho's place? Let's say eleven-thirty for lunch. I'll call him and get a quiet table."

"I'm going to come right to the point," Austin said. "Something has come up of national importance, and I need your help getting an appointment with the president."

"The president! Are you kidding me? What's this all about?"

"I can't tell you, except to say that I need to see him as soon as possible."

"Does this have anything to do with that birth certificate thing?"

"Can't say. But it's a big deal, and I'd stake my reputation on what I have to discuss with him."

"You really can't tell me?"

"No. Please trust me. I will fill you in after the issue blows over."

"What issue?"

"I told you I can't tell you anything. So will you help me or not?"

"Of course I will. I'm already in too deep with you. The other day somebody asked me if I know you personally."

"What did you say?"

"I asked why the question, and he said there were rumors about leaks from the senator's office to the press, and they wanted to know how close we were. I just shrugged it off, and there were no more questions."

"Actually, I just changed my mind. I guess you're entitled to know what I've been up to." In a hushed tone, he asked, "What would you say if I told you that our new Treasury Secretary is Vice Premier Guang's son?"

"Well I'll be hornswoggled!" he exclaimed, using one of his father's favorite expression. "That's pretty embarrassing! Was it really that evident? It slipped right past our brightest and best investigators. The nomination process was just going too fast, I guess. Does anyone else know?"

"Not yet. Not until you get me that appointment with the president."

"Are you going to print something?"

"I haven't taken it to my editor yet, but I'll decide on that after I hear what the White House has to say. The big meeting with the Chinese could present some major security concerns if this gets out. It could blow our relationship with them sky high. You know, father coerces son. Father asks for asylum. Son outwits father. I can think of a myriad of possibilities, so I've decided that for the sake of maintaining good relations I may be willing to remain quiet in exchange for some favor. I haven't thought of what that might be quite yet, but I'll come up with something."

"So you want me to approach the White House and tell them you need a favor? You can't be serious. You know I can't just call them and say, 'Hey, can my buddy come by for a chat with, say, the president!'"

"Come on Ben, I'm serious."

"All right, I'll pull some strings, or call in a chip, that sort of thing. You're not the first person to ask me for a favor, you know."

"Just get me a meeting with Logan Catalina, the new Director of Communications," Austin said. "I'll take it from there. I hear she has the ear of McNeill, and he can get me in to see his boss. Can you do that for me?"

"Austin, I think I can handle that, but you'd be making a mistake if you're thinking of using her as any sort of a messenger. She'll press you for details and she'll be hard to resist. Have you seen her?

"Just stick to your guns and tell her I need to see her."

"Of course," Ben said. "I'll try, but forget McNeill. Cut out the middleman. You're integrity is on the line, and the fewer people in the know the better. You even made the mistake of telling me too much in the beginning. I'll just ask her to find out if you can meet privately with the president. When do you want to see her?"

"As soon as possible."

"Austin, you can trust me to get the job done. Always remember that."

Ben thought about Austin's request and decided it would be best to follow protocol, not wanting to be too close to the action himself. The next day, Ben asked the senator to call the White House and request the meeting for Austin. The senator was only too happy to help, and he cleared Austin's request without a question. The press hadn't been overly kind to the senator lately, so he wanted to cooperate. And he trusted Ben.

Ms. Catalina was being bombarded with requests for meetings from people wanting to gain influence with the president, but since the request came with the senator's personal endorsement, she complied.

"So Mr. Cook, what can I do for you?"

Austin hesitated for a moment before answering. *Who's in charge of hiring around here?* he asked himself. *I'd love to have that job. That person must have had the same job at Fox.*

He cleared his throat. "I have information of the utmost importance that can't be shared with anyone except the president."

"Please don't waste my time," she responded. "I can't imagine anything that important, especially coming from you. I've read your stuff and find much of it to be somewhat tilted. And your questions in the press briefings can be quite irritating."

"I'm just doing my job as honestly as I can."

"Okay, get on with it. I am quite busy."

"Ms. Catalina, this information could affect the Treasury Secretary's meeting with the vice premier next week, and our national security could be involved," he said with authority. "I'll stake my reputation on it. If I'm wrong, you can ban me from any further press briefings."

"Mr. Cook, I'll run it up the flagpole and get back to you. But to be clear, I am personally intrigued with the thought of no more of your appearances around here.

After Austin left, Ms. Catalina almost went into orbit, thinking about the implications of what she had just heard. She caught her breath and immediately called Mr. McNeill and asked if she could see him on a matter of extreme urgency.

Walking down the hall, she felt a little queasy. After all, this could be a very important request, and she had been picked to receive it.

Austin hadn't really told her anything, but why would he bother to risk his reputation like this if there wasn't some truth to what he was saying?

Mac would know how to proceed, she thought, and it made her feel a little better.

"Keep this to yourself, Logan, and I'll deal with it," Mac said."Not a word to anyone. Understood?"

He considered the importance of the meetings with the vice premier and decided a short meeting with Austin might be worth the president's time. He'd heard of Austin's hunches and didn't want to take a chance.

"Mr. President, I need to see you."

"What's up, Mac?"

"Well, you know that pesky journalist who always has interesting questions in our briefings?"

"Yes, I certainly know who he is. He's the one who seems to have a corner on the business of challenging everything we're doing around here, right?"

"Yes, and now he wants to meet with you personally. He says he has highly important information with national security implications that bears on our meetings with the vice premier. Cook says he only needs five minutes of your time. He's even offered to put his career at risk if he's wrong about his information. I think it's worth your time to see him."

The president put his chin on his hands and shook his head. "Guang will be here in just a week. As if I don't already have enough to deal with, much less an adversarial journalist."

"Ms. Catalina, I'm calling to follow up," Austin said. "Did you get the meeting set up for me?"

"Mr. Cook, I'll be as blunt as I can. If you speak to anyone about whatever it is that you know or report anything about it, even if it's just an innuendo, you can kiss your career—and maybe yourself—goodbye."

"Why, Ms. Catalina … are you threatening me?"

"No, just making our position as clear as possible."

"I'll tell you what. I'll refrain from revealing what I know—now and forevermore—regardless of how the trade discussions go, provided someone else doesn't spill the beans first, if you promise to provide me with a full summary of the results of the trade negotiations before the final press briefing."

She jumped at the chance to take a little initiative.

"I'm going out on a weak limb, Mr. Cook, but I think your offer is fair and one that I can persuade the powers above to accept. I'll be back to you shortly."

"Thank you, Ms. Catalina, you may be excused," said the president.

"Please come in, Mr. Cook, and take a seat by the fireplace."

"Thank you, Mr. President."

"Now, what is this all about? I shouldn't give you the time of day because of your rather pointed comments about my administration and me. Yes, Mr. Cook, I've seen your tweets and blogs. However, I understand you've learned something of great importance that you can't wait to discuss. Is that correct?"

"Yes, Sir, Mr. President. I was told you only have a few minutes to see me, so I'm going to come right to the point. What would you say if I told you that your new Treasury Secretary is the son of Vice Premier Guang?"

"What? I'm sorry, Austin, if I may call you Austin, but that's an outrageous claim. If it were true, I'd be totally embarrassed. That couldn't have slipped past our people. We have the best and brightest investigators in the world. There must be some mistake."

"No mistake, Sir."

"The nomination process must have been going too fast. I suspect this would have never been found out if you weren't so ... so dang good at what you do. But what real proof do you have?"

"I met the secretary's mother, a lady named Sue Lyn Wong, and she confirmed what I learned when I investigated his background."

"Who else knows about this?"

"Sir, I don't even know if the vice premier knows."

"Really?"

"Really. I'll explain in a minute. I haven't taken it to my editor yet, but I'll decide on that after I hear what you have to say. Mr. President, we both know that your meetings with the Chinese would be jeopardized if this information gets out. If it were to leak out

198

before they meet, who knows how the vice premier or the Treasury Secretary might react? And if it came out after they meet, it might blow our relationship with China sky-high.

"I can see the headlines now," Austin declared. "You know, 'Father coerces son, or son outwits father.' The press can be pretty vicious. Now, to answer your question, Mr. President. At this point, there seem to be only four people in the world who know what I've told you: you, me, Sue Lyn Wong, and a confidant of mine. Mr. President, it's my job to investigate the facts of a story and see where they take me. Journalists have that responsibility in a free society. However, I've decided that it's in our national interest to keep quiet for now, until this plays out."

"Thank you. But before you continue, Austin, let me tell you what I already know. In our own investigation of the vice premier, we learned that he had a love affair with another student named "Su Lin" Wong while he was attending college here in the United States and that he returned to China, presumably without knowing that she was pregnant. We can only surmise that the potential embarrassment to her family led her to seek an adoption. We never pursued the matter of the child, since our effort was focused on learning anything about the vice premier that could help us in our negotiations. We did locate and interview Ms. Wong, and we were able to get her perspective on his political thinking, but little else. At least we learned something about what he thought back then when they were in school together."

"Mr. President, when I interviewed her, I told her that I knew about her son and who the father is."

"How did you learn his identity?"

"That's what I do for a living, sir. Anyway, now she sees an opportunity after all these years to acquaint Secretary Lee with his birth father. She has put me in a difficult position because, for some reason, she thinks I can arrange a meeting between them. That's way beyond my ability. Besides, I don't know what you plan to do with the information I'm giving you, so I'm really caught in the middle."

"Austin, I appreciate your coming to see me and being so forthright. Since I depend heavily on my Chief of Staff in all critical matters, with your permission, I'll enlarge the circle of those in the know to five people."

"Fine, Sir."

"Once I have a plan in place, we'll meet again, and I'll explain it to you and see where it takes us."

"Thank you, Sir. I'll look forward to your call."

Austin stood, shook hands with the president, and left.

Simon briefed Mac immediately after the meeting and summarized the case. They spent the long evening hours considering the issue, and neither of them got much sleep.

At their meeting the next morning, Mac asked the president to indulge him for a quick minute.

"You know my wife is into genealogy and all that kind of stuff so when I look at facts, dates pop out at me. No, I didn't discuss any of this with her. But when I compared the birth dates of Winston and Guang that I gleaned from our reports, I noted something very interesting. Many Chinese are big into the zodiac, so I checked it out. It's the curious nature of my intelligence background, I guess. It seems that both Guang and Winston were both born in Years of the Horse. Who knows if the vice premier believes any of that nonsense, or Winston for that matter, but you said you wanted to know everything about the vice premier, so all I can tell you what the Chinese Zodiac says about the personalities and compatibility of Chinese business partners born in those years. Guang is what they call a "water horse," and Winston is a "fire horse."

Water represents wisdom, and fire represents propriety: the advantage goes to Guang. Remember that Reagan embraced this stuff! They were well known to have consulted astrologers on certain things."

"Mac, spare me the rest of the personality and compatibility stuff. Right now, I've got some ideas about this dilemma, but I want to hear your conclusions first, so please go ahead."

"Well, Sir, here's how I see it. The first question has to be whether the vice premier, let's call him Jinli, or Winston are aware of their relationship. The next question is whether we should tell one or both of them, and when. I'm betting that they're both in the dark. We don't have any evidence that Winston has ever even raised a question about his birth father.

"You would think our investigators would have asked him about that, so, if they did, his answer must have been, 'I have no interest in finding out.' However, if Winston had otherwise learned that Jinli is his father, wouldn't he have told you when you discussed your intention to invite the Premier to come to Washington? And since Sue Lyn didn't even know she was pregnant when Jinli left for China, how could he have found out about the baby, unless she wrote and told him what happened? Regardless, if he became aware of a baby, he probably would have begged her to get an abortion. Children of unwed mothers are a disgrace to a Chinese family. There are many factors to consider: it's like solving a Rubik's cube or playing Whack-a-Mole."

"Go on."

"Every time we make one move, another one will pop up. We don't have the time to devise a comprehensive plan that takes every possibility into account. And we would have to get too many people involved to figure it out."

"So what do you recommend?"

"I say we do nothing, say nothing. The best outcome might result from neither of them learning the truth about the other. What they don't know can't hurt them, as they say."

"Okay, Mac. Now here's the way I see it. I agree with you one hundred percent. We don't know what crazy idea Sue Lyn might be thinking up about trying to contact Jinli, or spilling the beans to Winston for that matter. Regardless, we have at least one thing going for us. Remember that Jinli has a wife, and if he learns about Winston being his son, he may very well keep it to himself and say nothing to her or Winston."

"But Mr. President, what if Sue Lyn contacts Winston?"

"Well, then, we'll have to rely on his integrity not to say anything until later, or hopefully never at all. If Winston finds out about Jinli and says something, he runs the risk of failing to achieve the goals we set out for him and gets blamed for being soft on his father. Or worse yet, steamrolled by his father."

"I understand, Mr. President; however, there's another potential problem with this whole thing. If one of them learns about the other and doesn't disclose what he knows, the knowing party has a negotiating advantage. The conventional wisdom is that the best negotiations take place when both parties have all the facts. So, how do you propose to deal with that?"

"My boy, that's why I make the big bucks. I get paid to figure these things out. I'm not sure right now, so we have to be alert, and if we believe that either one has heard from Sue Lyn, we better be ready to act and make sure they both get the same information, pronto. You know, Mac, after this discussion I think this whole thing is simply in the hands of the Almighty. Let's just pray that Austin and Sue Lyn hold their tongues."

"Well then, Mr. President, have you decided on a course of action?" Austin asked.

"Yes, and to bottom line it, we plan to say nothing and let the chips fall where they may. Hopefully, nothing is ever said. Austin, you are the linchpin in this highly sensitive matter. You understand that the government would be ill served if this information got out. And my credibility and our administration's reputation would be destroyed.

"Ms. Wong has protected her son from knowing the identity of his father for all these years, and we have to respect her reasons. So, if we don't support her wishes, she might take things into her own hands and do something irrational. She could call the press to get the vice premier's attention, or reach Winston somehow in an effort to unite the two of them. Who knows what she might do?"

"So what do I tell her?"

"Just that we don't plan to do anything, but let her know that we will protect her public identity and, if she wants, deliver whatever personal message she has for either of them before the vice premier leaves. Please tell her she has my personal commitment to comply with her wishes to the best of my ability."

"Yes, Sir."

> Austin Cook @ OTP Apr 27 Simon – Only
> 18 days until the vice premier arrives. View
> on Twitter.

Austin paid another visit to Sue Lyn with an answer from the president.

"Sue Lyn, the president has considered the facts and has asked me to convey his best wishes to you that the matter can be resolved to your satisfaction. To be blunt, the concern is that if anything is said to either the vice premier or Winston, it could potentially create an international incident. There is no way to know how either of them would react, or the press or the Chinese government for that matter. It's possible the vice premier might feel he was invited here with the motivation that upon learning about his son, he would yield to our position on critical issues. He might easily call off the talks and go home and suffer the consequences of his past indiscretion.

"Or, Winston might feel that he was put in an embarrassing position without prior notice, and when the word got out, as it invariably would, his personal information would be revealed for all to see. The questions from the press and the opposing party would never stop, and his distrust of government might bring about his resignation. Neither side would win."

"Or, they might become overjoyed with the news, but never reveal it publically," Sue Lyn replied.

"Can we take that chance? There is too much at stake. We have to find another way. You told me you want to stay in the background, so can you think of a way I can arrange an introduction without compromising the talks and causing the possible furor I just described?"

"I was afraid that might be the answer, so yes, I have an idea. Let me explain it to you, and you can take my decision to the president."

"Fair enough."

"Hello, Mr. Secretary. Good morning and thanks for coming in," said the president.

"Good to see you, Sir."

"How is everything over at treasury?" "Busy, busy. But that's the way I like it."

"I won't take much of your time, but I thought we might have a little chat about the trade talks with our Chinese friends, since things are going to become a little hectic around here as we get closer to Mr. Guang's arrival on the fourteenth. I want to make sure you don't have any questions or concerns before then, especially as they relate to the vice premier."

"No Sir. Our Trade Representative's negotiating team and I are totally prepared. We've learned everything we can about his political history and his participation in China's economic growth. Of course, his reputation precedes him. We have our list of priorities and our discussion points clearly in mind, and we're ready to go. I just hope I'm up to the task."

"Winston, you have nothing to worry about. I have every confidence in you. That's why I chose you for the job. But remember, if you should stumble, it will be my responsibility and I will take the fall."

"Thank you, Sir. I appreciate your support but that wouldn't be appropriate."

"On another subject, what do you know about him personally?"

"Not much. I don't know if there's much to know. There aren't many clues in his dossier or on the Internet. The information I found was pretty inconsequential. He is somewhat of a mystery man. However, Mac did fill me in on a few things he learned from a colleague of his in Los Angeles who is writing an article on him for some publication. Apparently his friend found another Chinese student who knew him fairly well when he was in school, and he was able to get some answers to his questions."

"What did he have to say?"

"Nothing that we don't already know. Just that he was extremely bright, hard working, competitive, and loved to debate economic theories. That sort of thing. But he did make it sound like the vice premier's education in the states really stimulated his thinking about the pluses and minuses of capitalism. He had a chance to experience our way of life, first hand, and I doubt he ever forgot it, since he continues to be a real advocate of the free market and keeps pushing China in that direction. I suspect he may not be such a diehard communist after all."

"That's an interesting perspective. You mean he might be a closet capitalist?"

"You said it, not me."

"Sorry, it was just my feeble attempt at a bad joke. Humor has never been my strong suit. Anything else?"

"It's a small matter, but he apparently loves the game of Go. Actually, I play it myself, and I've taught my kids to play it, as well."

"Is that about it?"

"That's enough. I think I have a picture of the kind of man he is, probably somewhat like some of my professors back at Georgetown—very intellectual, but not stuffy."

"Thanks for the visit, Winston. Please stay in touch. If you hear anything else about the vice premier, please call me."

Winston thought about his conversation with the president on the way back to his office. *Well, it was rather strange,* he thought.

Simon was happy with the conversation and told Mac he didn't feel they had anything to fear from Winston.

"Mr. President, in all due respect, you may be satisfied that the Secretary is in the dark, but that still doesn't address the question about what Sue Lyn may do. We still haven't heard back from Austin about whether she has anything in mind, or not."

"True, but our plan stands until I hear something that affects our decision."

PART THREE

The Revelation

CHAPTER 14 ~ The Receptions

MAY 11, 2017

"Ladies and Gentlemen, this is your captain speaking," Captain Hal Krueger announced over the PA system. Thank you for your patience during the air traffic control delay. We'll be landing in Los Angeles in a few minutes on runway 24L and then taxi to the Tom Bradley International Terminal where you will deplane. Welcome to Los Angeles where the time is approximately seven thirty in the evening.

Then the First Officer repeated the message in Chinese.

The captain's voice awakened Shuchun from her sleep. She looked over at Jinli and sensed that something was bothering him. "What is it?" she asked.

"Oh, nothing in particular. I just have a lot to think about. You know how important this visit is, and I want to come away with a good result. I know very little about their new Treasury Secretary, but I'm hoping his Chinese-American heritage will help our relationship."

"What do you know about his family background?"

"I have his dossier. I know that he grew up in Virginia and that his father is a pastor. He excelled in school and has a distinguished academic record. At fifty-one, he is one of the youngest men to become Treasury Secretary. He is married with two children, a boy and a girl. And he was born in the Year of The Horse, the same as my father and myself, now that I think of it. Some coincidence don't you think?"

"Do you think the Secretary knows you were also born in the Year of the Horse? I know you don't believe in those things, but what if he does?"

"If he is a Christian, I doubt he does. In any event, I guess I can't take a chance. Since you raised the issue, I'll Google some Chinese Zodiac fortune-tellers and see what they have to say before we head to Washington, just in case it comes up in a conversation."

"Good idea, Jinli. You're always prepared. That's part of what makes you so successful."

The aircraft slowed and dropped in altitude, and as Jinli looked down, he noticed how the airport he remembered from back in 1965 had changed. In the distance, he made out the silhouette of the old Mines Field terminal that was still there.

As he heard the wheels drop and lock into position, he saw the famous four-legged theme building with a restaurant on top, right in the middle of a horseshoe shaped group of terminals. Then, the tall, shiny control tower now overlooking the expanded runway system came into view.

Jinli had seen a great number of airports throughout Asia and the Middle East in recent years, and this airport's arrangement certainly didn't appear to reflect the current state of the art standard for international airports. Nevertheless, he was somewhat impressed with its appearance.

It was all coming back to him now as he was returning to the scene of his lost love. He'd expected his homecoming would be rewarding, even if it were spiked with moments of melancholy.

As he considered the years that had passed, he wondered if Su Lin, or Tom, or another familiar face would appear at the graduation

210

ceremonies. If he saw Su Lin, assuming she was still alive, how would he react? In one sense, he hoped she would be there. But at the same time, he prayed she wouldn't show up and rekindle his feelings of their time together, especially with Shuchun by his side.

Then it hit him, as he considered the real possibility of seeing Su Lin again. Maybe this trip represented some application of "the future will reveal the past," the proverb she'd discussed with him back in college.

He had never forgotten that day or what she'd said.

Jinli and Shuchun were greeted at the airport by the university president, Thaddeus Wheeler, and his wife, Carol Ann. Their limousine ride to the hotel was pleasant, as the four of them became acquainted on their way to Pasadena. Jinli politely begged off Thaddeus' invitation to join them for dinner due to the late hour and extended his regrets. He was feeling the jet lag, and thought that a little something from room service and a good night's sleep at The Langham Huntington hotel where they were staying would better prepare him for the next day.

Jinli's U.S. Secret Service detail were in their assigned positions as he took his seat at the dais in Alumni Park the next morning. His own Chinese security guard, sent by the Counsel General for the occasion, blended into the fabric of the crowd.

It was a beautiful, clear day, and the crowd of several thousand graduates and their families in attendance were in a happy mood. The graduates were anxious for it to be over and their parents were anticipating a life with no more tuition payments.

Jinli had been told the main ceremony was planned to last for a little over an hour, so he was encouraged to keep his remarks fairly brief. After the ceremony, the graduates would be going to satellite ceremonies at their individual schools, where they would receive their diplomas and have their pictures taken. The processional started promptly at eight thirty a.m., and the graduates marched in under their school's flag as the band played "The USC Fight Song, and Conquest." The speeches began at nine a.m.

When it came time, President Wheeler presented the vice premier with his hood, acknowledging the honorary degree that was being conferred on him.

After a lengthy applause, Jinli walked to the dais and began to speak. "Confucius said, 'The will to win, the desire to succeed, the urge to reach your full potential … these are the keys that will unlock the door to personal excellence.' He also said, 'Choose a job you love, and you will never have to work a day in your life.'

"What I remember most about USC is that it gave me the opportunity to continue my education and practice the habits that I had been taught by my parents when I grew up in China. They gave me the will, the desire, and the urge to improve myself. If you haven't read your own Stephen Covey's, *The 7 Habits of Highly Effective People,* I recommend it to you, as it embraces the habits I ascribe to my own experience.

"For me, I was destined to follow my father with a career in government, and I have loved every day of my pursuit of excellence in my chosen field. You have that same opportunity, so continue to study and grow in a profession that you love. Find that profession and pursue it with all your ability. Learning is never over, so treat education as a lifelong pursuit.

"I miss the interchange of ideas I experienced here as a student, because that has benefitted me in immeasurable ways over the past fifty years. You all know that the economic system in my country was vastly different from the one that you enjoy in America, so I especially appreciate the lessons I received in my classrooms and the lively debates about competing systems that we had. They were stimulating, and I hope they allowed my classmates to learn a little something about a far away land that many Americans did not fully understand, just as I learned about the benefits and shortcomings of capitalism.

"Respect for one another's political and economic systems will continue to enable us to learn from one another in the future and allow each of us to make the best choices for our people from the available options.

"China is one of the world's oldest civilizations with a rich cultural past, but as an established multi-cultural country, the People's Republic of China is just sixty-eight years old. In fact, I was born there before my country was founded, and I've witnessed many changes from my youth to the present, especially in the field of education. An educational drive has become a hallmark of Chinese ideology in the twenty-first century, as our Chinese intellectual power base continues to grow. Student exchange programs between China and the United States, especially in higher education, are helping to bridge our cultural gap and strengthen our economic relationship.

"I am particularly pleased to see that China is consistently near the top of the list of newly enrolled international students here at USC. We Chinese are still learning and I am still learning, as I trust you will continue to do so, as well. In the future, I believe that we will accomplish more together than apart. The challenge for all of us is to find the right balance between our respective needs at home, and the assumption of a responsible role in the international community to meet today's challenges throughout the world.

"I challenge you to do your part, so go out into the world and make it a better place. I am truly grateful to our university for their kindness in awarding me with this degree today. I also want to thank the dean and staff of the business school for the education I received here. I will be forever grateful to USC.

"And finally, the USC Alumni Club of Beijing and I salute the graduating class of two thousand seventeen and their parents and friends. Thank you all for coming."

As Jinli smiled and waved during the applause, he scanned the crowd for any familiar faces but saw none. Tom had hoped to make contact with Jinli, but the campus security would not let him get near his friend in spite of his protestation.

After the ceremonies, the Wheelers and Donna Lucas, the new university Provost, escorted Mr. Guang and his wife to the USC University Club at Kings Stoop Hall, where the Chairman of the Board of Trustees hosted a lunch in their honor.

There was the ever-present group of protestors with signs about human rights that popped up along the way, but whenever they appeared, the university security personnel quickly removed them from the scene. Fortunately, they hadn't made a disturbance during Jinli's speech.

Jinli was always mindful of them wherever he went outside of China. He was sensitive to their human rights' cause, but he was powerless to do anything about it. He was a party man, always remaining true to his responsibilities, staying out of the fray.

That evening, the vice premier and his wife were feted at the Consular Corps Reception and Chairman's Dinner for the International Circle members of the Los Angeles World Affairs Council. They were special guests of the Consul General of the PRC, one of the Consuls General who represent ninety-eight countries in Los Angeles, the third largest diplomatic corps in the United States.

The Guangs thoroughly enjoyed their evening of conversation and camaraderie, and Jinli felt very comfortable being back in Los Angeles, albeit in a much different role.

The next morning, the driver provided by President Wheeler drove them back to the university for a quick look around the campus. Inconspicuous in street clothes, Jinli took out his map and studied it as they walked around.

Not far behind, but always out of sight, were the Secret Service agents assigned to protect them.

Jinli was impressed with all the changes that had taken place, especially the recent addition of the new USC Village, a mixed-use complex on fifteen acres, with its five-story residential colleges that reminded him of the pictures he had seen of Oxford. They were not as old of course, but he thought they were better.

Then they were off on a day-long journey for pleasure, passing by many of the places that Jinli remembered as he retraced some of the routes where Tom had taken him as a student. He was intrigued by the fact that many of those landmarks were still there, offering Shuchun a glimpse of Jinli's college experience. They stopped for lunch at El Cholo, where she ate her first authentic Mexican meal. She wondered why the rice was prepared in such a strange way, but she said she liked it.

Then, it was off to see more sights.

The day was full of excitement for both of them. As they arrived back at their hotel, she remarked that she loved Los Angeles, especially with the contrast of ethnicities in its old and new neighborhoods, and the vibrancy that filled the air.

Typical State Department planning for their visit to D.C. had taken place as the Chief of Protocol's office coordinated the transportation and meeting sites between the two governments. China had sent an advance team to scout travel routes, hotels and, of course, restaurants for the vice premier and his wife. It was the first visit to the United States for Ms. Guang, and she would no doubt want to see the typical tourist venues, so a tour was scheduled for her. No detail was overlooked.

The safety and security of the Guangs was all important. Any attempt at cyber intelligence would be thwarted. Their hotel room was remodeled in advance by the Chinese to prevent any electronic surveillance. The walls were papered with foil and jamming devices were installed to prevent the detection of any conversation. Even the guests at the official dinner would be surveilled.

China didn't trust the U.S. any more than the U.S. trusted China.

A protocol officer for visits met the vice premier and his wife at their hotel after their flight from Los Angeles, and a U.S. Secret Service escort drove them the short distance to the North Portico of the White House.

Upon their arrival, the Chief of Protocol ushered them upstairs into the Yellow Oval Room, where President Simon and First Lady Suzanne Simon greeted them.

"Vice Premier Guang, may I introduce our Treasury Secretary, Dr. Winston Lee, and his wife Pauline," said the president. After the remaining introductions, the Guangs were offered coffee and tea while they enjoyed a brief respite, and signed the White House guest book.

Shuchun whispered to her husband, "Yellow is our country's most prestigious color. They have thought of everything. Do you think it's just a coincidence that we were taken to this particular room?"

Jinli shushed her and whispered, "Later."

Meanwhile, the invited guests had received their table seating/ announcement cards upon their arrival and were being ushered into the East Room, where they conversed and enjoyed some refreshment.

As everyone heard the ruffles and flourishes resonating off the marble floors, followed by the marine band playing "Hail to the Chief," the president, his wife and their honored guests descended the grand stairway to the Entrance Hall for official pictures and formed the receiving line in the Cross Hall.

Guests proceeded through the receiving line following the Order of Precedence, established in advance according to the guest list, where they were introduced to the president, the vice premier, the first lady and the vice premier's wife.

The guest list included members of Congress serving on committees involving foreign affairs and trade, senior members of the Treasury and Trade Representative's offices, senior officers of investment banks with offices in China, and the principal negotiators of the vice premier's delegation. The president selected the other guests personally.

As a military aide introduced each guest to the Simons and the Guangs, the White House photographer took pictures to be mailed out later. All the while, members of the media, standing behind ropes, were also taking photographs and recording names.

Austin sent an associate of his to take pictures for OTP.

The official dinner, held in the State Dining Room, was a pro-forma affair.

On cue, the media entered the room to note the welcoming remarks by the president, followed by a toast to the evening's guest and his wife. Then the vice premier, seated next to the president, rose, returned the toast, and thanked him for his gracious invitation.

Then the media departed.

The four-course dinner was Chinese-American fusion. The chef from the Chinese Embassy had assisted the White House Executive Chef in selecting the menu and preparing the meal.

Seated with the president and the first lady were the vice premier and his wife, Shuchun, Secretary Lee and his wife, Pauline, the U.S. Trade Representative, Ambassador Aimee Remington and her husband, Howard, and the Chinese Ambassador to the U.S., Han Pu and his wife, Liang Li.

The vice premier's quiet conversation with the secretary was pleasant, but a little stiff at first. After all, Mr. Guang was Lee's senior by some twenty years and he was a significantly more experienced politician. He did not intimidate Winston, but Winston had expected to be on the defensive from the start. He was determined to avoid discussing politics until their meeting the next day.

The life experiences of the table partners were vastly different from one another. As the conversation somehow turned to recollections of growing up, Winston mentioned his mother's background as a missionary in China.

That was the icebreaker.

The vice premier chimed in to say that missionaries had schooled his father as a young man, and that missionaries aided his father in escaping the ravages of war, seeking a safe haven in the revolutionary stronghold in the mountains.

When the Chinese Ambassador related his early days as an educated urban youth sent to the countryside to start a farming operation as a "sent down," Shuchun related her own similar personal experience, and the conversations took off.

As the cross talk turned into a collegial discussion about growing up, they regaled one another with anecdotes from their past, and the vice premier remarked to the president that he had not had such an enjoyable evening in years.

Meanwhile, during the dinner hour, the Protocol Officer for Gifts was meeting with a staff member from the vice premier's delegation downstairs, and they exchanged gifts.

The president's gift to the vice premier was a framed copy of the joint communiqué of the United States of America and the People's Republic of China on the Establishment of Diplomatic Relations that was released on December 15, 1978, in Washington and Beijing, that read, in part, "… The United States of America and the People's Republic of China have agreed to recognize each other and to establish diplomatic relations as of January 1, 1979."

Below the wording was a picture of Vice Premier Deng Xiaoping with President Jimmy Carter taken in Washington, D.C.

President Simon had included an inscribed a note of good will, and signed it on behalf of the American people.

A press release would be sent out from the White House the following morning describing the president's gift.

The vice premier's gift to President Simon was a replica of one of four hanging scrolls from the Ming dynasty included in The Eighteen Scholars collection, hanging in their National Palace Museum, that depicts men playing a game of Go, one of the four arts of the scholar. It reflected, "… the meticulous appreciation of refined beauty in the life of upper classes in the Ming Dynasty."

During dessert, everyone was treated to music provided by the U.S. Army Strolling Strings.

After the ensemble finished playing their selections for the evening, they presented a special performance by a local artist on a zither like instrument called a "guzheng." She chose to play a famous Chinese song, "High Mountain, Flowing Water," which was said to have been written in three hundred BC.

The audience was spellbound by its unique style and beauty. She received a standing ovation at the conclusion of the piece, and the president and first lady stepped aside as the Guangs approached her with outstretched arms of thanks.

When the applause ended, the president turned toward his guests and invited them to join him in the Entrance Hall for dancing.

As Mr. Guang started to leave the Dining Room, he turned and stayed for a moment when he noticed the mantle above the fireplace behind his table. It bore an engraving of John Adams' famous quote, "I pray Heaven to bestow the best of Blessings on this House and all that shall hereafter inhabit it. May none but honest and wise Men ever rule under this roof."

The vice premier followed the lead of the president, and they withdrew from the room as their wives chattered away.

The Guangs had one glass of champagne and then politely excused themselves. The military aide standing nearby sensed the cue, and immediately called for their car. The president and first lady escorted them back to the North Portico, where the Guangs thanked them for their gracious hospitality and departed for their hotel.

They refrained from conversation during the ride back, waiting to discuss the evening until they were in the safety of their hotel room.

"Well, what did you think?" Jinli asked as they entered their hotel suite and closed the door.

"I had a marvelous time and enjoyed every minute of it," Shuchun said. "The ladies were so nice and comfortable to be with. How about you?"

"The president was everything I expected him to be: respectful, warm and very friendly. But you know, I became a little more fascinated with Winston as we got finally got into some deeper conversation. There is something about him that I can't quite put my finger on. Maybe I'll figure it out tomorrow."

CHAPTER 15 ~ The Clues

MAY 15, 2017

The vice premier arrived at the secretary's third floor office in the Treasury Building early the next morning, ready to begin the work at hand.

"Mr. Guang, may I show you some historical features of the building before we greet our teams in the conference room?" Winston asked.

"Certainly, I would enjoy that."

"I hope you noticed the statue of Alexander Hamilton as you arrived. He was our first treasurer."

"I did. Very impressive."

"First, let's go down to the second floor and take a look at the cash room and the vault.

"This is where our country began keeping its currency in the year 1869. In fact, we operated a bank here until 1976 when it was closed. Now, all of our money is kept in my office safe upstairs … just kidding, of course. It's all in a shoebox in my desk drawer."

When the vice premier stopped laughing, the secretary said, "Now, let's go back upstairs to the third floor to see the office suite of Samuel P. Chase, our Treasury Secretary during the Civil War. Then we'll visit the Andrew Johnson Suite. He succeeded Abraham Lincoln as president and used it as his temporary White House in deference to Mary Todd Lincoln after her husband's assassination."

As they entered the conference room, everyone stood up.

"Mr. Secretary," said the vice premier, "may I present Mr. Xi Wan, our Minister of Commerce, who will lead our negotiations."

After they shook hands, Winston said, "Mr. Guang, say hello again to Jack Donnelly, whom you met last evening. He will be your minister's counterpart."

"It's a pleasure to see you again," said the vice premier.

"Likewise."

After sitting and listening to the secretary's welcoming remarks, the members of both delegations rose and left, taking the short, eight-minute walk past the White House to the offices of the ambassador. Once there, they broke into smaller groups to discuss the issues on a list that had been predetermined by the parties.

The vice premier and the secretary stayed behind to meet privately. After the last delegate left the room, the vice premier extended his hand and said, "Mr. Secretary, your president's gift to me is very much appreciated. It signifies the profound relationship that exists between our two countries, and I will be proud to display it in my office."

As they crossed the hall, the secretary echoed the vice premier's confidence in their relationship.

When they entered the secretary's office, the secretary complimented the vice premier on his selection of a gift for the president.

"Well," the vice premier said, "it was a little surreptitious, given what I'm told is your interest in the game of Go, but it does represent a genuine thought about the need for more refinement in our lives. Politics has gotten rather ugly in so many ways that

I think we need to make an improvement in the way we approach one another."

The secretary was taken aback by the vice premier's statement. He had seen his diplomatic side at dinner the night before, but expected a tougher sounding opponent when they got down to discussing business.

"Mr. Secretary, I would like to dispense with all the formality between us when we are alone. I would be pleased if you call me Jinli?"

"Of course, sir. And please call me Winston."

As Jinli studied the room, getting a sense of Winston's persona in pictures, awards and other memorabilia, his attention suddenly focused on a Go board with a standard nineteen by nineteen grid, the type used in all worldwide tournaments. Winston had set it up on a table in a corner of the room next to a window.

"I understand you play?" Jinli asked.

"Yes, and there is a growing interest in the game here in the U.S. Even my son plays."

"Wonderful. Do you suppose we will have some time later to squeeze in a game or two?"

"I think we will."

Jinli opened the dialogue, telling Winston that there was little doubt in his mind as to the motivation behind the president's invitation. "We are holding a substantial amount of your country's debt, and the balance of trade continues to favor us. Do I have that about right?"

"I think that's a good summary," Winston replied.

"Let's cut to the chase, as they say. What do you propose?" Jinli asked.

Winston caught his breath at Jinli's straightforward approach before answering.

"Well, we both know that China's sudden sale of our debt would disturb markets around the world. There is concern about that possibility although a relaxation or elimination of Chinese import restrictions on the U.S. would ameliorate that debt accumulation problem over time. Second, the claim by some that you manipulate your currency has created a level of distrust that can only strain our relationship.

"If we can agree on a response to those negatives, it would generate a lot of confidence by our government in your policies. Our trade relationship is intertwined with so many areas of international banking and financial operations that I believe we would both benefit from a clearer understanding of our monetary relationship."

Jinli was impressed with his analysis. "Well stated, Winston. We are keenly aware of the issues you raised, but I think you'll agree that the growth in our economy is the envy of a great many folks. However, we do recognize the need to stimulate our domestic consumption that we sacrificed over the past several years in favor of that growth. Now we need to increase the standard of living of those on the bottom rungs of our ladder, and I think that the timing is right to make a course correction. That fits with what you have in mind, doesn't it?"

"Perhaps," Winston replied, "but I haven't made a proposal yet. I don't want to negotiate against myself, so I want to hear your solutions first."

"Ah, ha! You have learned your craft well," Jinli exclaimed. "Now that we have framed the issues, what do you say we take a break and have a little game to allow us a time for a little introspection?"

"That's an excellent idea," Winston agreed.

Winston had made sure the stones were counted ahead of time: 181 black stones and 180 white ones.

Jinli drew black, and placed the first stone, as is the custom. The first game lasted only forty-five minutes. Winston was fearless, but was no match for the more skilled player and so he lost.

"How does an early lunch sound?" Winston asked.

"All right, but I'll challenge you to another game this afternoon if you're up for it."

Lunch was waiting for them in the dining room. They consumed it slowly without much conversation while they considered their respective positions on the trade matters at hand.

When they finished, Jinli proposed that they hold a little afternoon tournament and resume their discussion the next day, giving them even more time to think. Even so, barring any surprises, Jinli felt they should be able to reach agreement on the terms of a policy statement fairly quickly.

"I suggest we play six games," Winston said. "The winner must be ahead by at least two games at the end of play. I'll include my first loss, of course. That will provide you with the ability to make a strong comeback from a three game deficit if that should become necessary."

"Winston, I like your style. I can see that you are a real competitor. I like that. I don't have much respect for pushovers."

They played until late afternoon. Alternating starts, Winston went first in game two. Winston managed to eke out a win, but Jinli quickly won games three and four, taking a three to one lead.

Winston somehow managed to win a lengthy game five, escaping disaster. "Jinli, one more win, and you'll be the champion," Winston confirmed, "but we can play it later. Right now your wife is probably looking for you to go to dinner. You should get going. We'll have plenty of time tomorrow."

Jinli thanked Winston for the games and left. His car was waiting downstairs to take him back to the hotel.

"How did it go?" Shuchun asked.

"Popo, it was a day to remember, and tomorrow may be even more exciting.

This whirlwind trip has really energized me. Where are we going for dinner?" "The protocol people selected a restaurant for us, but Pauline recommended a smaller place close by, and she thinks you'll love it." And he did.

Jinli was back in Winston's office promptly at ten o'clock the next morning, ready for more action. However Winston suggested they get their business out of the way before playing their final game.

After a two-hour discussion and a reasonable bit of negotiation, Winston beckoned his secretary to his office and dictated the wording of a Joint Communiqué for their review and approval. After a couple of tweaks to the language of the document, they were in agreement and Jinli signed it.

Winston instructed his secretary to hand carry it across the street to the White House for the president's approval and signature. It wouldn't be released to the press until Jinli was long gone on his way home. The press wouldn't like the delay, but Simon had a good reason for setting it up that way.

After lunch, it was time to get down to the real business of the day. Currently a game up on Winston, Jinli was feeling pretty confident that he could win it all. However, when play began Jinli's confidence started to wane slightly as he realized Winston's emotions were flying high. Regardless, he was careful not to show anything on his face. An international victory by Jinli would never make any headlines, but if he could pull off a win, he would note it in his journal as one of his personal accomplishments during the trip.

On the other hand, Winston considered the meaning of a loss. Winston's honor was at stake. How would he explain losing to his wife and kids? After all, he had never lost in local competitions. His reputation was on the line, and he could never hold his head up high if he succumbed to his counterpart from China. As the play moved along, neither player ever led by more than a couple of points. Winston began to sweat, but not noticeably. He was the more slow and deliberate player, but as the pace began to pick up he attacked with a flourish and deftly placed his stones on the board in a way that totally confused Jinli. Winston carefully concealed his final move and placed a black stone on the board with the guile of a grandmaster! A white stone must be played to end the game, and with no moves left on the board for Jinli, he conceded his move and the game went to Winston.

They had finished in a three-three tie.

"Quality play," Jinli remarked, resigned to the loss. "Quality play. I never saw it coming."

"GO"… a Chinese abstract strategy board game
dating back to the Zhou Dynasty in China

That afternoon Jinli returned to his hotel, pleased that the meetings were over, but disappointed that he hadn't put Winston away.

As he walked through the hotel lobby with his Secret Service agent in tow, the desk clerk came out from behind his station and rushed toward the vice premier. The agent stopped him in mid stride and asked what he wanted.

The clerk handed him a double-tied yellow drawstring bag and said it was given to him with strict instructions to hand it to Mr. Guang personally and say that it is a gift.

"Who delivered it?" the agent demanded to know.

"I don't know, sir. I didn't recognize the man," the clerk answered in a trembling voice.

"What did he look like?"

"He was a pretty normal looking guy I guess—maybe in his mid to late thirties." The agent untied the bag and peeked inside, looking carefully at the neatly wrapped little red box with yellow ribbon and a bow. It didn't appear to present any kind of threat or apparent danger, so the agent handed the bag to the vice premier.

Jinli let himself into his suite, and the agent stationed himself outside the door. Jinli was getting tired of the constant protection he had everywhere he went, but he knew it was a necessary evil.

He sat down and turned the little box over in his hands while he pondered the contents of the little gift. Without much hesitation, he removed the ribbon, unwrapped the box and removed the lid. A fortune cookie was stuffed in between some tissue paper. He cracked it open and removed the familiar little slip of paper with a printed saying on it that read: "The future will reveal the past; now your past has been revealed."

Obviously it was sent by Su Lin, Jinli surmised.

At that moment, Shuchun interrupted his thoughts as he heard her key in the lock. She was returning from Pauline's tour of the Washington monuments that she began the day before. He rose from his chair, embraced her and asked, "How did it go today?"

"Fine. Pauline is such a wonderful girl. By the way, I told her you really liked the restaurant last night. Her tour was great, and we stopped at the church she and Winston attend so I could meet his parents. They are such nice people. There were a lot more interesting sites to see, but we ran out of time. Anyway, I'm happy to get back here. My feet hurt, and I'm tired. How was your meeting with the secretary?"

"I have to say he turned out to be very easy to work with, and we reached an agreement on my recommended negotiating points that were approved at our last standing committee meeting before we left."

"That's very good news, dear."

Jinli and Shuchun had been entertained like royalty over the previous week, but they were ready to go home. They decided to order dinner in their room and retire early. Only a short meeting with Winston was on Jinli's schedule for the next day.

When Winston got home that afternoon, his kids were surprised to see him there so early.

"Hi, Dad," they chimed in unison.

"Hello. How are you guys doing?" he asked.

"Dad, somebody delivered something for you this afternoon," Henry said. "Hank," as his friends called him, was his twenty-one-year-old son, home from college for the summer.

"For me?"

"Uh-huh."

"A man brought it to the door a little while ago," Pauline said, as she entered the room and gave Winston a peck on the cheek.

"Who was he?"

"I don't know, but he seemed to know who you are," interrupted Tiffany, Hank's younger sister. "He said it was a gift from a close friend."

"Well, let's take a look see." Inside a double-tied yellow drawstring bag was a little red box tied with yellow ribbon and a bow.

"Open it Honey," Pauline said.

"What is this?" he said as he tore the ribbon and paper off the box and tossed the lid aside. He yanked on the crumpled tissue paper inside and a Chinese fortune cookie fell onto the floor.

"This is really strange. Why would anyone send me a fortune cookie?" When he tugged on the paper slip inside the kids asked him to read it out loud. It read: "The future will reveal the past; now your past has been revealed."

"What does that mean, Dad?" Henry asked.

"I don't have a clue," Winston replied, sounding confused.

"It says 'your past,' Pauline remarked. "And just what happened in your past that I don't know about?"

"I can't recall anything, honey, but you sound like a very suspicious wife," answered Winston, laughing.

Pauline went on, "Well then, it's apparently something you're totally unaware of."

"I suppose so," Winston said, "but regardless, the person who sent it knows what it's all about. Honey, should I ask my dad if he has any ideas? It sure sounds like a Chinese Proverb to me."

"You can check with him, but first you might ask Mr. Guang if he's seen it before."

Jinli tossed and turned during the night, lying there, wide-awake, thinking to himself. He had a suspicion that Su Lin might show up at some point, but didn't expect to hear from her this way.

He recalled the proverb and remembered Su Lin's explanation of its meaning when they were back in school together. She had used the example how the consequence of Christ's birth was revealed later on. But what about the second line on the slip? What happened in my past that has been revealed? Could it be something in my past that involved Su Lin? He paused for a moment.

"Oh brother!" he said out loud as he sat up with a start. "What is it?" Shuchun asked when his outburst awakened her. "Oh, I think I may have figured it out."

"Figured what out?"

"Oh, what I might say to Winston tomorrow morning before we leave. You know, this week has been quite revealing."

Jinli stopped by Winston's office early the next morning to say goodbye before catching their flight back to Beijing. The negotiating teams had wrapped up their work the previous afternoon and sent written summaries of their agreements to all the participants.

"Winston, I've thoroughly enjoyed our time together, and I hope to see you again soon."

"Thank you, Jinli. And next time we'll play that tiebreaker game if you're up for it."

"Of course I'll be up for it!"

"But before you go I have a question," Winston said. "Yesterday afternoon, someone delivered a gift for me at my house. It was a small box with a fortune cookie inside. The slip in the cookie read, 'The future will reveal the past; now your past has been revealed.' The message must be for me, but we can't figure it out. Absolutely everything in my past is on the table for all to see. The vetting took care of that when I was confirmed as secretary. Pauline asked me to find out if you've come across that proverb before and can help us understand it."

"Yes, I've heard that proverb before, and I'm relieved and excited to hear that we received identical gifts. Mine was waiting for me yesterday back at the hotel. Winston, that was no coincidence. I know who sent the gifts, and I can tell you that the messages hold a great deal of personal significance for us, especially given our respective roles in the negotiations. This isn't the right time to explain it to you, so if you'll bear with me, I want to collect my thoughts first and then write them down. I'll ask the protocol officer who takes us to the airport to deliver a letter to you after he drops us off. It will explain everything, and I think you should read it in the privacy of your office before you go home tonight."

"Jinli, this sounds as mysterious as the proverb itself."

"Trust me, this is the best way. After you read my letter you'll understand why. Only you and I will be able to appreciate the potential impact of what it may mean in the future, but the whole world need not know anything right now."

"I will respect your wishes even though I don't know much more than I did a few minutes ago."

As Jinli prepared to leave, Winston reached for his hand and said, "Pauline and I will pray for travel mercies on your way home. May God bless you and Shuchun."

Then, uncharacteristically, Jinli said, "Until we meet again," as he stepped forward and gave Winston a hug.

Earlier that morning, Austin Cook posted this blog:

My exclusive news from the White House.
POSTED MAY 17, 2017 by AUSTIN COOK

Yesterday, First Vice Premier of China Guang Jinli, and Treasury Secretary of the United States Winston Lee, prepared a Joint Communiqué to be released tomorrow by the White House that will summarize the results of their two-day meeting. The vital importance of their trade relationship is reflected in an agreement reached on two major issues: China's pledge to remove the peg of its currency to the U.S. dollar, and its removal of barriers to the import of American goods. The latter includes the adjustment of China's import tariffs to create more parity with American tariff rates. The stated goal of the agreement is to support the consumer needs of China's growing population. Dates for implementation are to be determined. A White House Press Release will be forthcoming.

Back home, the agreement reached in Washington was lauded in the newspapers and on television as a historic step forward in U.S.-China relations, while privately, a number of high-ranking party officials characterized it as a 'giveaway' that threatened to undermine China's attempt to overcome the U.S. as the economic leader of the free world. They wondered if the U.S. Treasury Secretary had bested the vice premier in their negotiations.

PART FOUR

The Consequence

CHAPTER 16 ~ The Aftermath

NOVEMBER 7, 2017

The months following Guang Jinli's trip to Washington put a terrific strain on him. He was constantly being called upon to justify the terms of the agreement he negotiated with the U.S. Treasury Secretary, which he said were intended to provide long-term benefits to China's economy from their increased purchases of American goods.

Guang Jinli and his wife quietly boarded the Hawaiian Airlines Airbus A330-200 at the Beijing Capital International Airport with non-stop service to the Daniel K. Inouye International Airport in Honolulu, ostensibly to begin a long-needed vacation in the Hawaiian Islands. Now, he would be free to pursue his suppressed goal of working for greater human rights for the Chinese people.

> Austin Cook @ OTP Nov 7 – Please check my blog for deets of shocking news. View on Twitter.

Austin Cook posted this blog:

My exclusive news from the White House.
POSTED NOVEMBER 7, 2017 by AUSTIN COOK

Today, Guang Jinli, the First Vice Premier of the People's Republic of China, accompanied by his wife, Yuan Shuchun, walked into the Honolulu office of the U.S. Citizenship and Immigration Services requesting asylum. They stated that they fear persecution by the Chinese government because of their underground support for Hong Kong's continuing right of democratic self-governance after year 2047 when that freedom will be lost upon Hong Kong's reunification with mainland China. Asked if they expect to stay in Hawaii, they said they plan to settle near his family in the Washington, D.C. area. More later.

APPENDIX

FAMILY TREES

FAMILY TREE OF CHINESE CHARACTERS

CHEN YONGMIN	GUANG HE	YU XIU	YAN XIA

CHEN (GUANG) WEI Born 11/3/1918 (Year of the Horse) In Shiling Town, China	YU MINGZHU Born 1920 (Year of the Monkey) In Shanghai, China

GUANG JINLI
Born 1/17/1943
(Year of the Horse)
In Yanan, China

FAMILY TREE OF CHINESE-AMERICAN CHARACTERS

WONG MIN	XING MEI	JONATHAN MONROE	MARY JANE SMOOT

JUN JIE (JIMMY) WONG Born 1920 In Waihiawa, HI	MARLENE (MONROE) WONG Born 1922 In Castroville, CA

SU LIN WONG
Born 1946
In San Francisco, CA

241

CHARACTERS

CHINESE CHARACTERS
(IN CHINESE NAMING CONVENTION)

Chen Yongmin	Father of Guang Wei
Guang Wei	Father of Guang Jinli
Yu Mingzhu	Mother of Guang Jinli
Guang Jinli	Son of Guang Wei
Yuan Shuchun	Wife of Guang Jinli
Ma Xing	Premier of China
Xi Wan	Minister of Commerce
Han Pu	Chinese Ambassador to the U.S.
Liang Li	Wife of the Chinese Ambassador

BRITISH CHARACTERS
(BY FIRST NAME)

Clarence Hopkins	Missionary
John Huckleberry	Missionary
Walter Harness	Missionary

AMERICAN CHARACTERS
(BY FIRST NAME)

Aimee Remington	Secretary of Homeland Security
Archie Jackson	Los Angeles resident
Austin Cook	Journalist with OTP
Benton (Ben) Elliott	Staffer for Senator Mickiewicz
Bill	Security Guard
Billy Eddie Phillippi	Beer and Wine Distributor
Bo Dugan	Private Investigator
Bob Fishback	Director of the FBI

Bragg Donaldson	Chairman of the Export-Import Bank
Brian (Mac) McNeill	Chief of Staff to The President
Brianna Norman	White House Press Secretary
Carol Ann Wheeler	Wife of USC President Wheeler
Cole Stickman	Special Agent of the FBI
Dan Rodriquez	Secretary of Customs, Immigration and Border Protection
David Lee	Father of Winston Lee
Donna Lucas	USC Provost
Eileen Stansfield	Adoption Counselor
Emma Legrand	Special Agent of the FBI
Glenn Boyd	Secretary of State
Grace Lee	Mother of Winston Lee
Hal Krueger	Air China pilot
Henry Lee	Son of Winston Lee
Howard Remington	Husband of the Secretary of Homeland Security
Isabel Villa	Nursing student
Jack Donnelly	Secretary of Commerce
James (Jim) Charlton	Vice President of The United States
Jane Appleby	Reporter with CNN
Jun Jie (Jimmy) Wong	Father of Su Lin Wong
Kate Summerville	Reporter with CBS
Leonard Murdock	Reporter with Reuters
Linda Snuggs	Girlfriend of Austin Cook
Logan Catalina	White House Director of Communications
Lucho Santiago	Restaurateur
Michael (Mike) Simon	President of The United States
Michael Angelo (Mikey) Gagliano	Restaurateur
Pauline Lee	Wife of Winston Lee
Peter Smith	Business School Dean
Russ McKinnie	Secretary of Energy
Sheng Tom	Retired Professor at USC

Stephen Mickiewicz	Senator Mickiewicz
Su Lin Wong	Girlfriend of Jinli Guang
Susan Charlton	Wife of Vice President Charlton
Suzanne Simon	Wife of President Simon
Dr. Thaddeus Wheeler	President of USC
Tiffany Lee	Daughter of Winston Lee
Tomas Retsuc	Secretary of Homeland Security
Dr. Winston Lee	Secretary of The Treasury

MEXICAN CHARACTER

Bernard Corvera	President of Mexico

ABBREVIATIONS

CHINESE ORGANIZATIONS

PRC	*People's Republic of China*	Sovereign state of China
CPC	*Communist Party of China*	Chinese political party
NPC	*National People's Congress*	National legislature of the PRC
PLA	*People's Liberation Army*	Armed Forces of CPC
ROC	*Republic of China*	Nationalist government of China before 1949 and current sovereign state of Taiwan
KMT	*Kuomintang of China*	Chinese political party
NRA	*National Revolutionary Army*	Army of the KMT before 1949

AMERICAN ORGANIZATIONS

AFDC	*Aid to Families with Dependent Children*	U.S. Federal and State program
ASAP	*As Soon As Possible*	Common phrase
BLS	*Bureau of Labor Statistics*	Unit of U.S. Department of Labor
CAMEX	*Canadian American Mexican Exporting Countries*	(Fictitious organization)
CBP	*Customs and Border Protection*	Agency of U.S. Department of Homeland Security
CBS	*Columbia Broadcasting System*	Network television service
CEA	*Council of Economic Advisors*	Agency in the White House
CEO	*Chief Executive Officer*	Highest ranking corporate executive
CIA	*Central Intelligence Agency*	U.S. Federal government agency
CIBP	*Customs, Immigration and Border Protection*	(Fictitious Agency)
CNN	*Cable News Network*	Cable television service
D.C.	*District of Columbia*	Capital of the United States

DNA	*Deoxyribonucleic acid*	Carrier of genetic information
EPA	*Environmental Protection Agency*	U.S. Federal government agency
FBI	*Federal Bureau of Investigation*	U.S. Federal government agency
FERC	*Federal Energy Regulatory Commission*	U.S. Federal government agency
FERPA	*Family Educational Rights and Privacy Act of 1974*	U.S. Federal legislation
GPS	*Global Positioning System*	Radio navigation system
GSA	*General Services Administration*	U.S. Federal government agency
HHS	*Health and Human Services*	U.S. Federal and State program
HUD	*Housing and Urban Development*	U.S. Federal government agency
ICE	*Immigration and Customs Enforcement*	Agency of Department of Homeland Security
LAX	*Los Angeles International Airport*	Airport designation
NAFTA	*North American Free Trade Agreement*	Agreement among U.S., Canada and Mexico
NSA	*National Security Agency*	U.S. Federal government agency
OPEC	*Organization of the Petroleum Exporting Countries*	Intergovernmental organization
OPM	*Office of Personnel Management*	U.S. Federal government agency
OPP	*Office of Presidential Personnel*	A White House office
OTP	*On-line-Truth-in-Politics*	(Fictitious media outlet)
PA	*Public Address*	Speaker system
PC	*Politically Correct*	Common phrase
PI	*Private Investigator*	Common phrase
SFO	*San Francisco International Airport*	Airport designation

TA	*Teaching Assistant*	Common phrase
USC	*University of Southern California*	U.S. private university
USITC	*United States International Trade Commission*	U.S. Federal government agency
VA	*Veterans Affairs*	U.S. Federal government program
WPA	*Works Progress Administration*	U.S. Federal government agency

ABOUT THE AUTHOR

After his retirement, Jim and his wife, Sue, moved from Palos Verdes Estates, California on the Pacific Coast to Palm Desert, California in the Coachella Valley.

With more time to travel, he developed an increasing curiosity about the history and culture of places around the world. That experience has evolved into a new endeavor: the enjoyment of writing novels that tell intriguing stories built around the lives of interesting characters. His first attempt resulted in a children's book he wrote for his nine grandchildren, *Gnorman the Gnorwegian Gnome*, which takes place in Svalbard, Norway.

The success of that book led him to take on *Consequences: The Future Will Reveal the Past*, a more ambitious project that stemmed from his experiences while attending college in Los Angeles. The story explores the relationship between a foreign student from China and his first love as their lives take vastly different turns. It is now available as a Second Edition.

Consequences was followed by *The Art of Chicanery*, a novel that tackles the subject of gun ownership, one of the most challenging civic issues being discussed in our overheated political climate today.

For more information, visit *Books by Jim Prock* on Amazon.